FROM HEAVEN AND BEYOND

He was male. No doubt about that. He was muscular, built like an athlete or soldier, with a line of puckered scar tissue visible at his neck. His nose looked as if it had been broken at least once. His features were strong and rugged, but not perfect. Brenna was obscurely glad of that.

There was no other word for him but male. What made him so, and how he was different from the other angels she'd seen, she couldn't quite pin down. She just knew that he was potently, appealingly masculine.

Cairn.

As Brenna felt her lips form his name in that instant of strange, perfect recognition, the figure in her vision snapped upright.

He tipped back the strong column of his neck, his thick, tousled golden hair brushing his shoulder. He searched the sky, looking upward into heaven as if the girl's soul had called out to him.

My soul, Brenna thought. *I called out to you.* She willed him to turn, to see her somehow. He stopped looking upward, started to turn his head toward the side. He would see her any second now….

The intercom in the living room buzzed loudly. Brenna's eyes flew open. The vision immediately dissolved.

☑ T5-BBV-185

Corinne Everett

Love, Remember Me

LOVE SPELL   **NEW YORK CITY**

LOVE SPELL®

March 1997

Published by

Dorchester Publishing Co., Inc.
276 Fifth Avenue
New York, NY 10001

The name ''Love Spell'' and its logo are trademarks of Dorchester Publishing Co., Inc.

Printed in the United States of America.

To David Engel, fellow cappuccino drinker, manuscript reader, and my favorite bon vivant;
and
To my husband Phil, who said this one would be the first to sell.

LOVE,
REMEMBER ME

Prologue

Scotland, 84 A.D.

Darkness crept into the remaining daylight, draining the air of light and warmth. The man and woman lay together in a tangled, bloody heap of arms and legs, holding each other in the face of death as they had so briefly in the full flow of life. Two hearts, two lives meant to be one.

As their blood leached away into the black soil, their lives also retreated in tempo with the sun sinking behind the low, rolling hills. Discarded broadswords lay forgotten at their sides. Their clan had convinced the Romans that this part of Scotland was not worth having.

But at grave cost.

Cairn and Brynna had run the Romans off in the

end, following fast and hard in the grip of a Celtic
fury, outdistancing even their companions. Together
in the last encounter, they had somehow had the
strength of twelve men.

If only they had as many lives between them, Cairn
thought.

There was a rendezvous point for the clan, but
Cairn knew they would not reach it in time. Instead
they would die here.

He thanked the gods that he could die with her,
regretting only that they had no more time on earth.
But together they would rise into the Light, someday
to be reborn in new lives.

"Promise to remember?" Cairn asked.

"How can I? We'll both be dead soon," Brynna
said.

His voice, though weak, was fierce. "I won't forget.
I won't let you."

"You're stronger than I am—you always have
been." Her low voice was husky with pain and thirst,
her skin cold. How he wanted to keep the life in her!
But Fate had not intended her to be a warrior queen.
He knew she led the clan because she had no choice:
the Romans had killed her father. Her lean frame,
though strong for a woman, did not have the physical resources his did.

Cairn had given her that much, at least: the
strength of his body. Rough, trained for battle, he
had been honed to maximum strength in the increasingly lethal battles of Celt versus Roman.

None of their people protested against the combined powers of Sight and Sword. Hers was the Sight
because she knew where the Romans were and when

they would attack; his was the Sword because no one had ever defeated him in battle, game, or sport.

That cooperation, necessary for battle, had become something else. They had not had the time to marry, not with war all around them, but they had handfasted themselves and lain together for the first time last night. Cairn shivered with the memory of her fiery, innocent sensuality, which had called a response from him that burned into his soul.

Now he knew the reason. She had known she was to die. He was not sure whether to shake her or kiss her. For allowing them so little time, or for giving them the one precious night that had been theirs.

Today, they had won for their clan but not for themselves. As he held her now, his temper eased. The Gift was not easily controlled; quite possibly she had only just known.

Such courage! She had not avoided the battle today, the one he had counseled in ignorance of her fate. She had not spared herself. Her choice to engage in battle today had been a wise decision tactically. A correct choice for their people's future.

But from victory had blossomed tragedy.

Clotted blood streaked Brynna's once-fiery hair where he stroked it. Cairn recalled when her inner fire and charm had set off its russet beauty; he ignored the way it looked now.

"We cannot lose each other. The Wheel turns, Brynna," he said. "Even I know that."

Her palm, callused after weeks of wielding a sword, squeezed his forearm. "I know," she whispered. "We will meet again."

"Did you see this?" he asked in a low voice.

"Yes," she said. "But Cairn, I . . . I will not remember."

So something deeper even than despair colored her words. She knew.

"It cannot be true," he rasped. "Knowledge of the Light is yours. I am only an animal with a sword, a crude man."

"No," she said, her voice sure despite its weakness. "You are much more than that."

In the slumping of her body between his hands, he felt her approaching death. Grief choked his throat as he forced the words out. "We had so little time. I regret only that. Surely the gods will not part us forever?"

Privately he despaired. By the gods, he could not even die with her. He could not risk forgetting by going with her into the Light where their souls would be remade, given new lives. If she, who knew so much more than he, would not remember, he had no chance at all.

He would remain here with her until her soul was gone. Then he would wait the rest of his life for her. *As long as it takes*, he thought fiercely, his hand trembling where it smoothed her hair. If only he knew when he would see her again, if he could only be certain that he would recognize her spirit.

But that certainty was not granted mortals, whose fragile lives were constantly made and remade on the Great Wheel.

"I will not die today, Brynna. I will wait for you." He shifted her gently in his arms. "Do you know . . . when?" he asked, his voice urgent against her hair.

This was near blasphemy. Their people believed

no one knew whom they might become in future. Thus the present life could not be manipulated or tampered with in expectation of future gain.

But in this moment, he dared everything.

"Cairn, I cannot say. I cannot see that far." Somehow with her Gift, she knew what he planned. "You cannot wait for me," she said in alarm.

"I will."

"You cannot defeat the purpose of the Light."

"I do not want to. But I understand this much. We are meant to be together."

"How did you know?" she asked, surprise coloring the remnants of her once-lovely voice.

"That kind of knowledge isn't necessary, my heart. A man knows. I love you," he said, his voice softer than he had ever allowed.

Brynna had hope, then, more than she had ever dared. She had known she was to die, known even that it would be in battle, but had never dared to think their love would survive death.

She had hoped they would be reunited one day, their love strong enough to overcome new lives, and that their souls would seek each other once more. But this was the stuff of dreams, of those who whispered in secret by the fireside at night.

Brynna wanted Cairn for herself, in her secret, well-guarded heart where the woman reigned still over the warrior queen. She had not enough time left to tell him her foolish dreams. Her sight was fading, her breath failing.

But she was not so selfish that she wanted him to die beside her. She strove to speak one last time. "Live, love . . . and remember . . . me."

Cairn bent his head down to Brynna to catch the dying words from her lips. The once-burnished gold strands of his hair mingled with hers, matted and blood-caked, his tears and hers falling freely on her pale cheeks.

The darkness surrounding her parted for a moment. A last ray of sunshine outlined Cairn's head and strong shoulders, the dying sun striking light off his thick, bright hair like a halo.

With her last bit of eyesight, Brynna saw his gray-blue eyes trying to bind her to earth with the force of his will.

For a brief moment, Cairn held her on the threshold. But he knew he could not stop the Power taking her. His strength was only of the earthly, physical kind.

As he watched, her spirit vanished from her green eyes, her body sagging limply in his embrace. He bent over the still form, grief invading his body, his soul.

Holding Brynna against his chest, he saw—felt—the light around them changing. Pure white Light washed over them, impossible from the human perspective, visible only to one who stood between worlds and time.

He balanced on that threshold. Brynna was gone. Perhaps he did not have a choice, but he would act as if he did.

Cairn rose with effort to his feet, pulling Brynna up with him. His ability to stand surprised him, his audacity even more. He struggled to draw breath into his failing lungs.

"No," he said.

14

The Light around him grew, overwhelming, blinding.

"I will wait," he said to the Light, Brynna's still form held protectively against his chest.

It was the last thing he remembered.

Chapter One

Washington, D.C., October 1997

He came to her in dreams. At first there were only his hands, stroking, caressing, gentle. As he aroused her senses and prepared her for his possession, more and more of him came into view. His arms, strong-muscled and dusted with golden hair. His hard, bare torso, sinewy and resilient, the skin bronzed by a life lived largely outdoors. His powerful thighs, gently pressed against her, urging her to open, to cradle him between her legs in a gesture as ancient as it was instinctive.

She could not see past the shadows that were all around them. Darkness shrouded the campsite, but the shadows she sensed were not physical only. They crowded in on dark wings of unease, brushing against her with unwanted foreknowledge.

She refused to focus on them, although she knew what they told her. She had only this night, this one night, to become one with the man she loved more than life itself. For that was what would be required of her. Tomorrow, before the waning of the sun, she would be in his arms again.

Dying.

"No!" Brenna cried, shaking herself free of the dream, her breathing fast and shallow. The wind rattled panes in her bedroom window, moaning around the corners of the old stone apartment building near the Washington Cathedral. She stumbled to the kitchen to fix herself a cup of coffee.

The clock on her wall read five A.M., one hour before the rush hour started in the nation's capital, but still two hours before she normally would have to wake up. Why did she have to wake up completely to escape the dream? Why couldn't she change her dreams, as the books suggested? "Confront your enemies. Turn the dream to your own purpose, and it will no longer become a nightmare."

That had sounded good when she was standing in the bookstore, leafing through books in the large self-help section. But who was the enemy? Certainly not him, whoever he was. Yet the dream came only with a sense of foreboding attached. Sooner or later, no matter how strong, no matter how loving, the fantasy man and the exquisite sensations he produced in her faded before the onslaught of the shadowed night.

Then she would wake up, her body on the edge of a glorious discovery, her mind confused and frightened.

This morning, driving through the crisp air blown in by last night's autumn storm, Brenna Sirin arrived at work, still mulling it over.

She was a journalist. She was a logical, practical person. Frankly, she had never recalled much about her dreams before.

The sensuality and intensity of these dreams, which had begun only recently, were unlike any she had ever known. Perhaps it was the recent change in her love life. Whoever the man was, he was not her fiancé. Make that her ex-fiancé. She had broken up with Jim over the weekend. If she had to dream of someone she'd lost, if her mind wanted her to regret choosing her heart, which had told her he wasn't the right man . . . well, shouldn't her brain have ordered up a dream of Jim?

There was no answer to that, just as there was no answer to the puzzle of the man haunting her sleep and the fear she had of never finding him again.

Coming in early to get a leg up on her article proved to be a failure. "I don't see how I'm going to do this," Brenna said. She shoved a folder into her desk drawer with unnecessary force.

"How you're going to do what, *cara?*" Marina, her friend and colleague, dropped her coat and purse on her desk, turning to face Brenna.

"You know what. This assignment. I don't believe in this stuff," Brenna answered, shoving a mass of reddish-gold hair behind her ears.

"Who said you have to believe in it?" Although Italian, Marina spoke nearly perfect English with a British accent picked up during years of school in London. Certainly Marina's voice was more cultured

18

than Brenna's own slight Southern drawl, even with the occasional mistake.

"I may not have to believe," Brenna amplified, "but I certainly have to write an article if I am going to get paid."

"To get paid," Marina echoed with a cheerful grin. "Anyway, why should you have to believe in anything? You, a tough-boiled magazine writer for one of the country's largest circulation—"

"—metropolitan magazines." Brenna and Marina finished in unison, laughing as they mimicked their editor-in-chief's frequent allusions to their magazine's prominence.

"And, *cara*,"—Brenna grinned back—"it's hard-boiled. Tough and hard-boiled."

"All right. If you were really 'tough and hard-boiled'," Marina said, enunciating with exaggerated care, "you wouldn't be losing sleep over this assignment." As usual the irrepressible Marina was right.

"It isn't the assignment." Brenna swiveled to face her computer screen.

Brenna felt Marina staring at her, even though she turned her profile away from her friend. She refused to meet the sympathetic look she knew would be on Marina's face, preferring to concentrate on the task at hand rather than her personal life, or lack of one.

She didn't need religious beliefs just to write an article. True, she acknowledged to herself, she would never have suggested herself to write about angel sightings for a feature article in the magazine. Especially when her taste ran more to investigative pieces such as why the city government had been so spectacularly ineffective at controlling violence despite strict handgun controls.

Yet their editor, Nora Leonard, deemed this topic important, and Brenna had written many pieces on subjects not of personal interest to her. What bothered her so much about this one? She didn't think the sardonic Nora put any great stock in angel sightings, but you could never tell with Nora. Her editor had explained in her typically cool fashion that the assignment was important because the subject was getting a lot of play in the papers and on TV. The clincher: it was a local story.

Brenna had dawdled uncharacteristically on this project. Nora had assigned her the piece weeks ago when word broke of the hefty advance and huge print run for local author Maud Barrett's book. Once launched, *Angels in Our Air* had provoked an immediate response among the buying public. Brenna had justified her lack of an interview so far by pointing out that the author had appeared on every talk show in the country and had only recently returned to Washington.

Unimpressed with Brenna's reasons, Nora laid down a deadline for the interview. Today. Trouble was, everyone seemed enthralled about the topic but Brenna.

"I don't know why this New Age stuff is so popular," she grumbled, turning back towards Marina. So far today she'd been unable to add a single sentence to her outline. "People who believe in this business kind of scare me, if you want to know."

Marina nodded, her mouth open to speak. The phone ringing shrilly interrupted her next words.

When the continued ringing made it clear the receptionist had vanished on yet another coffee break, Marina answered the phone. Nora hated unanswered phones.

"*Inside City* magazine," Marina said. She switched almost immediately into rapid Italian. One of her relatives, Brenna thought, then caught a phrase in English wafting by. "Thees ees thee Ponte Vecchio ristorante, we no do thee reservation in thee morning," she heard Marina say with the exaggerated accent of an Italian who speaks little English.

"Nice try," Brenna mouthed in English, knowing that answering "Inside City magazine" had already ruined Marina's gambit of trying to confuse the caller.

"It's for you," Marina mouthed back, a finger pointed in Brenna's direction. She drew a line under her chin with a questioning look. *Shall I cut this off for you?* she offered silently.

"Mother?" Brenna asked, still without sound, feeling her empty stomach start to churn. Marina nodded, making a sympathetic face. Brenna matched the slashing motion for "cut" across her own throat, raising her voice in her best restaurant Italian. "*Il conto por favor . . . uh, per favore.*"

She saw Marina roll her eyes at Brenna's Southern-accented Italian that no one would ever mistake for the real thing. Her friend cut off the phone call politely as if the "wrong number" had indeed been the Ponte Vecchio restaurant.

"And you correct my English?" Marina asked in mock outrage at Brenna's request for the check in mangled half-Spanish, half-Italian. "OK, what's go-

21

ing on with your mother this time?"

My fault, Brenna thought, annoyed that she could not hide her feelings from her perceptive friend. "It's this weekend, what else?" she replied, meeting her friend's warm brown gaze.

"Not that again. I thought you were going hiking in the mountains with Jim to avoid another dinner with your parents," Marina said.

"Jim?" Brenna pretended to consider, affecting a facade of unconcern that she doubted would fool her friend. "Let me see. That would be last week's boyfriend, *cara.*"

Marina, doughnut in hand, paused in mid-bite. Brenna knew she adored this junk food, unknown in Italy, for her morning breakfast. "I thought you were engaged."

"I was," Brenna answered, "until Mr. Air Force announced he was on his way to the Philippines and he'd be right back in two years."

Marina looked at her shrewdly. "You didn't want to wait?"

"For what? You know what pilots do on R&R."

"R&R?"

"Rest and recreation. Party time. Manila, Bangkok. Where the girls are easy and don't cost much." Brenna shrugged, hoping the hurt didn't show in her eyes.

"Are you still—what did he tell you—'holding out'?" Marina said, wrinkling her nose in distaste at the expression.

"Yes. I tried to tell him abstinence is 'in' these days. We even ran an article about it recently in the magazine, remember?"

Marina ignored Brenna's attempt at diversion. "Jim doesn't agree with this particular trend, hmm?"

"Well, let's just say I'm not making travel reservations." Brenna reached for her coffee cup, staring into the dark liquid as if it held the answers she sought.

"Are we talking about this 'R&R' or something permanent?" Marina pressed gently.

"The only way I could accompany him on military orders is if we were married. We're not, and he doesn't plan to be, not without 'sampling the merchandise' as he so delicately put it."

"Without what?" It took Marina a moment to figure it out. "Oh, really, what a pig."

"My sentiments exactly."

"*E tua mamma?*"

"My mother, the military wife par excellence? She'd never understand," Brenna said glumly.

"She wouldn't understand that you wouldn't have married Jim, even if he agreed to wait on lovemaking until you were ready?"

Brenna pushed back her thick, curly hair again. She *had* been having second thoughts about Jim recently, but she'd never spoken them aloud. Marina had somehow hit the nail right on the head. "What makes you think that?"

Marina snorted in a most unladylike way. "Please, *bella*, we Italians know love. This isn't it."

Brenna plunked the coffee cup down on the desk. "You're right. Sometimes, though, I feel as if I've been celibate for a thousand years. Like there will never be a Mr. Right. But I decided Mr. Half Right isn't enough."

She got to her feet, slinging a handsome black Prada bag over her shoulder, last year's Christmas gift from Marina. "And now it's time to go interview the half-baked," Brenna said in a last attempt at breeziness. "*Ciao.*"

"Maybe you aren't looking in the right places," Marina called softly after her.

Brenna stopped at the glass door that separated their open area, called the "fishbowl," from the corridor. "What do you mean?"

"Look up," Marina said.

"Things will be looking up, you mean," Brenna corrected automatically.

"No, look up," Marina repeated.

Across the space dividing them, Brenna stared back. "What for?"

"To see the angels." Marina grinned.

Brenna blew out her cheeks in exasperation, pushing the heavy doors open with one hand.

Remnants of last night's storm, like the turbulent residue of her argument with Jim, seemed to cling to Brenna. The wind whipped wildly around the car as she barreled up the George Washington Parkway in Virginia, shaking the little compact car. The folder of clippings threatened to slip off the seat and onto the floor of the passenger side.

No matter. She had read all the articles about Maud Barrett anyway. This angel business was not her style. She had other things to worry about. Was the nagging feeling right, the one that had whispered at her, saying Jim wasn't the one? She was almost thirty, and the biological clock she had denied possessing had started ticking relentlessly.

She had never found the right man. Something had always held her back. She didn't know why it was so hard for her to open up, to trust people. Especially men. After all, she'd never been "done wrong" or had her heart "stomped flat," as the songs had it. Before Jim, she'd never let a man get close enough to really affect her life when he left or they broke up. It scared her in a basic, fundamental way she didn't want to think about, the idea of being so close to someone that his departure or loss would break her heart.

Dragging her thoughts away from the unproductive track they'd taken, Brenna tried to focus on the task at hand. She had to interview the woman whose recent book claimed that an encounter with an angel had changed her life.

Not only had Maud Barrett lived to tell about it, she was raking in a nice profit as well, Brenna thought cynically, then felt suddenly ashamed at the thought. Living in Washington did this to a person—turned her jaded and cynical after a while. She didn't want to fall victim to the "insider's syndrome."

She reached for the foam-bottomed commuter mug, taking a swig of coffee. She hadn't been in the office long enough for the dregs to get cold, such had been Nora's ever-so-tactful insistence to Brenna to "get your butt in gear and get on the road." With September gone, Nora wanted the article wrapped up in plenty of time for the December issue.

As she drove, Brenna tried not to clench her jaw, remembering her dentist's latest injunction. "Now, Ms. Sirin," he'd said, "if you keep this up, I'll have to make you a night guard. You're wearing down your enamel, grinding your teeth at night. Do you have trouble sleeping?"

She hadn't responded to that. Her strange dreams caused the grinding, she was sure, but she'd admitted to only the usual Washington complaint, a hectic lifestyle and too much stress.

Brenna checked the address for the third time, wondering if Maud Barrett had bought the house in ritzy McLean before or after her book hit the best-seller list.

Two minutes later Brenna answered her own question. *Before*, she decided, pulling into the circular driveway. Definitely before. This was no McMansion, six thousand square feet of pseudo-Colonial on an eight thousand-square-foot lot, where two-foot trees and tiny shrubs instantly proclaimed the newness of the house. New money, those houses shouted.

No, this was old money. Old money and good taste. A wide expanse of lawn discreetly recessed the pale yellow brick Colonial from the road. Massive hollies, magnolias, and pines at least eighty years old further screened the place from curious eyes.

Brenna walked up the driveway, the quiet atmosphere putting her in a curiously relaxed frame of mind. The unusual peevishness dropped from her like a stone. Even the brisk October wind didn't reach in here. Brenna experienced a wild urge to take off the low-heeled half-boots she wore with her tailored wool trousers and let her toes sink into the deep, rich grass of the sumptuous lawn.

Ridiculous, she told herself. Abandoned and sensuous gestures were not Brenna Lindsay Sirin's style. She owned no high heels, nor feather boas. If she'd been sexier, more adventurous, wouldn't she have had lovers by now? The phrases echoed in her head, a composite of male voices over the years who'd called her quiet refusals "teasing" and claimed she'd "led them on." But they hadn't been leading her anywhere she wanted to go. It wasn't that she was against making love; she simply hadn't found the right man yet. And that included Jim.

Brenna straightened her shoulders defensively as she neared the large double doors. Those men had never stuck around long enough to see her cry over a hurt puppy, stood beside her when Handel's Hallelujah Chorus made her skin tingle with emotion, or offered a handkerchief when she cried at the end of *Casablanca* during its annual showing at a Georgetown theater.

She knew emotion ran deeply in her, but she'd begun to wonder about passion. After the way things had turned out with Jim, she questioned whether she was truly capable of it. When they'd argued and she broke off the engagement, he too had called her a prude.

Something must have shown on her face, something in her expression she couldn't quite control. When Maud Barrett opened the door, her first words revealed a shrewd intuition.

"Come in, Ms. Sirin," the older woman said. "The day will improve, I promise you."

Brenna couldn't contain her surprise. Maud Barrett bore no resemblance to the flighty New Age type Brenna had imagined. She looked like a typical

McLean matron, well mannered, well tailored, her face and figure well kept.

A subtle combination of brown and gold highlights graced her elegantly styled hair. Her unlifted face showed good living, only a hint of age around her eyes. Pale pink pearls glowed softly at her throat, while her pink-and-black woven wool suit completed the quietly elegant look.

She laughed, gesturing to Brenna to follow her through the mansion's marble-tiled foyer. "What did you expect me to be wearing?" she asked lightly. "A flowing robe?"

Knowing her expression must look guilty, Brenna tried to mumble something polite.

"Come this way, Ms. Sirin. We'll sit on the porch."

The porch turned out to be a slate-tiled room surrounded by floor-to-ceiling glass windows and filled with white wicker furniture topped by deep green cushions. The wind blew a set of Pipes of Olympus around outside, the deep tones more pleasant than the usual tinkly wind chimes.

Over tea and shortcake offered by a housekeeper, Brenna donned her best mantle of professional detachment. "Ms. Barrett, your book says that you owe your life to the intervention of an angel. Were you always religious?"

"No, and one doesn't have to be," Maud Barrett replied, her hand just touching the warm pink pearls at her throat.

"How so?" Brenna asked in what she hoped was a neutral tone.

"Since my experience, and the ones I detailed in my book, I've come to believe that angels are a universal phenomenon. The sightings occur across time, across cultures. Angels have important roles in the Jewish and Muslim religions as well as in Christianity. They appear to people who haven't been to church or temple in twenty years, or ever."

"Why do you believe you encountered an angel?"

"Because it could have been nothing else." Brenna cast around in her mind for the proof Maud Barrett had offered in her book, but could remember nothing concrete. She was relieved when the older woman began to describe her experience.

Maud's voice took on a fervent note, and Brenna paid closer attention. ". . . then I looked up," Maud was saying. "I saw the light in the sky. I saw wings. In my research, I found a great similarity among stories. A sense of peace and wonder, the glow of light, the sweep of wings. We all share some knowledge of this at a basic level, no matter who we are or where we come from. The encounter is like some of the near-death experiences. Are you familiar with them?"

Brenna, who had heard one of the first authors on this subject while in college, nodded. Her skepticism about such things had increased over the years, while her ability to believe declined drastically. As a student, she remembered excitement and enthusiasm after Dr. Weiss's talk. Now her memory was clouded by reports of the fake shamanism, channeling, crystal readings, and other manifestations of a society grasping desperately to find meaning in the approaching millennium.

"I know what you mean, but believe me, once you've crossed paths with an angel, you will never be the same," Maud said. "I come from a privileged background, as you can see."

She gestured self-deprecatingly around the elegant room. "I'd spent my life in genteel projects, charity balls where we raised money for noble causes, pretending that was the reason we held these black-tie affairs and bought three-thousand-dollar gowns. But since my encounter with angels, I found myself dissatisfied with all that. I volunteer my time now with the Samaritans."

Brenna nodded. The Samaritans were a nation-wide hot line for those contemplating suicide. Funny, she didn't recall seeing that in any of the articles about Maud Barrett.

"I've been hesitant to discuss it, because I didn't want to be written up as another rich woman dabbling in helpful projects. I'm not sure why I'm telling you now. I will sound even more self-serving if I tell you all my profits from the book are going to the Samaritans. So I haven't told you. This is just between the two of us, all right?"

Brenna found herself agreeing to something reporters never agreed to: keeping an important nugget of news confidential. But she understood Maud's position and sympathized. Celebrity involvement sometimes had a way of turning into more than a volunteer organization could handle. Publicizing Maud's involvement with the Samaritans could backfire, since the hot line pledged anonymity to the troubled people who called it.

Maud smiled, then thanked Brenna for her discretion. The conversation turned back to the topic of angel sightings. Despite her respect for the changes

Maud had made in her life, Brenna understood the woman's tenacious belief in angels no better now than when she'd arrived.

"The approach of the millennium may account for the angel-sighting phenomenon. We're either looking harder, or perhaps they're appearing more often. My dear . . ." Maud reached out to touch Brenna's arm in a friendly gesture.

The older woman drew back instantly, her voice faltering only a little as she finished the description of her own encounter with an angel. Brenna was so unnerved by Maud's reaction that she missed half of it. Had Maud sensed something strange about Brenna?

". . . so you must believe me when I say that I would have careened right off the road and into the telephone pole if I hadn't seen the Light."

"The Light?" Brenna asked, wondering why her heart pounded and the image of a blazing wheel in the sky popped into her mind. She never daydreamed during an interview. What was wrong with her today?

"You *do* remember," the older woman declared with an air of gentle triumph.

"Remember what?"

"Didn't you feel it when I touched you?"

"What?"

"Your past lives. Your love for him."

"Oh, please, Ms. Barrett," Brenna said, disappointed. She shut her notebook and brushed a stray curl off her forehead. "Is it such a short step from angels to channeling? I didn't think you were into all that New Age stuff."

31

"I'm no Shirley MacLaine, Ms. Sirin," Maud said, a bit stiffly. "I'm just a good old-fashioned Episcopalian. My church barely recognizes saints. Finds them rather embarrassing, in fact, along with all the other trappings of the old church. But I've also learned enough to admit how little I know about the spiritual realm. You'd be well advised to do the same."

Brenna rose, certain she'd antagonized her subject. Damned unprofessional of her, and after Maud had confided in her, too. For some reason she couldn't summon much guilt. The incident had unsettled her, badly, and she was by no means a skittish person. Right now she felt only a rising sense of panic, a need to run before something—someone—caught up with her. Someone who might break her well-guarded heart.

"I'm just a reporter, Ms. Barrett," she said, striving for detachment. "What I believe doesn't matter. I'm only here for the story."

They walked in silence to the front hall. At the door, Brenna paused. "I'm sorry if I've been rude. I didn't mean to be."

"It's all right. You're only fighting yourself, not me," Maud said calmly.

Brenna quirked a brow, knowing skepticism showed openly on her face.

"You've been waiting a long time, my dear, not knowing what you were searching for," Maud said. "And he has sought you for so long. I think the end of this millennium does mean something, even if it's not trumpets and the last call. No one can know that.

32

But for you two, at least, I don't think there'll be another chance."

Brenna gazed wide-eyed at Maud, until the housekeeper arrived with her coat and broke the spell.

"Thank you for your time, Ms. Barrett," Brenna said formally, reaching to shake the other woman's hand with trepidation, wondering if it would set her off again.

"You don't have a lot of time, dear." Maud's voice had taken on the same urgent note it had when she'd touched Brenna's arm on the porch. "You'll have to be open to hear what you need to hear, receptive to see what you must see."

She released Brenna's hand abruptly, her eyes clear and focused again. "I'm sorry. I've never spoken to anyone that way before. There's just something . . . I felt when I touched you."

"I'm sure." Brenna smiled grimly, politely, waiting for the story of some thousand-year-old Egyptian for whom Maud was the channeler to emerge as the woman's latest mystical experience. When Maud continued to look puzzled by her remarks, Brenna stepped onto the front walkway.

"Good-bye, Ms. Barrett," she said, heading for the car. She shook her head, trying hard to dismiss Maud's look of utter conviction as she'd told Brenna a man existed whom she had once loved and now must find. It was too ridiculous to contemplate, she told herself firmly, trying to suppress the curious thrill of apprehension and excitement that raced up her spine at the thought.

The brisk wind swirled around her in gleeful rediscovery as she exited the sheltered lawn. Halloween wasn't for another couple of weeks. Then why, Brenna wondered, did she feel as if someone had just walked over her grave?

Chapter Two

"We had ta jump from the burning building," the short, balding man across from Brenna said earnestly in his strong Brooklyn accent. "I wouldn't have made it inta the net if the angel hadn't pushed me."

Brenna wrote, "angel pushed," then looked at Arthur Walker again. His tidy, modest house in Arlington was a far cry from the tasteful luxury of Maud Barrett's, although it was not far away. It had taken Brenna less than fifteen minutes to get there.

Art Walker's down-to-earth statements didn't sound like the words of a man whose life had been forever altered. Even his little house was down-to-earth. Decorated in brown and navy blue, the rambler displayed a man's taste. Brenna remembered from her notes that Arthur Walker was retired and a widower.

Yet there was something of Maud's fervency about him. Beneath the modest, unassuming surface, a quiet assurance lurked. He had been touched by Fate, reprieved from death. Like Maud, he seemed to have made the most of it. A retired bookie from New York, Art Walker now volunteered almost every day at Martha's Table, a food service for the poor and homeless in Washington. On weekends, he joined the teenage girls and blue-haired elderly ladies as a volunteer at Arlington Hospital.

"Ah, the angel pushed you where, Mr. Walker?" she asked, knowing that while she would write up Art Walker's activities, she would respect Maud's desire to remain anonymous.

"Why, pushed me inta the fireman's net, of course," he said.

"The firemen held a net out for you and the other people on the tenth floor?" Brenna clarified as she scribbled notes.

"That's right."

"So you would have dropped into it anyway."

Mr. Walker took no offense at her statement. "No, that's the thing. I'd jumped out kinda wild, like. I wasn't headed for the net. I was way off ta the side. I would've missed it and probably ended up smack all over the pavement. Then I felt it."

"What did you feel, Mr. Walker?" Brenna asked, dreading what was coming.

"That hand. I felt a push, a gentle shove like, and I knew I was on target right inta the net again." He nodded his head for emphasis; wisps of his balding hair, combed over to one side, fell out of place.

"How did you know the push came from an angel?" Brenna asked, dutifully noting "angel's hand" on her pad.

"Well . . . well, I dunno exactly. I just knew I'd been helped, and when I heard about Maud Barrett—well, I knew that's what happened ta me too."

"Did you see a light, a halo, wings?"

"I saw a kinda light around me, I think, but I didn't see nobody. Nothing I recognized anyway. But I felt this strength, this sense I wasn't gonna die, ya know? That it wasn't my time."

"Well, thank you for your time, Mr. Walker. I appreciate it." Brenna shut her notebook and, rising to her feet, rolled her eyes while she still faced away from Art Walker. How could she write up his vague, but certainly heartfelt, declarations in any way that made sense?

She turned to face him. Now came the part where Mr. Walker would make strange pronouncements, as Maud Barrett had.

But Arthur Walker escorted her to the front door without another word. She stuck her hand out, expecting visionary transports and warnings once he touched her.

Absolutely nothing happened. A polite smile curved Mr. Walker's thin lips.

"Thank you again, Mr. Walker," Brenna said, relieved yet strangely disappointed. "You can expect to see the article in the December issue of *Inside City*." She looked at him curiously a moment, but only mild interest lit his faded brown eyes.

"That's nice, Miz Sirin. I'll look forward ta it. Good-bye now." And he shut the door to his little brick house, leaving Brenna on the stoop with questions racing through her mind.

Arthur Walker hadn't said anything like Maud Barrett had. Maybe she didn't attract crazies after all, Brenna thought. Maybe Maud was the only one with a screw loose. Yet Brenna couldn't bring herself to believe Maud was a charlatan. A crackpot maybe, but sincere.

Brenna resolutely forced her mind away from the puzzle of Ms. Barrett and her strange belief in angels and past lives. Half-baked—wasn't that what Brenna had said to Marina only this morning? That made her think of food. She consulted the clock on her dashboard, whose digital face indicated noon. Yes, she was definitely hungry.

She sighed, keeping her eyes peeled for a Chesapeake Bagel Bakery as she wound through Arlington on her way to south Alexandria. She hadn't eaten a single one of Marina's beloved doughnuts this morning. Besides, she wanted her friend to try something healthier, such as bagels.

Brenna looked at her list of interviewees again, noticing idly that they all lived in Virginia or the District of Columbia. Weren't there any angel-watchers in Maryland?

By the time Brenna returned to the office late that afternoon, she felt drained and just as unconvinced as she'd been that morning.

"None of these people can describe clearly what they saw," she told Marina. "They felt a 'presence.' Saw a 'light' or an 'unearthly glow.' One or two think they saw wings. But they're all sure an angel kept them from going off the road, or pushed them into the safety net, or made them look up in time to see the tower begin to fall. . . ."

"Why do they think they saw—umm, felt—an angel there with them?" Marina asked.

"That's the problem. They just 'know' they did." Brenna's voice reflected her frustration. She considered herself a pragmatist who liked to see, touch, and taste before she accepted things.

"Every one of these people has had one of those 'sixth sense' moments where you look before the tray hits the floor, or the vase falls off the table, that kind of thing. Heck, that's even happened to me. I asked them if this was like that. Yet they all insisted this wasn't the same thing. They were all sure they had experienced the presence or the intervention of an angel."

"Aren't we all supposed to have guardian angels?" Marina asked.

"Well, that's one theory, but none of these were particularly religious people. None of them ever thought they'd been near an angel before. In the case of Agnes Veer, a woman I saw this afternoon, she doesn't even believe in God. Now she believes in angels."

"I'll bet she does." Marina hesitated. Brenna looked at her sharply.

"Listen, *cara,* your mother called three more times. Saying you're out interviewing goes only so far with her, even when it's true."

"Used it too many times, have I?" Brenna smiled, knowing from the stiff muscles of her face that it didn't reach her eyes. No one could be as irritating as her mother when she chose to be, especially when she scented trouble in Brenna's love life.

Marina grunted noncommittally. "Why don't you have dinner with me Saturday instead of going to your parents'?"

"And ruin your out-of-town date? No way."

"Vincenzo is a cousin on my father's side. He's family. Anyway, he just lives in New York. He comes here all the time. You wouldn't be in the way."

"Listen to you. As if he comes from New York every weekend. No, Marina, that's not fair to you. Just because I no longer have a social life doesn't mean I'll horn in on yours."

Marina wrinkled her nose. "Horn in?"

"Interrupt, be in the way," Brenna clarified. "No, I'll go to my mother's. She'll have to find out about Jim some time. I want to see Daddy anyway."

Brenna reached for the phone reluctantly, letting her hair tumble over her cheek as she dialed so Marina wouldn't see her expression. "I wish I could interview the other people for the article this weekend," she muttered.

"*Dio*, but you are desperate," Marina commented.

"Umm-hmm," Brenna agreed. Then she directed her attention to the phone.

"Mother? It's Brenna. Yes, I have been out all day. Yes, interviewing. Yes, just like Marina said. What? The number for that new Italian restaurant?"

Brenna shoved curls out of her eyes, glancing pointedly at Marina. "I've no idea. Why?"

Choking with laughter, Marina fled.

"I'll be there at six-thirty," Brenna answered as patiently as she knew how. "How's Daddy? OK, see you then." She almost thought she'd made it through the conversation safely when another question emerged.

"No, Jim won't be able to make it," Brenna said. "I'll tell you when I get there."

Feeling anything but patient, she heard her mother out. "I said I'll tell you when I get there, Mother. Yes. Good-bye," she said stiffly.

Now would be a good time for this mystery man to find me, Brenna thought flippantly. Anything to distract her mother from the grim news—as far as Peggy Sirin was concerned—that Brenna was not about to marry the up-and-coming young Air Force officer her mother deemed so suitable.

Brenna spent most of Saturday at the Library of Congress, researching her article. Although she had taken her habitual morning run down Wisconsin Avenue past the National Cathedral, she hadn't found the sight of the towers of the grand Church as comforting as usual. Always before the stone building had reminded her of the solidity of faith that had built it, faith she didn't necessarily have to share to appreciate.

This morning, however, it had seemed like some looming sentinel. It reminded her of her strange week, her own unanswered questions, the odd but unshakable convictions of those she'd interviewed. So she fled into the safe confines of the womb of knowledge, where reason always ruled.

Dutifully, she started with angel sightings. She had read most of these articles before, so she scanned the pages of microfilm quickly. Then, remembering Maud's comments, she moved on to near-death experiences. Finally, on a whim, she looked under the heading "Millennium."

Brenna found more than she expected. What she hadn't known when she tossed in "millennium" as a search term was that according to some astronomers' reckoning, the turn of the century would actually occur in January 1998.

The strange convergence of planets, which many scientists believed was the astronomical explanation for the Star of Bethlehem, had actually occurred after what was called 1 A.D. These scientists claimed that the entire Christian calendar had been based on an incorrect dating of the birth of Christ. January 1998—a few short months away, not a few years—would usher in the third millennium A.D., according to these calculations.

Brenna remembered Maud's words about the millennium and time running out. A chill trickled down her spine. Then another shiver wracked her, this one tracing teasingly up her back like the dancing fingers of a lover's touch.

The microfiche blurred in front of her eyes. In her dream, there had been so little time. Her lover was tender yet urgent, driven by forces she didn't understand. *"So little time . . ."* Had he whispered that in her ear, tracing the sensitive curve of it with light, flicking touches of his tongue?

That does it, she thought, shutting down the microfilm reader and gathering up the microfiches. Even dinner at her parents' offered a better way to spend time than this. When her fantasies about her love life were better than reality, she figured she was in trouble.

*   *   *

Armed with a bouquet of flowers, Brenna turned up at her parents' door in Georgetown several hours later. Knowing her father's penchant for military precision—shared by her mother, the perfect military wife—she tried to arrive at 6:30 p.m.

Tried and, as usual, failed.

"Hi, Mom," she said, hoping the breezy greeting would forestall criticism.

She needn't have bothered. "You're late," her mother said, reaching for the flowers.

"Traffic," Brenna said, trying to suppress the special irritation that her mother always seemed able to rouse with a single sentence.

She barely heard her mother's belated thanks for the flowers because she spotted her father. "Dad! How are you?"

George Sirin strode forward, his hair as white as snow and as handsome as ever. Although her mother kept her hair a careful blond, never allowing gray to show, Brenna always thought her father looked incredibly distinguished now that his hair had turned completely white.

At seventy, he still possessed the bright blue eyes of a boy. Unfortunately, his personality had lately become somewhat childlike, too. Since her mother refused to have her father tested for Alzheimer's disease, there was no way of knowing for sure the cause of his increasing forgetfulness.

At his age, her mother claimed—twelve years separated her parents—a little forgetfulness shouldn't cause undue alarm. Brenna worried that her mother's attempts to hold back the tide of old age

43

might do her father more harm than good someday, but she held her tongue. Arguing with her mother always upset her father, because it put him in the middle.

"How's my favorite daughter?" he asked, enfolding her in a tight hug.

"You're such a charmer, Dad. I'm your only daughter." Brenna kissed his cheek.

"But still my favorite," he agreed with a wink. "Now where's that Air Force so-and-so you're planning to marry? Heard a good one the other day."

Her father, a retired Army general, delighted in needling Jim with jokes about the intelligence of jet jockeys and their penchant for fast planes and fast women. Brenna had already heard his latest joke half a dozen times, but for her father's sake, she would listen to it again.

As he finished, George looked around for Jim, obviously hoping to see the younger man's reaction.

"Jim's not here tonight, Daddy," she said.

"George, I told you that already," her mother said, untying her apron as she stood in the kitchen doorway.

"You didn't tell me the joke, Peggy. I heard it from Bob last month."

"No, not that," Peggy said with some exasperation. "I told you Brenna said Jim wasn't coming tonight."

"Oh." Her father looked lost for a minute, then turned to pinch Brenna's cheek. "On a deployment, is he?"

"No." Brenna took a deep breath. "Let's sit down and have dinner, OK? Then I'll tell you both."

Her mother summoned her to help put food on the table, while her father sat in the dining room, chuckling to himself occasionally. Presumably it was his joke he still laughed over, Brenna thought, but her heart contracted just the same.

Oh, Daddy, don't go away from us, she thought. By the time she finished telling an edited version of her breakup with Jim, her mother was fuming, her father was confused, and Brenna wanted only to escape the unwanted attention.

"What do you mean, you won't travel?" her mother demanded.

"That's not exactly what I said, Mother. I said I like my job."

"I'm sure you could find a job in the Philippines."

"Not as a reporter." Brenna knew her mother believed a good military wife made do with her lot, whether she liked it or.

"Mother, I don't think you helped put me through journalism school for me to work as a stock clerk in the post exchange."

"A military wife does whatever she has to, just as I did to follow your father."

Brenna had heard this a thousand times, and while she admired her mother's devotion and sacrifice, times had changed.

She knew the story by heart. Her mother had been poised on the brink of a brilliant modeling career. She gave it all up to accompany her father to an Army base deep in the Midwest. There, to hear her mother tell it, the latest fashion consisted of a new gingham apron.

Once Brenna came along, working had been out of the question. They had moved from Army bases all over the country to overseas and back. At about five years old, Brenna's own memories filled in the story.

Memories of settling in, adjusting, making friends, then moving again. Over and over. Brenna sympathized with her mother, but wished sometimes that Peggy Sirin remembered how hard moving had been on Brenna, too.

"Maybe I don't want to be a military wife, Mother," Brenna burst out when her mother paused. She had gone too far this time, she realized, watching silent tears start in her mother's eyes. Her father's mouth hung open slightly, working soundlessly as he tried to find a formula that would satisfy both women, and failing.

"Maybe you don't love anything enough to give up your own selfish life," her mother said, setting down the coffee cup in its saucer hard enough to make the wafer-thin porcelain tremble.

Regret fled Brenna's heart. Hurt and anger rushed in. She clenched her teeth hard to keep the words behind them. *Not in front of Daddy,* she thought, seeing how distressed he looked. *Not in front of Daddy.*

Her father reached out to pat her hand. "Nobody said you had to marry a military man, sweetie. We'd be just as happy to keep you right here with us, wouldn't we, Peggy?"

"Of course," said her mother, rising to remove the coffee cups, her figure the same slim size eight it had been all those years ago when the magazines had called her the "find of 1959." Brenna, who was a size ten with an occasional twelve necessary around the holidays, couldn't help but admire her mother's iron will when it came to self-indulgence.

Peggy took the tray into the kitchen, her posture ramrod-straight, her face stiff. The tap came on with a blast. Sounds of washing-up followed.

Shut out again. Brenna sighed. "I'd better help her with the dishes, Daddy."

"No, sit with me a minute, Brennabear," he said, using her childhood nickname. They sat, fingers loosely intertwined while Brenna tried to figure just how she and her mother always set each other off so quickly.

Her father started in on another long, rambling story about his experiences in World War II. Brenna listened with half an ear. ". . . and I don't think he'd work out any better," her father concluded, reaching for the wine goblet her mother had already removed from the table. His fingers closed on empty air before he looked to see why his hand was empty.

"Who wouldn't work out?" Brenna focused her attention on her father's face, handsome despite the inevitable sagging and wrinkles of age.

"Jim, honey. I don't think the two of you were any more suited than that master sergeant I inherited when I had my first platoon. That was the point of the story I just told you. You stick to your guns, sweetheart."

George patted her hand. "If Jim won't take you on your terms, don't think you have to meet his. That's what your mother always regretted."

"What did Mother regret, Daddy?" Brenna asked. Through the years, her father had never once spoken of the time her mother mentioned with such regret.

"She had to give it all up before she knew what she had. In those days women didn't work much, you

47

know. She could never have kept up that kind of career once she got pregnant. But she never got the chance to find out how good she could have been. It changed her, honey. I know you and your mother have these little spats, but you should have seen her. She was a high-spirited young thing in those days."

"What did I get from her?" Brenna asked quietly, knowing she was too level-headed and cautious to ever be called high-spirited. Nor did she own the mildly flirtatious manner of a woman who has every confidence in her attractiveness. A self-confidence her mother still quietly exuded.

In her dream, she hadn't worried about being attractive. . . . Brenna pushed the stray thought back, squeezing her father's hand.

"From your mother? You inherited the ability to think, and wonder, and regret," he said slowly. Brenna pulled her hand away from his, hurt, but her father caught it again, holding it with a strength she hadn't felt from him in years.

"Don't get me wrong, Brennabear. I only meant that you always look first before you leap. You examine every option and try to figure out where it will lead. It's made you a first-class reporter. But I don't know if it's always made you happy."

That led her back to Jim again. "You think it's something in me, Daddy?"

"No, no. I want you to be happy with yourself. You don't need to traipse halfway around the world after a man."

"You didn't want me to marry Jim?" Brenna asked, wondering why her father had decided to tell her this only now.

48

"You're as stubborn as your mother, hon. You would have gone through with it just for that, thinking it would make us happy?" He peered at her. "Good, I didn't think so. I didn't raise you on war stories for nothin', you know."

He mussed her hair in an old gesture. "It would have been fine if you'd married Jim. If that's what you really wanted. But there's someone else you're waiting for."

Brenna held her breath, but George said nothing more. The expression in his eyes retreated into the vagueness she had learned to hate, the uncertainty that meant he had lost his train of thought.

They sat in silence a little while longer. George Sirin patted her hand once more before releasing it. "Go help your mother in the kitchen before she complains about doing all the work herself," he said, as if he'd forgotten that he'd asked her to sit with him.

By the time the women finished, her father was deep into another complicated World War II anecdote. "Who's he talking to, Mother?" Brenna asked, peeping through the wooden shuttered door that separated the kitchen from the dining room.

"Who knows?" Her mother shrugged, untying her apron. "Better them than me. They have longer attention spans than I do."

The thought of her father talking to dead comrades made Brenna sad. Knowing it would be useless to start another argument with her mother about having her father tested for Alzheimer's, she asked what news Peggy had received from her friends overseas, other loyal Army wives like her mother whose

49

husbands hadn't yet retired.

Her mother's face brightened immediately, as Brenna had known it would, and they ended the visit on an amicable note.

Chapter Three

The Scottish Highlands, 1760

Cairn heard a crash, saw the woodland creatures scatter from the clearing where he hovered near a swiftly running stream. He dropped the heather he had been examining. One sweep of his massive wings brought him next to the girl's limp body near the stream. An empty water bucket lolled at her feet.

Had she seen him? Cairn wondered. He chastised himself. Did girls faint in the heather every day? Of course she had seen him.

What was he doing here anyway? He had been drawn here, drifting from place to place without thinking much about what he did. He was repeatedly drawn to Celtic lands, like those where he had been born. He and Brynna. He was not far from that area now.

Cairn looked more closely at the girl. Something about *her* drew him, too. She had red hair, streaked with gold, wrapped in long braids and pinned across the top of her head. Wild hope flared suddenly in his heart. Could it be, at last, after his waiting and watching, the long years of fervent hoping?

A hundred Scottish girls had red hair, he reminded himself. Probably ninety of them had eyes of hazel or green. He couldn't know for certain until she was awake, until he looked into those eyes. Looked beyond her present to see into her soul . . . assuming that he could, as Rapha-el had assured him so long ago.

He remembered the words first spoken to him by the Archangel Rapha-el when Cairn regained consciousness, wondering where and especially *what* he now was. Cairn had hovered in the air, massive wings moving without his volition to keep him aloft.

The unbearably beautiful being beside him spoke. "You were granted a special dispensation because your vow, your determination, moved us all." Rapha-el's beauty and power were unearthly, yet his face was remarkably human. He was the Healing Angel, he informed Cairn, and had the most contact with humans.

"But this search is yours. We cannot find her for you," Rapha-el had continued. "Your time is limited. We cannot sustain you indefinitely, for you are not truly one of us. Moreover, the Adversary is no fool. He seeks always to undermine our work, and what we have allowed you skirts the edge of the rules governing all. Should he learn of you, there will be trouble."

Cairn did not yet know who the Adversary was, but a chill ran through him at the words.

Rapha-el's face was stern and magnificent but no longer human when he made a final pronouncement. "No one can exist as you do, between worlds, belonging to none. We cannot protect you forever, Cairn, unless you become one of us."

They had flown then, Cairn testing his wings, up and up, beyond the realm of sky into the stars. "Nor can you exist as a man indefinitely," Rapha-el resumed, when the first blaze of wonder at his wings had subsided in Cairn. "That kind of power over the flesh is the bargain only those Below can strike."

Cairn looked at him uncomprehendingly. "The Faustian bargain," Rapha-el elaborated. "Selling your soul for longer life." Cairn did not yet know who Faust was either, but the shudder of revulsion that ran through Rapha-el similarly affected Cairn.

For an instant, he saw a vision of a Pit. Darkness engulfed his sight; unremitting despair filled his spirit. He heard the wailing of millions of trapped souls. His wings faltered.

"Stay with me," Rapha-el intoned, his voice deep. The image vanished. Cairn saw the welcome sight of stars again, anchored to the present reality by Rapha-el's gaze.

Rapha-el turned to look at Cairn as they moved ever upward, his silver eyes unearthly, intense. He gestured around him. "Those falling stars you used to marvel at in the night sky? Never think them a pretty sight again."

He reached out for Cairn, clasping his forearm. "Each time you see one, an angel falls from grace.

They follow the path of Lucifer, the Morning Star, once one of the brightest Lights."

Rapha-el released Cairn, who breathed again. With renewed breath came memory. The memories spilled out whole and terrible. And with them came pain, a blinding stroke stronger than any headache he had ever had.

Forged in the white-hot crucible of extremity and need, he remembered every scent, every sound, every touch. The night they had spent in each other's arms, the death that was not death but glory, the sharing that linked their bodies as closely as their hearts had already been.

His breath caught in his throat, remembering the day that followed, the death that was the end of life, the sundering of their bond, the separation. She was the reason he still lived. As he had vowed, he lived only to find her again.

"Brynna!" He flung her name into the heavens, an anguished cry that echoed off the moon and ricocheted from star to star. Earth itself might have heard his cry, but Rapha-el stopped him with one sentence.

"Her soul has not yet been reborn."

Cairn clenched his hand on Rapha-el's shoulder. He saw her lifeless body, remembered her last words, her last breath. His flame-haired, brave, loyal Brynna.

"I will find you," he had shouted then, not caring if his cry carried to the highest Heaven, where the angels chanted unceasingly in the presence of the Light.

* * *

Cairn shook off the pall of memory, staring at the girl lying on the ground in the chill October day. While he waited for her to come around, he could at least fill her water bucket.

Cairn swept up the bucket, hovered over the stream to fill it, then brought it back to rest at her side with a few motions of his wings. He would return it, and return her, too, to her cottage if he knew its location.

He wondered whether he could do anything to revive her. She murmured, moving on the leaves he had blown under her with his wings to cushion her. Cairn squatted at her side, adopting a soldier's posture of absolute vigilance. He would wait here all day if necessary. What was a day compared to the time that had gone by already?

He thought he had enough stamina to stay on earth for a day. The pain that had accompanied his strange transformation was never completely gone, but he had learned to master it for longer and longer periods.

The girl blinked, started to sit up. Cairn reached out a hand, then wondered if he could, or should.

He sucked in a deep breath, expelled it. There was only one way to find out how he interacted with ordinary folk. He put one hand behind her shoulders to help raise her. She felt warm, lithe. How many hundred years had it been since he had touched another human being?

She screamed in shock, alarming him. Her eyes started to roll back in her head. "Do not fear me, lass," he said. The Gaelic of this time was different from his own, but she seemed to understand what he said.

"Wh . . . what are you?" she asked in a shaking voice, her head on her knees as if she lacked the strength to look at him. Did she *fear* to look at him? Cairn dreaded the answer to that, so he concentrated on being pleased that this understanding of languages worked both ways.

He had not mastered the art of reading minds and did not know what she thought, but her emotions were not hard to read. Not for the first time, he wished for even a smidgen of Rapha-el's abilities.

Remembering his own initial shock on learning what he had become, awed by his own massive wings, he was not certain how to answer her. "I am a friend," he said finally.

Her head started to come up slowly. "Ye are the largest faery ever I have seen, if 'tis what you are in truth," she said.

Cairn remained silent, willing her eyes to meet his. He shook his head. He knew stories of faeries frequenting the glens, and no, he certainly was not one. "No, I am not a creature of magic," he said. At least, not as she thought of it, he added silently to himself.

She was getting bolder now. Slowly her gaze scanned his garments, lingered at his bare feet under his robe, then darted to his back where his folded wings lay motionless.

"Are . . . are ye a devil come to tempt me?" she asked.

"Why would you say that?"

"Because ye are handsome as sin and 'tis not right."

"What isn't?" he asked, growing more bewildered by the moment.

"How ye make me feel. My breath is short, I can't think straight, I . . . I want to touch you, I . . ." Her strong young voice had returned and was definitely irritated. She broke off, glaring at him.

"Look at me, Brynna," he said.

Her head jerked up at the sound. "Brianna I am," she said. "How did you know . . ." Her voice died as she looked him full in the face.

Clear green eyes gazed back at Cairn. He needed longer to look at them, because at first glance he saw only dark gray-green rimming the lovely green irises. He needed to see more deeply than that.

"You must be the devil," she cried, jumping up. Backing up, she moved backward until she bumped into her full water bucket. "Look at that," she cried. "You want to seduce me by helping carry water. I've heard that tale many a time."

So had he, Cairn realized upon reflection. The Evil One would often strike a bargain to help someone carry a heavy load. Someone far from home, alone in the woods.

"Why would you think I want to hurt you?" he said.

"I dinna think you want to hurt me," she said in a surprisingly thoughtful voice, stopping to hoist the rope of the heavy bucket onto her shoulder. "But you are trying to see inside me. Whyever would you do that, unless to tempt me with my weaknesses?"

So she had sensed his probing. Her sensitivity to it did not mean she was Brynna, although the similarity of her name with that of his beloved scarcely seemed accidental.

I could not do this worse, did I intend it, Cairn thought, splaying one hand through his tumbled hair. He did not want to tell her he was an angel— which in any case he was not—because then she would never believe he was a man. Yet what else could he say?

"I do not want to tempt you," he said. "I only want to see . . . to see if . . ."

But Brianna cut off his halting attempt to explain. "If 'tis Beltane the reason you're here, there be naught I can do about ye until midnight. But I dinna have to stand here talking to a devil, or whatever odd manner of thing you be." She turned and began walking away as fast as the heavy bucket would allow.

Cairn knew better than to offer her assistance with the bucket. Samhain? He cast back into his memory, found that he remembered the holiday, the belief that spirits walked abroad on this night. His own people had observed it. With the advent of the one God, the day was now called All Hallows, except, perhaps, in remote places like this. But the beliefs had been blended, and were still nearly the same.

Very well, then he would "appear" to her again to-night, when she believed the door between the worlds opened. Perhaps she would accept him then, and he would know for certain if she was Brynna.

What would happen after that, he did not know. His efforts had all been directed toward finding her. Trying to sense her spirit, wandering the world, wondering whether she had been born, where she might be.

Once he found Brynna, he had no idea what to do

next. He watched her retreating back, willing himself not to go after her.

One step at a time, he reminded himself, as he had down the years since Rapha-el had shown him how to maintain consciousness despite the stabbing pain. It came from the fact that he was neither one thing nor the other, neither true angel nor ordinary mortal, Rapha-el had said. If this was the price of temporary immortality, so be it.

Inactive for too long, his wings were now lifting him beyond the treetops. He let them take him, surrendering his active consciousness to a state that allowed him some respite from the pain without blanking out altogether.

How much longer? he wondered. How much longer until he met his beloved and love kindled the fire of remembrance?

"'Tis looking like ye have seen a ghost, Brianna," her mother said, when Brianna stumbled back into their small cottage.

"Oh, mother, I am damned," Brianna said, sinking onto the wooden bench.

"What is it, my lamb?" Margaret, used to dramatic statements from her strong-willed daughter, did not turn around. She had finished with the soap-making, and was now setting yarn in tubs to dye. Her hands, always busy, had not paused, but Brianna felt the comfort in her voice just as if her mother had enfolded her in a hug.

"Mother, ye'll never believe what I saw. I am not sure I believe it myself," she said. "I went down to the stream to fetch water, down a-ways, ye ken . . ."

"Where the water runs fast and deep. Aye, I know, my wildling." Margaret shook her head at Brianna's daring, her fingers turning the wool as it took the dye.

"I saw a man. A devil. An angel." She tugged her hair in frustration. "Och, I dinna know what he was, but he had wings. Wings, mother! He was no cowslip faery, wee and wise," she said. "He was as big as ever a normal man, and would look like one too but for those wings. And there was light shining around him. . . ."

Brianna tugged so hard that she knocked her braids off her head as the thought struck her. *His hair was gilt-bright, more beautiful than the maple that had just turned to yellow. Like the man in her recurring dream who kissed her so tenderly . . .* The persistent dream was the reason none of the local boys interested her. Her dream had come to life.

Margaret McKemie peeled off the thick gloves that protected her hands from the dye. She sat down at the thick wooden table that was the only one they owned. "What are you blathering about, lass?" she asked. "If this man looked like an angel—and angels be not man nor woman, ye ken—why d'ye think he was a devil?"

Brianna struggled for the right words. "Partly for that very reason, Mother. He was a man, with a scar along his shoulder where it joined his neck and tumbled golden hair that danced about his wide shoulders. How could that be an angel, I ask you, without smooth skin and a perfect face?"

Brianna smacked her forehead in frustration. "Och, listen to me, as if I know what an angel should look like. Who has ever gotten close enough to touch one?"

Brianna hugged herself, thinking of the shameful effect those blue-gray eyes and tousled hair had had on her. She had wanted to brush it off his brow, the better to see his long lashes that turned golden just at the tips. And his eyes! They had invited her to look into them until she went breathless.

"'Tis thinking you are bewitched, I am," said her mother, a frown on her lined face.

"Aye, I fear it myself," Brianna confessed. "Told him he was a devil, I did, and I would not be giving in to the likes of him." She tossed her head, her wild hair now completely unbound.

"Giving in?" her mother cried in alarm. "Did he try to couple wi' ye then?"

Brianna blushed until she was sure her face was as red as her hair. "No, no. But he looked into my eyes like he was trying to find my soul, to bind it to him. Then I told him I thought he was a devil come to tempt me."

"Ye'll not go out this night then, Brianna Mc-Kemie," said her mother. "For sure and ye will find him waiting for you. If the door is open so soon, in daylight, what chance will you stand tonight when the fires fan the spirits brighter?"

"I have never missed Samhain." Brianna started to rebraid her hair. She was hurt her mother would even think to forbid her the rare festivities.

"Ye have never been courted by a devil before either."

"He won't hurt me."

"How would you be knowing that?" her mother

scoffed. "Isn't that what any of them would say, all silver-tongued like they are?"

"Aye. But he won't. I just know it."

"Brianna," her mother said, bending over her where she sat at the beaten-up old table. "Dinna be telling anyone what happened. There's folk here who believe there be witches."

"Me? How could anyone think that of me, Mother?" Brianna said, laughing.

Margaret, remembering the call of owls deep in the night Brianna was born, held her tongue. Owls were held to be a sign of evil spirits.

Ill-omened, the midwife had called the difficult birth. A miracle, Margaret had thought, knowing babes emerging feet first almost always killed both mother and child. There were plenty among the crofters of Glen Avon who still remembered. Nor was her own Ian here any longer to protect them.

She looked at her daughter's glowing green eyes, remembered how hard it had been not to stifle Brianna's spirit by keeping her close to home. Her daughter had grown up free and happy. 'Twas too late to change that now.

"You may go," she said at last, running her rough hands over her daughter's shining mane. "But never be alone. Tell no one what happened today. And do not go near that . . . whatever he is."

Brianna hugged her mother fiercely. "Nay, I shan't. Nothing will happen, Mother, you'll see." She skipped happily out of the house, going to call the sheep home.

Margaret felt a heaviness weigh on her heart, but did not answer Brianna. She turned back to her dye pot. The cloth had been in the dye too long. It was ruined, no longer blue, but muddy and dark, almost black.

"This is only fit for mourning cloth now," she whispered. Then she bit her knuckle, stuffing her hand into her mouth as if she could take back the words. She ran to burn the cloth in the fire, but a terrible feeling inside told her it was already too late.

Chapter Four

Washington, D.C., October 1997

Brenna's article had to be wrapped up in two days. Nora had warned her that if she didn't hand it in November 1, she'd miss her deadline. Brenna didn't need a more explicit threat than that. She knew how many journalism majors were out there. Every one wanted to be a writer.

Unlike those aspiring to write the Great American Novel, however, Brenna had always prided herself on her professionalism. She didn't miss deadlines because she never waited for inspiration to strike.

The more you wrote, she felt, the better you got at it. It was that simple. Like tuning a piano or fixing a car. There were skills involved that could be learned. Learn those skills and you could do it.

Brenna occasionally spoke to high school English

and creative writing classes. The students always groaned when she got to this part, because they all wanted to believe that there was a muse out there with their name on it.

Just the way her dream wanted her to believe there was a man out there with her name already imprinted on his heart.

There I go again, Brenna thought. In the weeks since she had broken up with Jim, the dream of the rugged blond man came more frequently.

Was it long-repressed sexuality? She snorted; Jim would favor that explanation. Had she seen this guy on TV? On the cover of a novel? How could she know him, yet at the same time feel something tremendously important was missing, something she should remember?

Certainly his body belonged on the cover of a novel, one of those where the man and woman yearned toward each other and a splendid consummation was promised inside. She had felt his hard, strong body pressed against hers, her curves yielding, molding to him with a natural sensuality totally unlike her image of herself. His chest was broad and flat, his body superbly muscled. She seemed to know it very well, that body with its resilient textures of smooth skin and hard muscle, the sheer male vitality that emanated from him.

Her palms tingled and goosebumps rose along her arms. A melting sensation began deep inside. It would turn to throbbing soon, then an ache. Brenna smoothed her hands over her thighs, covered by sensible olive corduroys.

They lay in a glade. Stars framed his torso, and nightbirds called as he ran his hands over her thighs, smoothing away her tunic. He bent to place kisses from her ankles to her knees, then up to her hips. Meanwhile his hands worked seductive magic along her sensitive inner thighs to ease her legs apart.

"So little time . . ." he murmured, his head, his words, brushing against her sensitive flesh, his thick, bright hair just one more element in the riot he made of her senses. He positioned himself above her, his hard, hair-dusted thighs nudging hers open wider. A secret place in her throbbed in tempo to the blunt hardness preparing to breach her, moisture rising to dampen her and ease his passage. . . . Then the shadows swept in upon her.

Fear woke her. *Only I,* Brenna thought, disoriented, her heart still pounding, *could have an erotic dream with no ending.*

She shook her head, sending her hair flying wildly around her shoulders. Obviously her brain had turned to mush. That had to be the real meaning of the dream—how little time she had left to finish the assignment. It didn't matter how those words sounded in her dream, the form in which they came to her. She was never going to write this article if she kept dwelling on her increasingly compelling dream-lover.

She looked around the apartment she normally kept in orderly, but not obsessive, fashion. It was going to hell in a handbasket, just like her personal life. Articles were strewn from one end of the couch to the other, many of them reprinted from the microfiches she'd viewed. Reproduction prints of Renaissance angels playing musical instruments lay on the floor. An eight-inch Neapolitan angel in flowing robes, cunningly worked in papier-mâché, stared back at her from a tabletop. Marina's Christmas gift from three years ago.

She'd brought out the artwork to get her in the mood, and to help her think of ways to describe what her interview subjects had seen. None of them had seen anything resembling the classic depiction of an angel. Even Maud Barrett, whom she'd telephoned just yesterday to ask a few more questions, hadn't seen her angel clearly. But Maud did elaborate, saying she was convinced it was a male presence, something Brenna's research told her was unusual. Angels were supposed to be androgynous.

Light, wings, sensing a presence, a conviction that the origin was other-worldly, that the angel had special powers—these were the ridiculously small nuggets of information she had to go on. Pretty slim pickings, she thought glumly.

"Write the article about the people, if you can't believe in the angels," Marina had urged her when they had coffee after work. "Quote liberally from Maud Barrett's book, and make some observations about Washington people. You know, the usual." The trademark of *Inside City* magazine: follow national trends, feature locals.

Brenna nodded. What would Marina say if Brenna said she was being seduced in her sleep, and somehow, she didn't know how, it was connected to this angel story? "Quote liberally or literally?" she asked instead, fighting down the urge to confide in her friend. She stirred extra sugar into her cappuccino.

"Both," Marina said. "*Cara*, this isn't like you. You don't usually wait for Mother Nature." She frowned, her dark brows furrowed in concentration. "Wait, that's not the right expression."

"Do you mean 'wait for the muse to strike'?" Brenna asked, hiding a smile.

"*Ecco*, that's it. That's what you tell the children, isn't it?" Marina knocked back the rest of her latté with practiced Italian speed.

"The teenagers," Brenna said. "Yes, that's what I tell them. Now I'm the victim of my own propaganda. I don't know what's blocking me, Marina. Shoot, listen to me. I don't even believe in writer's block."

"Let's go watch a movie then," Marina suggested suddenly. "Isn't there a video store just around the corner here?"

Wondering why Marina had changed the topic so fast, Brenna found herself out the door of Starbucks, keys in hand. She was on her way to get the car while Marina went into the video rental store.

Brenna looked idly at the boxes on her floor after Marina left. She had told Marina she would take them back. The idea had been worthwhile, but it hadn't worked.

The tape still sitting in the VCR was *It's a Wonderful Life*. Marina had never seen it before, knowing only that in the story an angel saved someone's life, and it was popular on American campuses at exam time. She had thought it might help.

Clarence's adventures in becoming an angel hadn't helped Brenna, although she had enjoyed seeing the movie again. He didn't look much like an angel. He wasn't well-built with golden hair.

Why would she think an angel looked like . . .
Brenna clenched her teeth. Now she had her dream-
lover mixed up with her project for work. Angels
weren't men, she reminded herself.

Yet Clarence the apprentice angel hadn't been androgynous. Neither was Fred Gwynne and the little
boy he'd helped in *The Littlest Angel,* which they had
watched next. Fred Gwynne was tall, but not blond
and certainly not handsome. He had a kind face, but
that was about as far as you'd go.

Brenna pulled the clip from her hair, letting the
weight of her hair tumble down her back. The wall
clock displayed midnight. This was truly ridiculous.
She'd be worthless tomorrow if she didn't get to bed
now. She had only tomorrow left in which to finish
the article.

She didn't bother to pick up her assorted "research" materials. Marina had laughingly called it
"angel dust" when she was there. At least the movies
had left Brenna in a better mood, even if they hadn't
provided any inspiration.

After a quick teeth-brushing and face-washing, she
slid into bed wearing an oversized turquoise T-shirt.
For once, sleep came quickly. But not gently.

Brenna had dreamed about flying before. In those
dreams, she had never been able to rise above the
treetops. Something—her fear of heights, the ac-
companying vertigo—always held her back, kept her
earthbound.

Tonight, she dreamed she stood under a huge tree.
There was a swing high up. It looked enticing, sparkling in the bright, crisp air, promising no limits to

freedom. Brenna knew she could swing from that high perch, but first she had to reach it. Looking up, she spotted Marina already there.

"Come on up, *cara*, it's beautiful up here," her friend called down from her position on the swing. The weather was sunny and warm, even though the leaves of the tall oak had begun to change. The dream-weather was like Washington's just now, glorious fall shades of orange, red, and yellow.

Orange . . . The color of Halloween. She remembered, even in her dream, that her article was due on Halloween. Tomorrow. But in her dream, she wasn't anyplace that she recognized.

Marina swung high above her head, sailing in a clear arc against a limpid blue sky. "Come on up," she called again. She was so high up, it seemed impossible to ever reach her.

"I can't, I'm waiting for my muse to strike," Brenna replied.

Then Marina abruptly disappeared, as happens so often in dreams. Brenna found herself lifted high, held securely in warm, strong arms she couldn't see, until she reached the high perch. She wanted to thank the man who had brought her, but she didn't see anyone.

She forgot about finding him for the moment while she experienced the most wonderful sensation of freedom.

There was no fear. She wasn't afraid. She couldn't fall. Brenna was at the top of the world. The swing was made of gold, warm and yielding under her weight, yet so responsive that she hardly had to pump her legs.

Brenna looked out over valleys, mountains, streams. She felt for a moment as if she could see the whole world from there.

Then, without warning, she felt a push at her back. She fell from the high, fantastic seat. Over and over she tumbled in the air, an exaggerated fall that seemed to go on forever. Curses followed her in the chilly air, the brilliant light fading even as she fell.

"Witch!" they cried. "Save yourself if you can. Damn yourself if you do." A lethal version of the dunking stool test for witches, Brenna thought wildly, unable to escape the reality of the dream and wake herself up.

She remembered that if a woman accused of witchcraft could float, she was considered guilty. An innocent woman sank to the bottom like a stone. But the woman would be dead before she could be pulled from the water.

"Why do you hate me?" Brenna called out, still tumbling, knowing now the cause of her fear of heights. "What have I done?"

"Consorted with the devil. Fly if you can," the voices called.

"I don't want to fly," she cried out.

"You do," came a deep voice beside her. "But not like that." Strong arms caught her and swept her away, far away from the hateful, frightening voices. Somehow the two of them flew, but the night was dark and cold now.

She could not see her rescuer or the means of her rescue. But his voice was warm and reassuring. Though she had heard few words from him in her previous dream, somehow she knew this was the voice of her dream-lover.

He set her down on a pile of rocks and wrapped her with softness when she trembled and could not stand. Light blossomed between them, cool and pale and reassuring. She looked into the face of her rescuer, saw the gilt-bright hair, and knew. The softness enveloping her came from wings that sheltered them. They rose from behind his shoulders, were curved around them. She caught one glimpse of intent gray-blue eyes before she fainted.

When she came to, Brenna knew with the strange intuition only found in dreams that she was now looking through someone else's eyes.

"Brynna," she thought she heard him say, the man who had rescued her from the terrible fall. It sounded so close to her own name. But she felt a spark of indignation. She was not Brynna, she was herself.

She wanted to assert who she was, but could not. Everything around them was dark. Where was the light he'd caused to shine?

Dimmed, she realized. The girl whose eyes, whose dream, she now shared, was afraid. Terrified, in fact. This girl feared his light, his wings, his differentness. As the people who had shouted at the girl had been afraid of her.

Not me, Brenna wanted to say. *I'm not afraid of you.* But she was only an observer, helpless to speak to him or to reassure the girl that she had nothing to fear from him. The words were not hers.

"Brynna, will you not speak to me?" he asked again. "Why did you jump?"

"Did ye not see?" she asked, trembling away from him as if she wanted him to withdraw his wings. Brenna liked the whisper of them around her, but she knew the girl who had spoken did not. Or if she did, the feeling was buried so deep beneath the terror that Brenna did not think the girl could find her way back to it.

"They made me jump!" the girl cried. Brenna felt it, the fear that clawed at her, the strangeness of her position. This girl had never been so frightened before. Brenna realized the sharp differences between herself and the young woman . . . this Brianna.

That was her name, Brianna. This girl had never before been afraid of falling, never been afraid of heights. Feeling the coltish, strong young limbs of her body, Brenna realized that the girl was athletic and fearless.

Or had been until now.

Brenna used the girl's frantic glances to take note of what she wore. Brenna wanted to look into his eyes, but her young companion did not. The girl wore a long heavy wool skirt, a woven woolen blouse, a long length of dyed-over plaid across one shoulder. Scottish, then. Nineteenth century? No, earlier. When folk still believed in witchcraft.

Brenna was drawn out of her own thoughts, back into the girl's pain by the jolt of fear that went through her body when she felt the feathery caress of a wing against her cheek. It was meant to be reassuring, but the girl was afraid. She was afraid of those who'd tried to kill her, but sadly, she was even more afraid of the man—or whatever he was—who held her.

Worst, she now feared herself. The girl Brianna questioned her own sanity.

No, Brenna longed to tell her, *he will not hurt you*, but she had no power here, no voice. The girl wasn't even aware of her, and Brianna's growing terror was somehow pushing Brenna out. Brenna tried to hang on, wanting to help, but things around her began to fade.

The winged man tried to clasp her cold, cold hands, but Brianna pulled away from him. "They saw me this afternoon. Fiona and Davey s-s-saw me. They heard me call you a devil. Then they saw me carry away the water."

"Is that all you think there are on earth, demons?" he asked in a voice laced with pain and anger—most of it directed at himself, to judge from the tightly drawn expression on his face. Brenna saw it as her sight faded, but she did not think Brianna noticed.

"'Tis what they tell us in the kirk," she said in a timid voice that Brenna knew had once been high and lilting. As the man opened his mouth to respond, Brenna felt a wrenching, her spirit plucked from the girl. She did not think either the man or the girl noticed.

Cairn could not bring himself to say the words to her, to force her to acknowledge him. *Do you not believe in angels?* It hovered in his mind, tantalizing with possibilities. Surely she would not turn away from him then. But he was not an angel. Not truly. He was a man. And he held a woman who was not yet a woman, not ready to accept what he was.

Love, remember me. As she had foreseen, she did

not remember him. He wanted to groan aloud. He knew now that he had found Brynna. But he had come too soon. Whether too soon in her young life, or too early, in a century that would not accept his strangeness, it did not matter.

Cairn forced himself to concentrate on the here and now and not the fruitless centuries. He knew she felt fear, and it sickened him. She had been so different at the stream this afternoon. Healthy, lively, playful. She hadn't really been afraid of him, despite her words. But now, like a good horse badly handled, she trembled away from his touch.

Her scream as she fell had reached him. He had been miles above the village, waiting for the blazing exultation of the Samhain fires. His ability to hear her scream from so far away had convinced him she could only be his Brynna, because he could not have heard her otherwise.

Without stopping to think, he had folded his wings and plunged to earth to reach her in time. He had saved her, just barely, but he wondered if it was not already too late.

"They said I enticed an evil spirit," Brianna continued, her voice now heartbreakingly timorous. "That b-b-because they saw you in daytime, they said I must be able to conjure well, that I was a powerful witch. Davey said he kn-knew now why I was never interested in him. Because I—I consort with you."

"For this, they forced you to the cliff?" Cairn asked, unable to comprehend the savagery of the crofters' response. In his time, the Celts had honored and revered wielders and holders of the Power—what these people reviled as witchcraft.

"Aye. They took me there for a witch-test. If I was a witch, I would fly to save myself. They would not believe me, would not listen to Mother. The older folk told of strange things about the night I was born—omens, signs. They talked about owls. 'Tis foolishness," she said, a shred of normal indignation back in her voice. "What d-do owls have to do with anything?"

Cairn knew that owls were held to be the incarnation of female spirits, but did not tell her so. She needed no information that might further undermine her already fragile state of mind.

He lifted a hand to her cheek, unthinking. She shrank back, bumping into the wings in which he had enfolded them to protect her.

"Release me!" she screamed.

"What will you do, Brynna?" he asked, wondering if he could let her go. Surely if he had enough patience, if he let her mature, he could talk to her someday. What did a few more years matter to him now, after so much time?

Yet he wanted desperately to tilt her head back and blaze the knowledge into her with his eyes until her soul recognized him. Holding her lightly, saying nothing about their shared past, took more restraint than he had ever possessed as a normal man.

"Brianna! My name is Brianna. Just let me go, dinna touch me!" She struggled within the shelter of his arms like a wild thing.

He unfurled his wings from around her. Maybe if he did not touch her, she would calm down. He thought of Rapha-el's healing hands and wished for that kind of power.

Brynna ran the moment he dropped his arms. Ran like a woman possessed, truly possessed, of evil spirits. There was no demon in her, however. She ran from fear, from ignorance, from a destiny too soon forced upon her. His fault.

Cairn felt the pain attack him as soon as he set off after her. The sudden call, the mad plunge from the sky, had drained every slight angel-power he did possess.

Now he would be lucky to catch her as she fled wildly from him.

His wings would not carry him. He was not strong enough to lift them, to lift himself. Cairn stumbled along, running when he could, trying to avoid rocks as she ran away from him into the night.

Concentrating on his footing, he did not see the danger until too late. She veered away from the area where the villagers had gathered. Some were descending even now to search for her body.

She skirted the forest edge, avoiding the woods with the stream where they had met. She ran through meadow and moor, down into the cleft of the glen and up again. Cairn kept up pursuit behind her, lacking the strength to speak, to beg her to stop. Not that she would have heeded him.

After she'd been yanked out of the dream, Brenna drifted, half-asleep, always on the verge of waking up, but never quite able to. Then her breathing suddenly accelerated, adrenaline hitting her chest and tightening it until she could barely breathe.

The dream seized her again. Suddenly she was seeing again through the eyes of the frightened Scottish girl. The nightmare was as sharp as reality. Brenna realized the girl's intent and fought to escape the dream's hold on her. She tried to communicate "stop" to the girl, whose long, thick hair whipped into her eyes as she ran.

Brenna tried urging the girl Brianna to slow her pumping legs. They were fleeter than Brenna's own had ever been, so sure-footed. But Brenna was only an observer again, along for a terrifying ride.

Then the young Scottish woman reached the edge of a cliff. She could go no farther. Brenna threw all her efforts into making the girl turn to face her pursuer. Brenna knew he was there and that he offered safety, but the girl Brianna could not see past her terror. But she turned and for one brief instant, Brenna looked out of those eyes and became the young woman again.

The woman who was Brenna recognized something about the man who stood before her in the dark night, his arms reaching for her even as he stumbled in utter exhaustion.

"Brynna, no," he called hoarsely, the name that was like hers and the girl's, but not quite the same. "No, I beg you."

But even as she watched his blue-gray eyes flare wide with shock, the girl who was Brianna turned away and jumped.

Brenna snapped bolt upright in bed, her T-shirt drenched with sweat. Her heart pounded rapidly, and her breath came in gulps. She could not suck enough air into her lungs.

She cried shaky tears for the dream girl who had jumped to her death. Still overwhelmed by the feeling of reality about it that she could not shake, Brenna wondered where dream and reality met and separated.

She recognized the man who had rescued her. How stupid of her. Of course she recognized him. He was her creation, the creation of her overactive imagination.

But he knew her first, he had been looking for her.

Oh, how she wished that could be true. Her practical nature rebelled instantly. Still, wouldn't it be wonderful to know she was so important to someone that he would do anything, go anywhere, search through time, to find her?

As she slipped back into sleep, the tears that slid down her cheeks were for herself, for the foolishness she could not shake, for the myths and miracles that did not exist—if they ever had—in this modern world.

Chapter Five

"I have never had a dream like that, never. It seemed so real." After a bracing shower and a hot breakfast, Brenna downed the last of her coffee while talking to Marina. Her fingers still trembled slightly. She'd been this way for the better part of an hour, waiting for Marina to get to work. She had already left a message on Nora's voice mail saying she would finish the article at home today.

Brenna gave Marina an edited version, telling her that she'd dreamed about an angel; then she told her she'd dreamed of seeing a girl jump off a cliff. She did not mention the connection between the two. "I tell you, Marina, it felt like I was seeing something that was really happening in another time and place."

And to another self, she wanted to add.

That would mean she had a past life, as Maud Barrett had told her. No, she couldn't accept that. Why not just write it off to the strangeness of dreams?

Brenna balanced a pencil on her index finger to see if she could make it stay, aware that she had fallen silent.

"Did you finish the article last night, *cara?*" Marina finally asked as silence stretched thickly between them.

"No," Brenna admitted glumly.

"Well, don't you think that's it then? You were all tied up with that article that's been leading you crazy . . ."

"You mean 'driving you crazy,'" Brenna interrupted.

"No, it's driving *you* crazy, not me." Marina laughed. "So you dreamed about an angel. That's not so strange, is it?"

Brenna wasn't up to any introspection. "I'm not firing on all cylinders this morning," Brenna warned her.

"If that means you're cranky, I agree. Look, finish the piece, then we'll go out for a nice Italian dinner and talk about this. We'll celebrate getting it off your chest."

"I may need to get the dream off my chest, but it's the article I have to get off my back," Brenna responded, more tartly than usual. The pencil fell off her finger.

A puzzled silence reached through the phone. "Did I lose you?" Brenna asked.

"*Sì.*"

"Sorry," Brenna said. "I meant it's taking longer

81

than I thought to finish up this piece. Let's not plan for tonight. I think I'll be too tired. How about tomorrow?"

"*Va bene*," Marina said.

"OK. *Ciao*. And thanks for listening." Brenna hung up.

Brenna sipped at her third cup of coffee, staring idly at one of the angel prints. Weren't angels supposed to save people? Some Guardian Angel he was, she thought. Then her modern cynicism choked in her throat. Her brief period of detachment from what she'd witnessed shattered like flawed glass.

She had seen the anguish in his eyes, knew his grief was terrible. Worse, she could not shake the feeling that the terrible events had really happened.

Without warning, thoughts that weren't her own flowed into her. *Oh, my beloved. I did not save you. Did not protect you. Could not stop you leaving me. You left me . . . again. Love, you did not remember me.*

They were *his* thoughts. Brenna shook her head, trying to clear her head of the staccato sentences that pricked her like sharp needles of truth. Goosebumps rose on her arms.

"Too much caffeine, kiddo," she said out loud, rising to plop her mug in the sink. She turned back to the laptop computer on her kitchen table, seeing the article for the first time as a way to rid herself of the unpleasant residue of the powerful dreams.

She plunged in, rewriting the opening in a flash of inspiration. "Maud Barrett of McLean wasn't sure what she saw, late that night in the driving rain. But she knew what it wasn't. It wasn't anything she'd ever seen or experienced before. . . ."

The sun had fallen from its chilly peak before Brenna looked up again. She stared at the clock in the living room, dazed. It was five-thirty. Scrolling through what she'd written, she realized she was a page away from completion.

Maybe there was something to this muse business after all.

Half an hour later, she clicked on SAVE and rose to massage her numb behind. She was walking around picking up and organizing her angel debris when the phone rang.

"Hi, Bren," Jim said. "I've been thinking." Typical, thought Brenna, that he didn't stop for her to respond. "I said some stuff I'm not proud of. I . . . Uh . . . Oh hell, I can't do this over the phone. Can I come over and see you?"

"Where are you?" she said warily.

"Just flew into Langley. I can be there in two hours." Only a jet jockey could turn the three-hour drive from Langley Air Force base into two, Brenna thought.

"I don't know, Jim. I'm finishing this article. I'm off deadline and—"

"You're behind deadline?" he asked, amazement evident in his tone.

"This has been an extremely difficult piece and—"

"Jeez, I didn't think I'd upset you that much." The smug note in his voice was too much for Brenna.

"If you'd let me get a word in edgewise here, Jim, it has nothing to do with you. Sorry. It's about this angel story I'm working on."

"Uh-huh," he said, sounding unconvinced.

"Oh, just come up here." Brenna conceded defeat.

"I guess we can go to the Cactus Cantina," she said, naming a popular southwestern-style place a few blocks away.

"Most pilots think they've seen one at some time or other, you know, Brenna," he said, his tone devoid of innuendo for once.

"Really?" she said, her interest hooked. "Have *you?*"

"I . . . uh, I'll tell you when I get there. Hey, why don't you order some pizza in for us?"

She didn't really want to see him in her apartment, but this subject had to be pretty personal for a man who considered the words "wanna get married" the depths of profound emotion.

"All right." She sighed, one hand going automatically to her hair to check how wild it had become in the past few hours. She had a tendency to pull at it while she was writing, and by now, it probably looked as if it had been through an encounter with a wind machine.

"I'll be there by seven, babe," he said.

The minute she hung up the phone, Brenna started frantically cleaning up the apartment. She stopped after a while, realizing Jim would neither notice nor care.

When she went to fix her hair, Brenna stood a long time, watching herself in the bathroom mirror as if she expected to see that other girl appear through her eyes. She saw only her own green eyes and untamed red-gold hair. She closed her eyes for a moment, remembering.

In dark relief, a picture formed against her lids. But it wasn't anything from her earlier dream.

He knelt at the cliff edge, looking down into the night. Although Brenna saw only a picture and heard no sounds, she felt the unutterable agony in him, the despair that had driven him to his knees, robbed him of the strength to stand. She appeared to be back in the dream where it had left off last night.

An angel, brighter than he, clad completely in cloth of gold, hair like a waterfall of shimmering gold down its—her—back, alighted beside him.

Even as Brenna tried to work out how she knew the angel was a woman, the angel swept wings like molten gold around the man-angel, enclosing him within the circle of her compassion. When she unfurled them, he stood, unbearably sad but no longer despondent.

The golden angel kept her hand on his shoulder as yet another angel flew past them, up into the star-strewn sky, where a huge wheel of fiery light revolved slowly in the air. The flying angel, whose wings were gray and silver, held a burden lightly in strong arms, flying past the pair on the cliff. A belt of heavy silver links glowed against the night-dark sky as he flew.

Brenna's angel raised one arm in supplication as the silver angel flew past without stopping. Then he dropped to his knees again and bent his head. Brenna saw what he looked like up close for the first time—through her own eyes, which were wide and wondering, not afraid as the girl Brianna's had been.

The brown-and-gold-clad angel's massive wings were light tan, blending into brown and gold feathers near the tips. His robe was light brown edged in gold, his thick hair wavy and bright like that of the angels in Renaissance paintings.

But he was male. No doubt about that. The Renaissance angels were ethereal, perfect. He was muscular, built like an athlete or soldier, with a line of puckered scar tissue visible at his neck. His nose looked as if it had been broken at least once. His features were strong and rugged, but not perfect. She was obscurely glad of that.

There was no other word for him but male. What made him so, and how he was different from the other angels she'd seen, she couldn't quite pin down. She just knew that he was potently, appealingly masculine.

She longed to comfort him, but he was so far away on the cold hilltop. She had no way to reach him. Brenna watched helplessly while silent tears rolled down the face of the grieving brown-and-gold angel. Although in her culture, men were not supposed to cry, he was no less masculine in his grief. The tears turned golden as they fell, rolling down the side of the cliff. They tumbled, rolled, and finally bounced, becoming harder, not dissolving.

What had been teardrops hardened into quartz-like crystals. They had something of the rough-hewn look of the man himself. Most came to nestle in cracks along the cliff face; others slid beneath tree roots or fell into nearby streams. They gleamed briefly. As they hardened and settled, they turned darker, smokier.

Brenna recognized the golden-brown stones. She had a necklace that had been her grandmother's, made of cairngorms, the smoky quartz found in the part of the Scottish Highlands known as the Cairngorm Mountains.

Cairn. His name was Cairn.

Caught up in the realization, she barely noticed that a hand, hidden at the bottom of the cliff wall, snaked out to catch some of the falling crystals. A face filled with unholy glee appeared briefly. Bat-like wings flashed once; then the creature vanished.

Back at the cliff top, the golden angel looked down at Cairn, who appeared as if he could no longer fly. Once again Brenna knew things she had no reason to know, no way of knowing. The golden angel took mercy on the man, as was her nature. She was Gabrielle, Angel of Mercy and the Annunciation.

The knowledge flowed into Brenna, who was not sure she wanted to know it. She paid it no more heed than she had the strange creature she'd seen at the bottom of the cliff.

Brenna had room in her mind for only one name, one thought.

Cairn.

As Brenna felt her lips form his name in that instant of strange, perfect recognition, the figure in her vision snapped upright.

He tipped back the strong column of his neck, his thick, tousled, golden hair brushing his shoulder. He searched the sky, looking upward into heaven as if the girl's soul had called out to him.

My soul, Brenna thought. *I called out to you.* She willed him to turn, to see her somehow. He stopped looking upward, started to turn his head toward the side. He would see her any second now. . . .

The intercom in the living room buzzed loudly. Brenna's eyes flew open. The vision immediately dissolved.

Disconcerted, she blinked twice, looking in the mirror again. It seemed that she had been inside the vision for hours, but only a few minutes had gone by. God, it had been so real!

Her eyes were wider than usual, greener than normal, but that could be the moss-green sweater she had on. Otherwise, she thought wryly, she didn't look as if she were losing her mind.

Brenna shook her head, undoing the effects of the recent brushing.

Angels? Visions? Dreams at night were one thing. But dreams in broad daylight when she was awake—not a good sign.

The intercom buzzed impatiently again. Brenna scooted out to answer it. "Yes?" she said, out of breath.

"Pizza, ma'am," the nasal teenage voice said.

"Of course," she said, alarmed by the intense surge of disappointment that rushed through her at the words. *Get a grip, girl. Angels don't buzz intercoms.*

"Fourth floor," she said, pressing the entry button. Now that the pizza was here, Jim could not be far behind.

She leaned her head against the wall by the intercom. So she had dreamed when she was wide awake. It was better than the alternative suggested by her recent experience: that she had lost her marbles.

For once, reasserting her skeptical and practical nature failed to make her feel better.

"Light of my life, here I am," said Jim when she opened the door for him a few minutes later. In one hand he held a bottle of wine, in the other a bouquet of flowers.

For some reason his words irritated her, although it was only one of a number of easy, affectionate expressions he frequently used.

"Going for the gusto?" she asked wryly, figuring two could play the cliché game.

"Baby, I came to throw myself on your mercy." Somehow that grated on her, too. Brenna accepted the flowers and the wine, ducked under his arm to avoid the kiss, and headed for the kitchen. This was a mistake, she thought.

On the other hand, she mused, taking the pizza out of the oven while Jim deftly opened the wine, a little company right now might not be such a bad thing.

Jim knew where the wine glasses were, of course. He'd made himself quite at home at the table in her oriel window, the closest thing she had to a dining room, by the time she emerged with the pizza and a green salad.

"Hey, cheer up, kiddo," he said, reaching out to tap her chin lightly. "This isn't supposed to be a wake, you know."

He polished off three slices before noticing she hadn't even picked up a piece. "Is it this article, Bren? You sure sounded strange over the phone."

"It's a lot of things, I guess," she said, taking a sip of wine. "I didn't want to write it, then I dawdled over it, so I got behind. Dad hasn't been in the greatest shape, and Mother . . ." She broke off.

"Your mom's bugging you about the grandkid thing, right?"

"Not exactly." Boy, wouldn't it feed his ego to know

her mother thought breaking up with Jim was a bad idea? Oh no, she wasn't going to tell him what her mother's views were.

"I know, Bren, she called me," Jim said, startling her.

"She what?" Brenna stared at Jim, noting how his straight dark hair always stayed neatly in place. "How dare she?"

"Easy does it, kiddo. She was upset, thought maybe you were working too hard or something. Said the Old Man missed seeing me around." Since he used the standard military term among younger officers for the general, she didn't mind.

"Did you tell her why we broke up?" Brenna asked.

"Are you kidding? I can be a jerk, but I'm not that big a one. That stuff is between you and me." The look in Jim's limpid brown eyes showed she'd offended him.

Brenna started to apologize mechanically, then cut herself off, reaching again for the wine. He was right. He could be a jerk. She had nothing to say "sorry" about.

"Thank God for small miracles," she said finally.

They spent the rest of the meal trading small talk. Jim didn't mention his orders once, which surprised her. He was always bursting with excitement on the eve of a deployment, and this assignment was a big one for him. If he was working on being sensitive for a change, she thanked whoever had pounded it into him.

Brenna didn't object when they took the rest of the wine bottle and their glasses over to the couch. When he commented on her stack of clippings and prints, she loosened up and told him a little bit about the project.

"That Barrett lady sounds wacko," he said, topping off her glass with a keen look at the flush on her face.

"She's not wacko," Brenna said, thinking of Maud's new approach to helping people. "But the project has been driving me around the bend."

"Yeah? Why?" Brenna didn't protest when he settled her against his shoulder. It felt comfortable, the way it had in the early days of their relationship when she hadn't worried that he would trespass on her boundaries. Frankly, it felt good just to lean on someone strong and male. She hadn't realized how much she'd missed the contact, the strong hands rubbing softly at the nape of her neck, the broad shoulder to snuggle against.

"Well, my dreams have been getting stranger and stranger. I think I even had one today before you came."

"You mean you took a nap?" Jim lifted the glass out of her hand. It had started to tilt at an angle as she relaxed more completely against him.

"Hmm? No, I was standing right there in the bathroom, combing my hair, when it happened. Then the buzzer went off, scared me half to death. It was the pizza guy."

"Lots of people daydream," he offered, stroking her hair.

"This was more than a daydream. It was like I was right there. Like I was seeing something that had happened, that had really happened in the past."

"What does this have to do with your article? You know you've always had weird dreams." Yes, and one

91

of their familiar themes of argument had been his assertion that if she'd sleep with him, he'd make sure she wouldn't have such dreams.

Or, if she did, he'd counter, he would be there to cuddle her in the night. Knowing how Jim's hormones were routinely in overdrive, she always declined. She didn't doubt that his initial intentions were good. But he just wasn't that altruistic and she knew comfort was not the reason he wanted to spend the night with her.

He didn't seem inclined to run through all that again. Good, she thought gratefully. Maybe they could get their relationship back on a better footing after all. "One of the things I was most frustrated about while writing this article was that none of these people had actually seen any angels. When I dreamed, the one last night and the daydream or whatever I had today, there were . . ." She trailed off, wondering if she sounded as stupid as she felt.

"There were what, hon?" he whispered, kissing the top of her head where it rested against his shoulder. "You can tell me."

"My dreams were full of angels."

He didn't say anything for a moment, and she wondered in a brief panic if he was thinking of some smart remark. But all he did was shift her so that she was lying in his arms looking up at him.

No alarm bells went off. They'd done plenty of kissing and cuddling in the two years they'd been together. She just wouldn't make love with him. *Just*, Brenna thought. It was a big thing to him. As it was to her. But for different reasons.

When the time was right, she would know it. It

wasn't that marriage was her goal or that she had some kind of religious hang-up about it. She simply hadn't met the man she was ready to give herself to. The engagement to Jim was partly out of a sense of guilt he had managed to induce in her. If she knew he was committed to her, he'd said, they could work their way up to a full sexual relationship. His reasoning, not hers. Then she realized she hadn't answered the most important question: Did she love him?

Brenna tried to concentrate on just being with him. Jim leaned down to brush a light kiss across her lips. He tasted of wine and smelled of aftershave. It was nice and male and definitely real.

"So were these the angels you'd heard about from your interviews?" he asked.

"No, that was the strangest part. My dreams had nothing to do with the stories I'd heard. These people had all been saved from an accident or some life-threatening situation. In my dream, a girl died and the angel blamed himself."

"Himself?" Jim said, running his hand lightly up and down her arm. "I thought angels were chicks."

"Women. And no, according to most legends, they're not. I think because they're perfect, they're some kind of combination of male and female. Or most of them, anyway."

"Androgynous?" he asked.

"My, what a big word," she said teasingly.

His arms tightened around her. "Don't patronize me, baby."

She was just starting to say "I'm sorry" when his mouth came down on hers hard, in a way that told her she'd angered him. He'd probably been mad since she broke off the engagement. How many handsome fighter pilots ever got jilted? Her comment just now had been snotty, she had to admit, but she'd had her own anger, too, at the pressure Jim had placed on her.

Her hand was on his chest, to push him back, to get some air, to try to talk, when he slipped his arm under hers to settle it on her breast.

He misread the sudden panic shooting through her that gave her goosebumps. The adrenaline rush also tightened her nipples, which he felt through her sweater. Naturally, he interpreted it in his own favor. Jim eased back on the kiss. He didn't remove his mouth from hers, however, as he immediately slid his hand under her untucked sweater.

Brenna started to struggle. She wasn't enjoying this. Big jerk, didn't he know that? Obviously not, because one hand continued to knead her breast, while with the other he dragged her sweater up to expose her torso.

"Jim, no," she said, the instant he pulled his mouth away from hers. But he fastened it onto the lacy cup of her bra instead and she didn't even think he heard her. His breath was coming heavily now and he was clearly aroused. She could feel the bulge in his jeans against her arm. His hand cupped the shell of her bra to push it aside.

She tugged hard at his arms, pushing them away from her, trying to yank her sweater back down. She'd never felt such a tearing sense of panic. She wound one hand into his hair and yanked, grabbing his wrist with the other when he tried to move his hand back to her chest.

Her strength wasn't enough to stop him, of course, but she finally captured his attention. His head came up, eyes heavy-lidded with passion. "What's wrong, babe?" he asked.

"This isn't college and I didn't give you permission to paw me."

Anger blazed in his dark brown eyes. "Damn straight it isn't," he said, breathing hard. "This is worse than college. It's like high school. Why can't you be like every other woman I've—" He clamped down hard on his next words in the nick of time.

"Like every other woman you've slept with?" Brenna said, hauling herself up and out of his lap.

"All right, yes, if you want to be crude," he said. "What is your problem, Brenna? We've cuddled before. You've never acted like you thought I was going to rape you. Jeez, I've never forced myself on a woman before. I've never had to."

"Oh yes, Mr. Air Force Pilot, gift to American womanhood. Go ahead, tell me how every other woman loves it, how good you are. Isn't that what you told me last time? It must have been the thrill of the chase that attracted you to me. You finally got tired of it when you saw you weren't going to get what you wanted."

"Man, you're really on some tear tonight," he said, reaching for the abandoned wine glass. "I did want to marry you, Brenna. But I've seen too damn many military marriages go down the drain. Your parents are from a different generation. They're still together. I don't know a single married guy in my squadron who hasn't been divorced or isn't about to be."

He sucked the last of the wine from his glass. "I planned to be faithful to you, damn it. Was it too much to ask to make sure we were compatible first?"

Brenna had to unclench her teeth to answer. "Planned to be faithful, you mean, if I was good enough? It was too much for you to make the commitment first?" she said.

"Jesus, we're back to that again. Forget it, Bren. Tell your mother I tried. I'm sorry you're having bad dreams, but don't say I didn't offer."

He moved toward the door. "You know that 'frustration' you mentioned, baby? It's called sexual frustration, and I'd say you have as much experience in that as you do at writing. No wonder you don't sleep at night."

He grabbed his leather bomber jacket. "I'll be at the base the rest of the week. Call me if you change your mind."

"Hell will freeze over first," she snapped.

He turned, his hand on the doorknob. "And I thought you hated clichés." His smug, superior expression told her he thought he'd won the war of words.

"*Hasta la vista*, baby," he said as he let himself out.

Only after Jim left did she realize they hadn't gotten around to discussing his knowledge of angel sightings. Brenna sighed. Probably it had been no more than another ploy to get back into her good graces.

She threw the flowers in the trash, not wanting

additional reminders of Jim around. Then she went in search of her grandmother's necklace.

"My lady Gabri-elle, I killed her," Cairn said. He stood at the cliff top, Gabri-elle motionless by his side. They had stood thus the better part of a day. Yet she waited patiently.

"No. You did not kill her," she said.

"I finally found her," Cairn continued, hardly noticing what Gabri-elle said. "When I did, I overwhelmed her. She wasn't ready. She was too young."

Gabri-elle interrupted his litany of guilt. "She was young, I will grant you," she said in her voice like chiming bells. "But she lived in primitive times. These folk believe more readily in evil deeds and spirits than in good ones."

Suddenly a golden trumpet appeared in her hands. She blew three notes on it. Winging toward them from the east came an angel even more splendid than she. Garbed in emerald green, wings composed of iridescent feathers like those of a peacock, Micha-el, mightiest of angels, answered the summons.

He bowed before them, his mighty wings keeping him aloft imperceptibly. "You sent for me, Gabrielle," he said in a voice like quiet thunder.

They conferred then. Cairn had difficulty following their conversation. To him, it sounded like a duet between the deep golden chimes of bells and the long, slow thunder that rolls across the sky before a storm.

When they turned to him, he did his best to bear the weight of their combined gaze. He did not drop his gaze, though holding it took more courage than any he had possessed when wielding a sword.

Micha-el nodded approvingly. "You have learned much in your time with us. We can still help you, although not in finding she whom you love. She has returned to the Light."

Cairn glanced up. The blazing Wheel, where silver-winged Rapha-el had taken Brianna's soul, was no longer visible.

"When she emerges, or as who, none of us can say," Micha-el said. "Even though she does not remember you overtly, a part of her still seeks you. Were you to descend in earthly form, it will be much more difficult to find her."

"In earthly form? Is that possible?" Cairn asked.

"It is, but I do not recommend it. You have none of the protections we possess. You will be vulnerable to the Adversary. He might even offer you help in finding her."

Cairn's heart leaped at the thought. Thunder tolled abruptly in the heavens, rolling across the sky while clouds swirled and roiled beneath them. Thunder appeared in the Archangel's eyes. "Put not your hope in Darkness," Micha-el boomed. "Such power is gained only at the highest cost."

He waved his arm, in which a blazing sword had appeared. The clouds formed into a tableau. Two bright, powerful beings faced each other across a battlefield of clouds. Then the cloud-angels leaped at each other, grappling and rolling.

The heavens and the earth shook with the force of the two angels' combat, which seemed at times as though it would tear the fabric of heaven itself.

More clouds boiled up, hiding the contest. Then

the cloud-curtain parted with one mighty clap of thunder. One angel fell, while the cloud-angel that was Micha-el stood with arms and legs akimbo, breathing hard, spent.

The sword he held blazed undimmed, throwing out a beacon of light that lit the darkness through which the vanquished angel fell.

"Behold Lucifer, the Morning Star," proclaimed Micha-el.

Then Micha-el appeared to grow until he towered above Cairn and Gabri-elle. In one hand he held the flaming sword, in the other the Scales of Judgment.

"Behold Micha-el, Angel of Judgment," Gabri-elle said, and even her golden voice sounded awestruck.

On the Scales of Judgment, a life-sized Lucifer balanced on a platform, which sank slowly beneath his weight. As it sank, he turned dark, like tarnish covering silver. His magnificent multicolored wings turned black and leathery, like bats' wings. His face shriveled, his features malignant.

A tear dropped from the eye of Micha-el. It fell on the face of Lucifer. Where it touched, the fallen angel remained untarnished. One eye, one ear, half his face and hair remained bright. Coppery with fire and sunlight, his undamaged side served as a reminder that he had once been as magnificent as Micha-el himself. The rest reflected the darkness of his soul.

"Be cautious if you choose to walk among your own kind again, for temptation walks with them," Micha-el thundered. "In so doing you risk falling into the hands of the Enemy. You will lose everything you struggled so hard to find."

Before Cairn could so much as blink, Micha-el disappeared. A long, last roll of thunder rippled across the heavens, a flash of green from far, far away the only evidence that he had been there at all.

"Come," Gabri-elle commanded gently and took them to somewhere greener and warmer than the land where the girl Brianna had lived.

"You understood his message?" she asked.

"I would have to be blind and deaf not to," Cairn responded. He bent over and plucked a blade of grass, its prickliness a welcome respite from so much power and glory.

"A humble thing, a blade of grass," he remarked. One effect of Micha-el's visit, he found, was that he no longer felt so daunted by Gabri-elle. By contrast with the stern Archangel, the greatest of the guardian angels, she seemed positively gentle. He was not foolish enough to assume she had any mortal weaknesses, however.

"Oh, I have my weaknesses," she said, laughing.

"Someday someone will tell me how you do that," he muttered, tired of the ease with which they read his mind.

Then he realized why Gabri-elle was still with him. Suddenly confidence filled him, more than he had felt since the day he awoke to this existence.

"Despite what Micha-el said, my lady, you are going to help me, are you not?" Cairn leaned towards her, the blade of grass crumpling in his fist. "But I do not want to be reborn."

"How do you know you will not remember?" she asked.

"Not even the Archangel Micha-el knows when Brynna will be reborn. How can anyone assure me I will remember who I am? Yet if I do not remember, we will never find each other again."

"There might be less pain if you did not," she suggested. He knew Gabri-elle was thinking of the girl Brianna's fate and his own reaction.

"I will never stop searching."

"I know." She sighed. "Cairn, she will be born again. She will seek you, however blindly. Not even we know when. But she may be somewhat less than she was after this experience," the golden voice warned. "The results of one life often accumulate. Some things are passed on, often in ways that cannot be anticipated."

The blade of grass shredded. "Then I owe her still more, not less. She is the other half of my soul."

"Listen, then, Cairn. Here is what you can do."

Chapter Six

"Brilliant piece, Brenna." At five minutes to twelve, Nora dropped the edited article on Brenna's desk. Brenna quickly flipped the pages, seeing far fewer pencil marks than usual.

"Captures exactly the right spirit," Nora said out of the corner of her mouth. Unnaturally thin and a ferocious chain-smoker, Nora was hard to impress and gave praise sparingly. "Somewhere between description and acceptance, skepticism and belief. Nice job."

Nora started to walk away, then stopped at the next row of desks. "Especially for a late piece." As she had intended, everyone in the newsroom heard her.

Marina, whose back was to Nora, rolled her eyes and smothered a laugh. Brenna merely saluted. "We who were about to die salute you, O Caesar," she said tiredly.

"What did you say?" Marina said, her hands shaped into a classic Italian gesture of incomprehension. Brenna envied Marina her ability to express so much emotion merely by waving her hands in a certain way.

"C'mon, I'll explain the mangled reference over coffee. My treat. I don't have time for lunch. I've got to make the corrections." Even knowing Nora had given her the piece back at lunchtime deliberately, a petty punishment, Brenna felt her spirits lifting.

"So where are we going to dinner? Do you still want to go tonight?" Marina asked a few minutes later as they cradled hot Styrofoam cups in the cafeteria.

"I'm too tired. Let's go tomorrow, OK? Jim came over last night."

"Oh?"

"It was a disaster. I kicked him out."

"Then why aren't you feeling better about it? You look like something the dog dragged in, and it isn't just staying up late to work on your article."

Brenna didn't answer directly, not even to correct Marina's latest charming slip of the tongue. She was thinking of Jim's criticism. "Sometimes I wonder why I've never been able to keep a relationship going. I feel like I've been waiting for something for so long that I don't know what it is any longer."

But her dream-lover's feelings for her were so intense, she had woken up and cried to find the dream wasn't real.

"You and every other career woman over the age

of twenty-five," Marina responded. "Washington is full of bright, attractive women like you who haven't found the right man."

"But this town is full of men."

"Do you remember that cover story on 'Dates from Hell'?"

"Of course. We both contributed experiences for it, as I remember."

"Exactly. All those bright, handsome men out there are putting on fourteen-hour days. They don't have time for anything else."

Brenna was just punchy enough to find Marina's last statement hilarious. "Putting *in* fourteen-hour days, kiddo."

"The point, O Tired One, is that you're not alone. You're part of the sisterdom . . . sisterhood." Marina corrected herself this time.

Brenna pushed away from the linoleum-topped table. "Then why do I feel so alone sometimes?" she said, too low for Marina to hear.

She caught up with her friend after executing a perfect rim shot ten feet from the trash can to dispose of her coffee cup. "Listrani's for dinner tomorrow, *va bene?*" she said.

"*Va bene,*" Marina replied. "Get some sleep tonight, all right?"

"I'll try."

Scotland, 1880

"For seven days only, Cairn. Remember that. You cannot stay long on earth, not and remain what you are now." Gabri-elle's parting injunction still rang in

Cairn's ears. Time did not pass in heaven as it did on earth, so he had not even been certain in what time period he had arrived.

He had been given a "sennight." He had already heard the ancient expression here in nineteenth-century Scotland when he booked his stay at a hotel in the small Highland town of Braemar.

Seven days was an impossibly short length of time in which to find Brynna, especially in this remote part of the world. Yet any more time and he risked attracting the attention of Lucifer. Scotland still drew him, despite—or perhaps because of—what had happened here so recently.

No, not recently, he reminded himself. One hundred and twenty years had passed by the reckoning on earth. Among other skills, he needed to recover the knack of measuring time.

He was determined not to dwell on the difficulty of finding Brynna. At the very least, he would see the state of the world in this century, so distant in time from the one in which he had been born. His people had come from here. The girl Brianna had been born near here, in Glen Avon. Perhaps she even lived here, born again in this time.

Luckily, the gift of speaking so that others understood him in their own vernacular had not left him along with his angel form. In fact, he did not feel much different. Pain continued to be a factor, except that now it manifested as physical pain throughout his limbs, rather than in his head.

Had he not looked the same as so long ago, he would have said it was his age. But he looked no older and felt no older than his twenty-eight years the day of his last battle. Except for the painful experience he had gained.

Hiking and climbing, he found, had no effect on the constant bodily pain, nor did hot-water bottles or such medicines as were available in this day and age help. Other than that, he was normal in every way.

He became hungry and thirsty. He had to wear extra clothes when it was cold, take off layers of clothing when it was hot. It was summer now, a summer like those long ago—pleasant, even warm in the daytime, cool at night.

He also dreamed, not certain of the difference between curse and gift. For now that he had a physical body again, he suffered its consequences. Over and over, he relived his short time with Brynna, their one night together.

He remembered how her kisses had swiftly turned skilled after her initial hesitation and sweet, inexperienced awkwardness. How the smooth white skin beneath her tunic, untouched by sun or calluses, felt beneath his hands. How she had enclosed him hotly, tightly, sapping his control, demanding his response. How they had learned each other and loved each other until dawn.

Over and over that night, he had murmured to her, "so little time," using desperately the time they did have while knowing the sun would rise all too soon on another day of bloodshed. Not knowing the day would bring her death and end all happiness.

Cairn woke every morning in a fever of need, daylight crushing him with its cruel clarity of loneliness, revealed in the empty bed.

In retaliation, he pushed his body as hard as he could, with all the discipline of the soldier he had once been. Thankfully, in daylight at least, his body did not escape the rigid control imposed by his mind. If a week was all he had in this century, he would make the most of it.

He visited small Highland towns, roamed rocky glens, hiked along lochs so blue his eyes ached. As he walked in the Cairngorm Mountains, he found pale purple crystals, often imbedded inside thick crusts of rock. The amethysts reminded him of the Scottish national flower, heather, which in turn reminded him of the girl, Brianna.

One day at the foot of a cliff, he found golden-brown crystals. With a surge of emotion, Cairn looked up. There was something familiar about this place.

Shading his eyes, he scanned the rock face, the peak above. This was where the girl Brianna had jumped. He looked up at the cliff where he had stood for so long with his grief, the guardian angel Gabrielle at his side.

His hands tightened on the stones. He gathered them until his hands and pockets were full.

Later, back at the hotel perusing a guide to the region, he discovered that the stones and the mountains were both named "cairngorms." With the name so similar to his own and the knowledge of what had transpired there, he understood the source of his interest.

These mountains and those stones were part of him in a way he did not fully understand. His family had long since vanished from the earth. His clan had passed into the mists of history. His beloved, separated from him for centuries, was perhaps forever beyond his reach.

Yet here he felt at home. He tumbled the rough stones in his palm. It seemed this was all he had to anchor him to earth.

After that, he carried the stones in his pockets, a token of love and life from the distant past. Only once did he wish for his wings and that was when marking his travels on a map forced him to realize just how little territory he had covered, just how little he had accomplished.

Meanwhile, time rushed forward, the fragile, rushed pace that belonged to mortals. Soon time would devour him.

He had two days left when he met Mrs. Graham. Cairn had seen the old lady in the hotel. She took afternoon tea regularly at four. Cairn was usually back in the hotel by then, planning his evening walk.

His night vision had not completely disappeared, he had discovered. He could still see at night, although not as far as when he had worn angel form. Once he realized that, he wasted no moment of his time.

He paused only during the afternoon. The hot brown liquid called tea revived him, eased his aches, and gave him more energy. He had become as regular a devotee as the tiny bird-like woman who usually sat two tables away.

Today she perched on a seat at the table next to his. Cairn politely tipped his hat and said "Good afternoon," as always. Her eyes, sharp as a wren's, scrutinized his hat, his tweeds, his walking stick, then fixed squarely on his face.

"Have ye not found what you came for?" she said, pouring tea from the china pot set under a quilted tartan cozy at her table. Tartan plaids had become all the rage since Queen Victoria had begun to take holidays at Balmoral Castle, built for her near Braemar.

"Madam?" he replied politely, startled at her direct address.

"You may be looking in the wrong place," she said, stirring lumps of sugar into her cup. "Or you may be here at the wrong time."

He remembered a line from a French philosopher who had lived some time ago. Pascal. *The heart has its reasons which reason knows nothing of.* Was this coincidence? Or a message for him?

Mrs. Graham wasn't an angel, or he would have known, he was certain of that much. Whoever she was, there was no idea too small for him to pursue, no glimmer of hope he would turn his back on.

"What would you suggest, madam?" he asked.

"Stop using your head. Follow your heart." At this vague advice, Cairn reconsidered. Perhaps she was just a batty old *grande dame*.

"The Sight, young man," she said, stirring her milk into the tea energetically. "Have ye forgotten where you are?"

He moved his chair closer to hers, looking into her eyes when she turned her wrinkled face to his. Her eyes were faded blue, ringed round with darker blue at the edge of her irises. Brynna's hazel-green eyes had been ringed with the sign of the Second Sight too.

"You have not long, lad," she said. "Create a link, a connection. Leave something you might be able to retrieve, or follow, later on."

"How?" he asked. Despite the centuries of watching earth from Above, he felt as knowledgeable as a newborn colt here. "What is there of me that I can leave behind?"

"Ye'll know," she said confidently, carefully picking currants out of her scones and setting them to one side of her plate.

"You do not like those," he noted, making polite conversation as he wondered if he dared reveal who he really was and ask her to help him.

"I take them up to my room. Lay them on the windowsill for the birds. They make a lovely necklace, all strung out in a row." Her blue eyes twinkled.

His hopes were dashed again. She could not be of any help, he decided. Oh, she was a sweet old lady, even if she was a little dotty, but what could she know that would be of any use to him?

Cairn reached absently into his pocket to finger some of the stones he had collected during the week.

"That's it, laddie," she said, her gaze going to his pocket, even though he had pulled nothing out. "Leave something of yourself. It will find its way to her. Then ye can find your way to her." She dusted scone flour from her hands and started to stand up. He rose politely to help her from her chair.

"She isna so far away as all that," she said in a confidential tone. "But I cannot see how far. Godspeed, lad." Mrs. Graham lifted her head, standing on tiptoe. Cairn bent down, receiving her kiss on his cheek with surprise and pleasure.

She pocketed the currants, then whisked out of the dining room in a rustle of full skirts.

Cairn pulled out a handful of stones out of his own pocket. He had found the stones, true enough, but how could they be something of his? The amethysts were pretty enough, but . . .

His fingers tightened on the cairngorms. They seemed to vibrate in his palm. *This* was what she meant. The connection he had with these crystals was unclear to him, but he felt them call out to him every time he touched them.

He stared at her table as if something there would yield her secrets. How had she known? What was he supposed to do with the smoky cairngorm quartz?

Cairn hurried out of the dining room in search of Mrs. Graham. Although he asked the desk clerk, no one had seen her. She seemed to have vanished.

"Dad, do you remember that necklace of yellow stones that was Gran's?" Brenna had stopped by her parents' house on her way to Thursday's celebratory dinner with Marina.

"I thought your mother gave you Grandma's jewelry," her father said, looking around as if he expected Brenna's mother to materialize.

"She never gave me the necklace. I looked all over my place. I remembering wearing it one year to a White House reception, but I must have given it back to her. You remember the reception for the armed forces I went to with you?"

Her mother hadn't wanted to submit to the indignity of a metal detector, so Brenna had gone in her place. "I wore that yellow silk dress."

"Hmm. Yes, I'm sure you did. That was the night we saw General Lefkowicz. Do you remember?" Her father launched into a story about the legendary general's tactics during a WWII battle in Europe. In the middle of his recitation, Brenna caught the smell of something unpleasant and rubbery. Something was burning, whatever it was.

"Daddy, where's Mom?" she interrupted. She'd thought her mother would have emerged from the kitchen by now, but Brenna had been enjoying the time with her father too much to seek out her mother right away.

"Your mother went out shopping. Or to the grocery store or something," her father replied vaguely.

"At dinnertime?" Her mother never went out after three o'clock in the afternoon because she hated traffic. And she went to the commissary for groceries only when it first opened, to avoid crowds. Moreover, Brenna couldn't imagine her father cooking his own meal. He was a traditionalist of the old school.

"Did you say dinner? Damn." Her father spun on his heel, his straight military posture intact despite the slow, inevitable spread of arthritis.

Brenna trailed her father into the kitchen. As she did, the rattling sound coming from the microwave on the counter reached a high pitch. With an ear-splitting squeal, the door burst open, spattering its contents all over the ceiling, floor, and countertop.

Brenna and George had retreated, and were untouched. She saw that her father was unhurt and began to giggle. Her father turned to her with a wounded look on his face.

"Oh, Daddy, what have you done?" Brenna asked.

"Mother is going to kill you."

"She left a note saying to put the potatoes in the microwave and to reheat the lamb chop in the oven. Oh, hell," George Sirin muttered. "Do you think it was the potatoes in the oven and the lamb chop in the microwave?"

Brenna opened the oven door gingerly. The plastic dish holding the meat was beginning to melt onto the oven rack. "Since the potatoes were wrapped in foil, and the chop was in a plastic dish, I'd say so."

Her father looked aggrieved, but his eyes twinkled. "Always said I couldn't be trusted in the kitchen. We don't need to tell your mother about this, do we?"

"We don't have any choice, Daddy. That plastic is going to be murder to get off the metal rack, and those bits of foil are going to take you until Christmas to peel off the ceiling."

"Hell and damn. I don't suppose you want to go out to eat with an old man, do you?"

"Of course. Come eat with me and Marina. Where is Mom anyway?"

"I don't know, but she isn't here, is she? So she can't complain." As a temporary solution, Brenna couldn't fault her father's reasoning, but they both knew he'd catch hell later. No wonder he wanted to get out for a while.

After poking around for a few minutes, Brenna found the note her mother had left on the refrigerator. It said that her mother was at a museum reception until eight p.m. and gave explicit instructions on how to heat up the meal.

"Daddy, you really are hopeless," she said after reading it. "I must have inherited it from you. The

113

man I marry has to cook better than you, or we're going to be in trouble."

As they drove to the restaurant a few streets over, her laughter faded. If her father had been closer to the microwave, he might have been seriously injured when the foil-wrapped potatoes exploded under high pressure. She didn't suppose he would have set the oven on fire with the plastic dish that melted, but for the first time she began to wonder if her father should be left alone.

Suppose there had been a fire, or he'd gone out without a key? There were any number of things a forgetful old man could do. She'd heard of Alzheimer's patients walking away from their houses in bathrobe and slippers in a thunderstorm.

Brenna tucked her arm through her father's as they walked from the parking lot to the restaurant. If she hated the idea of thinking of her father as old, how must her mother feel about it? For the first time, she understood a little of her mother's reluctance to admit old age was taking its toll on her father.

There was not enough time. "Damn," said Cairn, clenching his fist on the counter of the jeweler's store in Braemar.

"Sir?" said the burly man handling the stones and jeweler's loupe with astonishing deftness, considering his size.

Even now Cairn felt his vision lengthening, the pain shifting from his limbs back to his head. He had felt no hunger since yesterday. This was his last day. Any hope of prolonging the transformation back to angel form was being dashed by the changes his body was undergoing even now.

"The necklace. Are there enough stones to make a necklace?" he asked, forcing himself to concentrate on the task at hand.

"Absolutely, sir. Once these are polished, they'll have a fine glow to them. Nice size. I'd suggest a graduated style."

"What is that?"

"You see this large one here, the size of my thumbnail? You put that in the center. I can cut and facet it as an ovoid sphere. It'll shape up to about six carats, I shouldn't wonder. Then these other pieces will make bonny three- and four-carat round spheres that will lay against the collarbone. These smaller two-carat stones will taper round to the back. A gold clasp, and there you have it. Will that be what you were wanting, sir?"

"It sounds fine . . . just right. How long will it take?" Given the work the man had just described, tomorrow was out of the question, Cairn realized.

"The cutting and the polishing will take longer than stringing the actual necklace. That's no work at all. But—hmm, give me six weeks and I should have it for you at the end of next month."

Seeing Cairn's expression, the man pursed his lips. "You're not from here, are you? You'd be wanting it sooner, I suppose. I canna do it in less than three weeks."

"Two weeks, three weeks, it's immaterial. I have to leave tomorrow," Cairn said, his heart heavy at the prospect. Not only had he not found Brynna, not the merest trace of anyone like her from Braemar to Grantown-on-Spey, but this was not going to work out either. Although what he would have done with a necklace once he had it, he had no idea. Certainly he could not take it with him.

The jeweler wiped sweat from his brow, his fair Scottish complexion turning red with anxiety. "Is there somewhere I could be sending the piece after I'm done, sir? Aberdeen, Edinburgh?"

Send him the necklace? In spite of himself, Cairn laughed. "No, that's quite impossible, I fear. I shall not be in this area again for a long while." If ever.

"Is there someone I can send it to, who can pass it along to you?"

About to say no, Cairn remembered the old lady. The one who had suggested it in the first place.

"Do you know Mrs. Graham?" he asked. "Mrs. Laura Graham," he added, wondering how he knew that. He shrugged, enjoying the feel of his shoulders moving under the brown wool frock coat he wore. Regaining a sense of his body and its capabilities had been one of the most pleasant aspects of this entire sojourn. Except for the nights.

"The Widow Graham who has her tea up at the Fife Arms Hotel every day at four?" the jeweler asked.

"You sound as if you know her," Cairn replied, watching the man's face grow even redder under his thin brown hair.

"Been courting that woman for an age, I have. That sly boots. Did she send you?" he asked hopefully.

"No, I am afraid not. But she's the only person I know well enough to entrust this to. Why don't you take it to her as a gift when you have finished?"

"I couldna do that," the jeweler said, lapsing into

a stronger burr in his agitation. "You want this for your lady."

"Aye, I do, but I shall not be able to get it to her on this trip," Cairn said. He pulled out some banknotes, counting them out until the jeweler's expression passed from keen observation to satisfaction. "This should pay for the necklace. Take it to your Mrs. Graham and tell her the visitor from the hotel sends it to her. It is hers to do with as she likes. I trust her as to the disposition of it. Take as long as you like on this. I want it done well, not quickly."

"Absolutely, sir, absolutely. It will be a labor from the heart," the jeweler said, his florid face beaming.

"Then I shall be content," Cairn said soberly. "For it comes from mine."

Chapter Seven

"Where did this come from, Mother?" Brenna asked, her fingers curling around the old necklace. She'd given in again, after her mother's fourth phone call that week, and had arrived in time for dinner on Saturday night. Her father was in his workshop in the basement, his favorite refuge when her mother was in a snit. The microwave incident apparently hadn't gone down too well, but her mother said nothing to her directly.

Brenna did not want to argue with her mother right now anyway. They were upstairs in her parents' bedroom. Seated at a window seat that looked out over the small back garden, Peggy Sirin held an old leather jewelry box on her knees.

"Was the necklace in our family?" Brenna fingered the stones, admiring their polished smoky-gold gleam. The facets were just slightly irregular on close inspection. If they were hand cut, the necklace was probably fairly old.

"No, actually it wasn't," Peggy Sirin answered. "My mother liked to collect jewelry, especially semi-precious stones. She loved all that big, clunky stuff. That's why I gave you most of it."

You liked the diamonds well enough, Brenna thought, but dismissed her catty thought. She knew the diamonds reflected her mother's pale blond beauty better than the earthy glow of topaz. The yellow and brown undertones favored someone of Brenna's coloring.

Brenna didn't particularly like "big, clunky" jewelry herself, but she did love semi-precious stones and unusual pieces, and her grandmother had owned several of those. The cairngorm necklace had a large center stone in it, a sparkling oval. The other stones were round, but all were lovingly cut, faceted, and polished to bring out their intriguing color.

"Do you know, I believe my mother's housekeeper actually gave that piece to her," Peggy reflected.

"Who was she?" Brenna asked.

"Who?"

"Gran's housekeeper," Brenna said. "I don't remember her."

"You wouldn't. She died long before you were born. Came over on the boat with some of the Irish who emigrated to Boston in the twenties and thirties. She was Scots-Irish, or so she said. Worked for your Gran from the age of fifteen."

"How did she die then, if she was so much younger?"

119

"I came home from boarding school for the Christmas holidays. It was 1944. She died in our house. Mother was quite upset, I can tell you. Wanted to have that sailor hauled back from Europe and shot, I think."

"What? You've never told me all this, Mom. You just told me it was Gran's jewelry."

Her mother drew her sweater closer around her in a defensive gesture. "You never asked, and as I said, you never knew her."

"What about the housekeeper?"

"She got knocked up by some sailor before he went to fight in the war," her mother said bluntly. "One of the last ships over. Megan died in childbirth, the child with her. Silly thing wouldn't get rid of the baby."

"Mother," Brenna said, shocked. "If she was Irish, she must have been Catholic. No Catholic girl would have had an abortion back then."

"I suppose. She said the strangest things before she died. She knew my mother liked the necklace, for I heard her say, 'You must have this, Mrs. Lindsay. It was my auntie's and she was Scots. Your family was from Scotland, too, even if they came over to America much longer ago.'"

Her mother's recall was perfect, Brenna reflected. She could hear the echo of a lilting accent in the words her mother recited. "You were there when she died?"

"I wouldn't have been allowed," her mother said indignantly. "Young ladies weren't supposed to know about such things." Then she had the grace to look sheepish. "I was horribly fascinated by it all, of course. Mother tried to keep it a secret, told people Megan had gone away to work for another family. Though how Mother expected to keep a baby a secret, I don't know. Maybe Megan was going to give the baby up for adoption," her mother said, half to herself.

Brenna found herself leaning forward, as if on the point of some discovery. "Go on, Mother," she encouraged. Her mother so rarely talked about her childhood.

"Father was out for the evening with business associates, and the midwife called my mother upstairs when everything went wrong. Apparently Megan had started hemorrhaging. I tiptoed upstairs after my mother, lurking outside in the hallway. Nobody else was around. My mother had given the other servants leave for the weekend. She had Megan up in the farthest guest room on the third floor, one we hardly ever used."

Brenna saw the scene as her mother described it, in the old Beacon Hill mansion that had belonged to her grandparents. Her mother's voice faded. Brenna saw the two women, one a middle-aged, prosperous matron, the other a young servant girl with the accent of Ireland in her voice.

"Mrs. Lindsay, you've been so good to me," Megan said, clutching her employer's hand. "I've done nothing but cause you heartache, and now I'm after paying for it."

"Nonsense," Edith Lindsay answered. "You've been a good girl and very loyal."

"Och, but I have not," she said. "If I hadna done what I did, this baby wouldna be taken from me now."

"You're not the first girl to have a child out of wed-lock," Edith said. *"I don't believe in that kind of pun-ishment, and you shouldn't either. It's a load of superstitious tripe."*

Megan's voice was growing fainter. *"Maybe,"* she said, *"maybe things just happen, but I'm after doubt-ing it. I know this baby was special, even if her mum and da weren't married as we ought to have been."*

Her voice took on an odd, prophetic tone. *"But now this little soul will not be born."* The midwife stepped in as the young woman's voice faltered, but Megan waved her away.

"Take this, Mrs. Lindsay," she said, pressing the golden necklace into her employer's hand. *"Maybe she'll come to your family, this soul that has waited so long for her happiness."*

Megan's dying words made no sense, but Edith Lindsay took the necklace anyway.

Her mother's voice trailed off. Brenna found her-self clenching the stones so tightly that they dug into her palm. "What did she mean?" Peggy said in a quiet voice. "To this day, I've never understood."

"I don't know either, Mother," Brenna said, al-though she had goosebumps. "The necklace is spe-cial anyway. Thank you for telling me the story."

"Well, as I said, it isn't my style of jewelry," Peggy replied, and the intimate moment disappeared as if it had never occurred.

Sitting a moment silently, they heard a bellow from below them. Brenna was the first to run down the two flights of stairs. "Daddy!" she called.

"George, if you dropped that engraving tool . . ." her mother began, moving down the stairs at a less unseemly pace. The women stopped on the threshold of the workshop.

Brenna put a hand to her mouth to stifle a gasp. The wooden jewelry box her father had been working on now had huge gouges dug out of its lid, marring a once smoothly finished top.

"George, that was for Christmas," Peggy said in a shocked voice.

"Daddy, what happened?" Brenna asked.

"I was just down here finishing this and . . ." Her father didn't meet their concerned looks. "I forgot . . . I mean . . . Who is it for?" her father asked with quiet despair.

Stepping closer, Brenna saw that her father had started to write several names, scoring out each one, apparently as he realized it wasn't correct. None of the names was hers.

"Oh Daddy," Brenna said, tears in her eyes. She hugged her father fiercely. "It's all right. I don't need my name on it. I know who I am anyway, right?" she said, making a stab at levity.

"Sure, honey," her father said, but he didn't smile. They all knew it wasn't all right.

12:30 A.M. "Oh-dark-thirty," her father would have called it after the military 24-hour clock. Brenna did not want to think about her father now or the argument she'd had with her mother in private afterward. She had begged her mother to take George Sirin to Walter Reed Army Hospital for tests.

Now the clock read half past midnight and Brenna was in the bathroom, reaching for the cold medicine, desperately hoping it would help make her sleepy.

She swallowed the medicine, snapping off the light quickly without looking at her reflection in the mirror.

Hands stuck in the pockets of her old flannel robe, Brenna wandered around her living room in the semi-dark. She ended up on the couch, looking at a print of a cherub and wondering how these tubby babies ever came to be considered angels. Her interview subjects would have been appalled, she was sure, if they'd thought a little flutter-winged "putti"—as Marina told her they were called in Italy—had been the instrument of heavenly intervention.

She didn't want to think about angels now either. All she wanted to do was sleep. But that hope still seemed far away, given how tense and keyed-up she felt.

Brenna tossed the print aside, reaching for the bookshelf where her big world atlas lay flat. She turned on a lamp, deciding to look at Ireland. Maybe she'd see where her grandmother's housekeeper, Megan Graham, had come from.

Ireland and Scotland shared a page on the atlas. As she cast her eyes over the topographic map, sounding out the wonderfully lyrical and evocative names, she spotted the range in the Scottish Highlands named the Cairngorm Mountains. A shiver ran up her spine and the hairs on the back of her neck rose.

Cairn. The image of the angel in her vision, the one she'd been trying so hard to forget, rose before her. Then she thought of the necklace. Could there be some link between the gold-and-brown angel and the cairngorm quartz? She recalled his grief, how his tears had tumbled into smoky golden stones at the base of the rocky cliff.

She had a necklace made of those same smoky stones.

Silly, Brenna chided herself. *You have some weird dreams and you expect all these fragments to link up and make sense. Where you have rocks is in the head.* She'd be out in McLean next, asking Maud Barrett to help her get in touch with this angel. Or channel for him.

In a dark cavern lit by hot, licking flames, a dark being sat. "Beloth!" roared the former Morning Star, Lord of the Dark, and a hundred other names he could use when he so chose. For the moment Lucifer would do.

"Your Lowliness?" replied one of his more recent acquisitions. One of his lazier ones, judging by his activity in the last few hundred years. Or lack thereof.

"It's Lord of Evil to you, varlet," Lucifer growled. "What the hell have you done about that mutant ang—that mutant you told me about?"

"I have the yellow quartz I captured. The stones resonate to his harmonic frequency, just as you said. I didn't think you'd particularly enjoy hearing them, as they are most robustly melodic, but if you wish . . ."

"It's been 1,200 years and you haven't found him on earth." Lucifer flapped his wings menacingly, then folded them. He hated the damned ugly things, if the truth be told—something he did rarely. The

125

truth was so unsatisfying compared with a well-crafted deception.

He still despised the wings, and appeared without them in public as often as his powers allowed. It was one thing to rule the Underworld, but the cost to his vanity of losing his magnificent appearance still rankled him privately.

And damned if having part of a radiant face remaining wasn't worse than being ugly as sin all over, because it only reminded him of what he'd lost. Whether that had been Micha-el's intention or not, he'd never know. But if it had, his archrival had an almost . . . diabolically . . . clever mind.

The Prince of Lies chuckled at his own little word-play. Then he stopped smiling. To owe his appearance to the tears of one of *them* . . . how disgustingly quaint.

Well, he was determined to have the man-mutant they were protecting. How fitting to use the man's tears to help track him to his destruction. Lucifer would love throwing that up to Micha-el.

Remembering his business, he resumed his ferocious expression. "Twelve-hundred years, *Duke* Beloth. You acquired that position long ago for a reason. You fled Above, bringing me news of this half-man, half-ang . . . One of them." As usual, he couldn't say their name, the name that had once applied to him as well.

"I beg your pardon, my Lord of Darkness, but it's only been one hundred and twenty years since I captured these stones. Seventeen-sixty was the mortal year, and it is . . ." He pulled a pocket watch out of his waistcoat pocket and consulted it. ". . . now eighteen-eighty."

Beloth spread his coat lapels. "By the way, I'm told this is the latest fashion in Europe, my Lord of Darkness."

Devil below, he was stuck with a dandy! "Pay attention to me, Beloth," Lucifer snarled. "Every year in Heav . . . up there is like a day on Earth. Every year on Earth is one hundred years down here. Have you forgotten?" To his credit, Beloth failed to cringe, although Lucifer deliberately turned his baleful side toward his foppish subordinate.

"Hear me well, Beloth. Since you like to indulge yourself in your besetting sin of vanity, you may now exploit it. Take your mortal dress with you." He indulged in his best evil smile. "You're going topside."

The starch on Beloth's perfectly turned-up collar was wilting, his cravat with it. Lucifer willed the heat in his chamber to rise. "You're going to take those damned stones and set up some kind of resonating frequency to alert you to the winged mortal's appearance," Lucifer ordered.

Beloth fingered the collar as his cravat drooped still more in the heat. "If he dares touch wingtip to Earth again to interfere in a human's life, I want him," the greatest of the fallen angels continued.

"I deserve him, damn it all. He cannot flout me." Lucifer was shouting now, his voice ringing off the damp walls of the cavern that was his office. He could carpet the walls in expensive Oriental rugs— even the magic kind—or line them with gold. Yet it remained infernally hot in here, and the walls dripped with sweat. They would forever.

"Yes, my Lord." Beloth bowed deeply, then turned to go. "One question, Master."

"Yes?"

127

"Should I wear the bowler or the top hat?"
"Out!" Lucifer roared.

The cold medicine kicked in finally. Brenna slept, but not dreamlessly. She saw a flying creature circling Earth in her dream. Her view seemed to be from a great distance. Her sight followed it lower and lower.

At first she felt a desire to attract its attention, to call out. As her vision drew closer to the creature, she bit down hard to keep from crying out. This creature was nothing like the shining ones she had seen before, although it twisted and looped in the air as if trying out its wings. The wings were dark and leathery looking. The creature seemed to absorb light rather than reflect it.

The creature flew all around the world in what seemed like minutes. It passed over Europe twice, three times, turning and swooping suddenly as a long-necked island swam out of a sea of clouds.

Brenna recognized the distinctive shape of Britain. As the creature's tail began to vibrate, she experienced a shock of recognition. The rocky landscape, the heather blooming on the moor, the icy blue waters of a loch. This was Scotland, a country she'd never visited in the flesh, but one that called to her strongly in her dreams.

In her dreams of the girl who'd died. Her dreams of him, of Cairn. The low, rich voice that she knew was his seemed to be urging her wordlessly toward it as well.

The creature homed in swiftly on the cliff, turning to and fro, like a dog looking for a scent. As it turned back and Brenna caught a glimpse of its face, she tried to wrench herself out of the dream, but she could not.

The creature had once been beautiful, powerful. It was still powerful, she sensed, but no longer beautiful. Yet even as she watched, it changed. The dark scales fell away, the wings disappeared.

A perfectly groomed gentleman suddenly appeared, walking down a path toward a small town. There was no tail visible, just a dark-haired man with dark eyes who had a neat little beard. His attire was straight out of the high Victorian era, a turned-up collar, tweed suit, and spats. A bowler hat. The very picture of an English country gentleman.

In his hand he cradled two stones that Brenna recognized. In a flash of sudden intuition, she knew that he held Cairn's quartz and that his intent, which she could not yet fathom, was dark.

The man entered the High Street, taking in the sights with apparent interest, walking neither too slowly nor too fast. He kept his hand in his pocket. She could no longer see the stones he carried.

He came to a storefront under a sign that said "Jeweler and Manufacturer."

Brenna's vision stopped at the shop door. She had no idea how much time had passed, but when he emerged, the man was smiling. He brushed a speck of dust off his lapel, then set out, whistling. As before, her vision stopped when he walked inside, entering a place called the Fife Arms Hotel.

Brenna's sense of unease grew. She did not see the man emerge again. The landscape of her dream shifted abruptly and she found herself on a modern-day bus traveling toward the Scottish mountains. The bus stopped to pick up passengers on a flat road that ran beside a loch. Her father got on at the front. She called to him but he didn't seem to hear or see her.

He fumbled with money in his pocket, but when he pulled it out, the driver said he didn't accept American money. "Doesn't this bus go to the Pentagon?" Brenna heard her father ask in a confused voice. She tried to get up to go help her father, but suddenly her mother appeared, blocking her way.

"He's fine. Leave him alone," her mother scolded.

"I have to help him," Brenna replied, helpless to move past her mother, watching her father stand forlornly at the front of the bus as the driver opened the doors and told him to leave.

"I'll take care of him," her mother said.

"You can't. He has to be warned. Someone wants to hurt him. I have to help him." But it wasn't her father she meant any longer. She wanted to warn Cairn.

"You can't help him," said her mother, whose voice didn't sound at all normal. "I have plans for him." When Brenna looked at her mother in concern, she saw that the dark man in the wool suit had taken Peggy Sirin's place.

He doffed his bowler, bowing. Brenna pulled back in horror. Her mother and father had both disappeared. Brenna was alone on the bus.

She walked forward to ask the driver if he could take her to the mountains. "Certainly, my dear. Love to help." He turned around and Brenna saw the same sinister man in the driver's stead.

Jerking herself upright and awake, Brenna discovered she'd fallen asleep on the sofa. The heavy atlas dented the soft cushion to her right. As she stared at it, disoriented, the clan names and mottoes that ran around the edges of the Irish-Scottish page jumped out at her in bold relief. Gordon, Graham, Grant.

Graham. *Ne oublie.* Do not forget.

"Do not forget," whispered a hoarse, dying voice.

"I will wait," came the faint echo from a distant past.

"Love, remember me." Was that voice, raw with pain and anguish, his . . . or hers?

"No," Brenna cried, stumbling into the bedroom, her hands over her ears. But the voices were locked inside her heart, not her ears.

Chapter Eight

Gabri-elle and Phanu-el, Angel of Hope, met Cairn on his return Above. He was drifting, yearning stronger in his heart than at any time yet during his long search, when he felt a tendril of hope brush his shoulder.

Looking up, he saw the ethereal angel whose sky-blue garment was as insubstantial as dreams, yet whose face was eternally reassuring. The sleeves of its robe were long and full in the medieval style, trailing down to the floating hem. It was a corner of this gossamer-light yet tensile-strong fabric that had touched Cairn.

"Useless," Cairn said, refusing comfort. "I failed."

"I think not," said Gabri-elle. "Look." She waved a hand over a section of sky, and a portion of the earth below appeared as through a telescope. Within the circle, rimmed by gold like a porcelain plate, Cairn saw the inside of the jeweler's shop he'd visited in Braemar.

A glistening necklace lay on the counter, cradled in a box lined with deep brown velvet. The burly jeweler had on his Sunday-best clothes and appeared to be ready to go out. He was smiling.

Phanu-el smiled serenely. "You see? You did leave something of yourself on earth. As your faery friend said, it calls you and it calls out to others." Phanu-el frowned a moment as if ready to say something more, but Cairn interrupted.

"Faery?" he said.

Gabri-elle's laugh carried the pleasing sound of chiming bells. "Yes, faeries. A group independently associated with our kind, shall we say. Composed of an unpredictable mixture of Light and Dark, they are subject to earthly fits of pique when so moved. Yet they can help mortals when they choose, interfere with them when irritated. The Celtic lands are full of faeries, although they are not so numerous as they once were. Your Mrs. Graham is just such a one."

Then Phanu-el waved a hand over the tableau. The scene changed. Cairn saw Mrs. Graham unwrapping the necklace carefully, the beaming jeweler at her side.

Phanu-el's sleeve brushed across the glowing picture once more. Cairn saw Mrs. Graham again, dressed in the garments of another time, thirty or forty years later, he thought. Yet she looked just the same as when Cairn had met her in 1880.

A young girl, dressed in similar clothes, her hair short under a bell-shaped hat, wearing a calf-length dress with a dropped waist, stood at the embarkation ramp of a mechanized ship.

A cargo ship, it was called. The girl was one of the passengers destined for the cheaper, crowded spaces bought with hard-earned money by those who wanted to emigrate across the water. Mrs. Graham was her aunt, giving her the necklace as a farewell gift.

Cairn glanced at Gabri-elle, who nodded her approval. He had understood.

The girl and Mrs. Graham embraced. Cairn saw a small brown box in the girl's hand. She clutched it tightly.

Although he strained to see her, he could not see or sense any apparent affinity between this girl and his Brynna. He wondered how this young woman was linked to his long search.

Then the blue of the ocean filled the glowing circle, endless blue sky and sea. Cairn's last sight was of a dark-haired girl standing at the railing looking west, toward a new life.

"Faery magic cannot pass over the water," Gabri-elle said softly.

"You don't know where the necklace has gone, who has it now?" Cairn asked, disappointed as the gold rim faded until the blue he saw was merely the blue of the air around him and his companions.

"That is your task," Gabri-elle answered. "The quartz will respond to you. You and Brynna, whose soul you seek." At his uncomprehending look, Gabri-elle continued. "You created these stones from your grief for the girl who died, Brianna," the golden angel said.

Cairn was not certain he understood how he had created the cairngorms, but it explained his sense of connection to them. He felt hope flare in him suddenly, like a match to tinder. As it took root and blossomed within him, Phanu-el smiled.

"Is she the one? The one with the necklace?" Cairn asked.

"Look within yourself and feel the answer," Phanu-el answered.

Cairn strained his senses towards the necklace, then fought down disappointment. The girl who boarded the boat was not Brynna.

But as he extended his senses, something tugged at the very edge of his awareness. Cairn caught the merest glimpse of a pair of wide green eyes, a hand clenching a gleaming necklace. Recognition jolted him.

"Yes," Phanu-el encouraged him. "Hold to that. Find her."

Cairn closed his eyes tightly, but the flash of vision was gone. He felt cold and empty again, the only being in this realm who did not belong, who did not want to belong.

His heart was on earth, somewhere. "But when is this? Where is she?" he asked in anguish, his voice low.

"Look ahead," Gabri-elle suggested. With a silent sweep of mighty wings, the angels departed from him.

Cairn was left to wonder and wander, focusing his vision until he narrowed it like a beam of light in a determined search for the necklace. Where the necklace was, there she would be. Or so he hoped.

If he found the correct time period. *If* she lived again on earth in that time period. *If* he found her before the Enemy found him. This time he wished for Phanu-el's unshakable hope rather than Rapha-el's healing power, for he feared the tender shoots Phanu-el had planted in him would wither from lack of nourishment.

"Ms. Barrett, thank you for agreeing to see me on such short notice," Brenna said as she entered the foyer of the elegant mansion in McLean. Two weeks had passed since she had held the necklace and wondered why she felt she had to go the Cairngorm Mountains.

During that time, her strange, restless dreams had intensified. Her dream-lover came to her still in tantalizing, arousing fragmented dreams that left her always on the verge of knowing something she had never experienced. Or of relearning something she'd once known but knew no longer.

Knowledge of herself, of him, his body. No, more, much more. His heart, his soul. Which were hers, as hers belonged to him. As soon as they found each other again.

Wound through it all was the name. Cairn. The man. The angel. Some mornings she woke feeling as if she had a hangover, so strong were the echoes of a memory she could not quite recall. Urgency permeated her dreams, his voice echoing "so little time" over and over. Through it all, she knew someone else searched for Cairn. Someone who hated him and wanted to destroy him. She had to help him, because he could not stand against the Darkness alone.

The Darkness? The dreams and thoughts were driving her mad. She couldn't confide in Marina, or anyone else she knew. They would think she was nuts. Brenna was beginning to think so, too.

At the end of her rope, she had called Maud Barrett. Considering the woman could have tossed a peck of "I told you so's" at Brenna, she had been amazingly gracious to agree to Brenna's request to see her.

"Please, Brenna, call me Maud. You sounded a little agitated on the phone." The December day was cold, but Maud looked warm in a wool suit of winter white, her pearls gleaming palely against a blush-pink silk blouse.

"Ms. Barrett . . . ah, Maud, I feel foolish," Brenna said, tugging nervously at the neck of her yellow turtleneck. At least she'd worn nice wool pants, but Maud looked so elegant, Brenna still felt underdressed. "Maybe I shouldn't have come. I . . . uh," Brenna knew her teeth were clenched. She ordered herself to relax.

Maud Barrett touched her arm. "No, it's all right. I don't have all the answers you seek, but maybe I can help you understand a bit more. If you are more open to these fanciful things?" she inquired without a trace of sarcasm, her brows arched.

Maud led her to the well-insulated Florida room once more. The cold outside had turned the air a crisp, clear blue. "What troubles you, my dear?" Maud asked after making sure Brenna didn't want anything to eat or drink.

"I haven't been sleeping well," Brenna confessed. "I'm worried about my father's health, I recently broke off a four-year relationship with the man I was supposed to marry . . ."

Maud stirred in her chair. "Forgive me for interrupting, Brenna, but there's something much deeper going on, isn't there? Something stronger, perhaps stranger, that's upsetting you?" she probed gently.

"I . . . Well, yes." Brenna took a deep breath. "I've been having dreams—daydreams, nightmares. I don't even have to be asleep to see these things. I thought I was just having worse dreams than usual, but now I'm scared." She gestured helplessly.

"What is in your dreams?"

Brenna blushed. "There are two kinds. One—the, ah, nicer dreams—are ones in which I . . . we . . . well, there's a man who loves me," she said in a rush, aware of the ambiguity. She wasn't going into any more detail than that.

But she met Maud's gaze as she continued. "There's a man. Or not a man, but an angel. He looks like an angel, but more rugged, more masculine. I don't think he is really an angel. Somehow I seem to know his name. It seems he knows me. I feel like I have to find him." Brenna wasn't having much luck relaxing her jaw, but she felt foolish talking on and on about such strange things to a woman she barely knew.

Nevertheless, the sympathetic look in Maud's eyes encouraged her. Brenna plunged onward. "The other kind, the dream that was the hardest to take . . . I suddenly felt like I was seeing from the eyes of this girl. She was afraid of him, the angel, afraid of Cairn. I knew she shouldn't be, but it was in the past when they still believed in witches. She thought he was a devil."

How could this make any sense to Maud Barrett? Brenna hardly knew what she saying herself. Maud only continued to look at her steadily, no disbelief apparent in her warm gaze.

"But then I had another dream, and I saw a real devil. He was disguised as a man, but I had seen him with his horrible wings and tail and—"

Brenna broke off, appalled at how this must sound. It seemed so much crazier out loud. "Maybe I'll have that hot chocolate you offered, Ms. Barrett— Maud—if it's still available."

"Of course." Maud rose and called for the house-keeper. Brenna took several deep breaths, but they didn't help much.

When Maud returned to her chair, Brenna sat with her head buried in her hands. "Listen to me, I sound like a perfect loon."

"Did you think we were loony, the people you in-terviewed?" Maud asked quietly. She held up her hand, smiling. "Wait, don't answer that. Do you *still* think we're loony?"

"I don't know what I think anymore," Brenna an-swered in a muffled voice, her cheeks still hot. "But what's happening to me seems a lot wilder than what you and the other people I interviewed described."

"I think our cases were simpler. We were being helped by an angel, a fairly clear-cut case of a helping presence."

"And me?" Brenna raised her head, looking straight at Maud.

"I told you that day, Brenna, that in your past lives

you might learn some answers. I still believe that. In fact, I think that's what you experienced with the girl you talked about, one of your past lives. The question is, are you any more open to the idea than you were before?"

Brenna groaned. "I don't know. It still sounds crazy to me, but in the dream, I really thought I was seeing out of that girl's eyes. As if what happened to her had happened to me. And at the very end, just before she jumped, she turned to look at him, at Cairn. Something in me recognized him."

"What do you want to happen, Brenna?" Maud asked intently, setting aside her tea.

"Well, I'd like to sleep," Brenna said, her voice barely above a whisper. "But I also want to know what connection I have to him. If he's . . . if he's real."

She sat up straighter in the comfortable chair, squaring her shoulders. "Or if I'm a single woman with an overactive fantasy life who's sublimating the need for a flesh-and-blood boyfriend."

Maud's laugh rang out, clear and warm and reassuring. "Your psychobabble is very good, my dear. But if you will believe me, I am quite certain that you are not going mad. Something is definitely going on. But it isn't up to me."

"What do you mean?" Brenna was sure she would get help from Maud Barrett. If she couldn't help her, who else could?

"It's a question of what you believe."

"All right. What do I have to do?"

"I can't claim to be very good at inducing a trance, but as I found out with you and have explored since,

I am sensitive to the aura of past lives. Have you ever been hypnotized?"

"No."

"Have you ever driven to work and forgotten where you parked your car?"

"Well, yes, of course. What does that have to do with hypnosis?"

"People are often on auto-pilot. Reading a book when your mind is on something else. Driving to work in the morning not fully awake, maybe listening to the radio or a favorite tape. Somehow you get there all the same. Fragments of the music you weren't paying attention to stick with you to be recalled later. That's the same as being in a light trance. In effect, when you are doing something without being aware of it, most likely you are in a trance, one you've induced yourself without even knowing it."

Brenna had never thought of automatic behavior in that way before, although she certainly knew what Maud meant by auto-pilot. It was how she got to work most days, unless she had to take a different route because of traffic. "I see what you mean," she said slowly, nodding her head.

"Let's try it that way since the idea appeals to you and you understand it. Now. Relax back into your chair. That's it. Feet on the floor, hands relaxed on your knees." Brenna complied, letting the comfortable wicker chair embrace her.

"Imagine yourself in your car," Maud's voice continued softly. "You take your normal route to work. Close your eyes and feel yourself in the car, the familiar setting. Try not to think of anything else. Feel

141

the rhythm of the car as the gears shift smoothly under your hand."

Afterward Brenna had no idea how long she'd been in the trance. But as she relaxed and became accustomed to the darkness against her eyes, to the soothing voice, she began to feel open. Less tense, less troubled by the idea that her dreams or visions or whatever they were, were bad. Or that she wasn't normal.

Gradually the darkness gave way to shades of gray. A cool wind blew over a field in late afternoon, a shiver touching her with icy fingers. Brenna sucked in a gasp as she saw more, beheld the pair in the clearing. Before the fright could jerk her out of her trance, Maud's faraway voice urged her to relax again.

As before, her view seemed located somewhere far away. She saw the two figures huddled together. As her vision focused and drew closer to them, she saw they were a man and a woman, dirty, battered, injured. They were clinging to each other for support, their swords laid to one side, one gold-chased, the other inlaid with finely worked copper.

"Promise to remember?" said the man, his once-rich voice thick with pain and exhaustion.

"How can we? We'll both be dead soon," the woman said.

"I won't forget," he said. "I won't let you."

"You're stronger than I am. You always have been."

"The Wheel turns, Brynna. Even I know that."

"I know. We will meet again."

They murmured soft, broken words. They were both dying. Tears misted Brenna's vision.

"... I understand this much," she heard the man say when Brenna pulled herself together, fighting to stay with the vision. "We are meant to be together."

"How did you know?" asked the woman, whose red-gold hair was caked with blood.

"A man knows. I love you," he said.

"Remember for me," she whispered.

He leaned over her. With the suddenness that characterized her dreams, Brenna was now looking up at him, cradled against his hard, muscular chest in the same position Jim had once held her. But she felt no panic, not even at knowing that she was seeing from the dying woman's eyes. She felt only an intense ache at the doomed love she felt for Cairn.

Her vision blurred again, but now it was not due to tears. Brenna's—the woman's—sight was fading.

"Love, remember me," she murmured. His arms around her tightened, but Brenna no longer felt them. As her eyesight faded to black, a ray of sunlight emerged from the gathering twilight, framing the man's head and shoulders. The sunlight formed a halo around his head. His hair was blood-streaked, but it had been fair. His eyes were blue-gray.

She knew him, knew his voice. He was her dream-lover, the brown-and-gold angel. They were the same man.

Cairn. She loved him.

He was trying to keep her with him through the sheer force of his will. Brenna longed to stay but knew she could not. As the woman died, Brenna was pulled up and out of the other woman's body.

Brenna's long-distance viewpoint returned. A mist-shape of the dead woman rose from the body, wavering. A hand reached down toward her from the sky. The mist-figure of the woman looked up. A silver-robed angel tenderly gathered the mist-form of the woman in its arms to carry her into the Light that suddenly blazed from the sky.

Cairn remained bent over the woman's body until the Light enveloped him. He clambered to his feet despite the blood flowing from the wound in his neck, still holding her.

"No," he said, determination firm in his voice. "I will wait." The Light blazed brighter, hotter, wiping out Brenna's vision. She retreated swiftly, instinctively, opening her eyes.

Blinking in confusion, she stared at the woman across from her with a blank look. Several minutes passed before Brenna could bring her mind to acknowledge that her body sat here, on a comfortable loveseat of white wicker, and that the woman across from her was Maud Barrett. Some part of her remained on that battlefield, wanting to reach for the man, to comfort him, to say, "I'm here."

"You have remembered," Maud said gently.

Brenna was not at all convinced that the woman was herself, but she knew she had seen Cairn, and now she knew what he searched for. The power of a love that strong, that deep, awed her.

"How long?" Brenna asked Maud, willing to accept that he existed, that he suffered, even if she still refused her own role in the drama. "How long has he been waiting?"

"I do not know how long he has searched. But you died almost two thousand years ago. As I told you

144

the first day we met, his time is nearly up. As is yours if you mean to find him."

"Your time is nearly up."

"How much longer do I have?" Cairn had asked Phanu-el, suspecting, fearing the answer he had just received. He had sought out the Angel of Hope when a long stretch of time had passed. He had made no progress finding the necklace.

After the Scots-Irish girl's travels, it seemed to have gone dormant. He had exerted his senses to the maximum, eventually found the girl who had crossed the ocean with Mrs. Graham's gift. He had seen her at her duties in the country across the ocean, but she had not been granted a long life.

At the moment of her death, Cairn experienced a wrenching sensation and flew close to earth. He saw through the elegant mansion, watching the dark-haired young woman named Megan Graham give the necklace to an older, expensively dressed woman as she died.

He withdrew as Gabri-elle came to take the girl's soul with her. She flew past him as if he wasn't there, but she carried more than the woman's soul. Then he knew why Gabri-elle, the Angel of the Annunciation, of birth and mercy, had come rather than Rapha-el or Cama-el.

Cairn saw the extra tiny burden of the unborn child Gabri-elle carried. He staggered back under the dark weight of pain. Brynna's was the soul of that unborn child. He had lost her again. She would not be born in this time.

After that, the new owner put away the necklace

145

for a long time. Cairn had been too grief-stricken to look again for many years.

Now he felt a sense of urgency such as he had never experienced. He remembered Micha-el's pronouncement that his strange condition could not last forever. The millennium approached.

Forcing himself out of his reverie, he met Phanu-el's gaze with unflinching determination. Phanu-el looked at him with a face no longer comforting but ineffably sad. "Your time with us nears its end," the angel said again. "You must descend to earth to find her. This will be your last chance. After that, you must remain with us, or else join with the Light to be reborn."

"Has she now been born?" Cairn asked.

Phanu-el shook its head, the fullness of the medieval-styled gown swaying under the beat of the massive wings. "I cannot say for certain. Look within, Cairn. You will find her. The time, the conditions are right." The serene face had brightened at these hopeful words. Then the angel's expression sobered.

"It would be better if you did not go to Earth, because I fear the Darkness will find you. But I also know that you will want to go, no matter what I or any of my cohorts say."

Cairn also knew he would take whatever chance he had, no matter how risky. "How much time do I have?" he repeated.

"Very little. This millennium draws to an end."

"Should I look in the land across the sea, in America?"

"America? I believe you will find her there, yes. But you must choose where the meeting ground will be.

Your past lives resonate most strongly in Scotland, the place where you had the necklace made. However, realize that you might go there and not find her. Then there would not be enough time left for you to travel as a mortal to find her."

Phanu-el's ineffable optimism could not be stifled for long. "Choose wisely, Cairn. I offer hope that you will succeed. I wish I could guarantee it, but that would be more than I am granted."

Feeling confidence flood him now that he knew he was to return to Earth, even with the odds against him and Brynna, Cairn could not begrudge the angel its attitude.

"Say good-bye for me to the others, would you?" he asked, eager to be off. Somehow he knew he wasn't coming back. Or if he did, it would be as a soul reborn into the Light as Brynna had been, with no overt knowledge of his past existence.

His search would soon be over, whether he had found her or not. Knowing that, he would take any risk.

"Stay a moment, Cairn. Gabri-elle comes to bid you farewell herself." From far off, Cairn heard the chiming he associated with Gabri-elle.

The golden being flew towards them. She backswept her wings as she halted in front of them.

"My lady," Cairn said, bowing deeply.

"You must not go unaware into this last search, Cairn," she said without preliminaries. "I offer you neither hope nor certainty, for they are not mine to grant. But there are some things you must know, if you are to have any chance of prevailing against the Dark when it finds you."

Chapter Nine

"*Sei pazza. Sei proprio pazza, cara.*"

"We've established that I'm crazy. You don't need to add to the chorus," Brenna replied lightly, staring fixedly at a rack of down jackets. "What do you think? The parka that goes to ten below, or the lighter one that protects to ten degrees above?" she asked, trying to distract Marina.

"Why would you go to Scotland at Christmas?" Marina demanded, not willing to be pacified. "The coldest place south of the Arctic circle and you want to go there now? How about June or July? I've heard it sometimes gets to oh, fifteen or eighteen degrees in those months."

"Do you mean centigrade or Fahrenheit? Never mind. If you want to be useful, then help me pick out a jacket." Brenna looked up, fixing Marina with a determined green stare. "Because I'm going. Nobody is going to talk me out of it."

"Your *mamma* must be scratching the ceiling."

For once, Brenna didn't bother correcting her friend's mistake. She dragged the hunter-green parka trimmed in thick fleece off the rack. "See if there's a wool hat that matches this, would you?" she asked, pretending to be totally absorbed in looking at herself in the mirror.

Marina headed for the salesman, muttering dire imprecations about Brenna freezing her butt off. At least that was what Brenna thought she was saying. It was hard to tell with all those Italian words mixed in.

Ten minutes later, a green wool leather-banded fedora in one hand, a bag with her parka in the other, they moved on to look for a thick wool muffler.

"You know," Marina said after they'd pawed through a selection and found nothing that went with the jacket, "this is exactly what you should buy in Scotland."

Brenna stopped, one hand in mid-air. "You know, you're right. All those Highland towns sell woolen goods, according to my guidebook. It just goes to show how distracted I am."

"If I were going off in search of a past life and a man I'd seen only in my dreams, I'd be distracted too." Brenna had finally broken down and told Marina what she'd learned at Maud's, although she left out the physical content of her dreams of Cairn.

"You really do think I'm crazy, don't you?" Brenna said, more amused than exasperated.

"Hmm, *diciamo mezzo-pazza.*"

Brenna snorted. "Half-crazy. Thanks a lot. Why don't you come keep an eye on me then?"

"I can freeze perfectly well in Milan," Marina retorted. "But the difference is, I don't have to do it with sheep."

"I beg your pardon?" Startled, Brenna looked up from her contemplation of long underwear.

"Isn't that how they keep warm up there, bring the sheep into the cabin?"

"In the eighteenth century maybe. For heaven's sake, I'm going to a hotel, Marina, not a hut. There'll be central heating. Hot water even. I just want warm things for hiking."

"Are you going to miss Christmas?"

"I have to. Do you like the pink or the ivory wool camisole?"

"Ivory, *cara*. What does your mother say?"

Brenna grimaced, carrying the thermal underwear over to the counter. "You don't want to know," she said. "The worst part is, you know all the arguments we've had over Daddy and her refusing to get him tested? Now she's trying to make me feel guilty by playing on his health."

Marina wrinkled her nose as always when she didn't understand one of Brenna's expressions. "Playing on his health?"

"You know, now she's trying to tell me this isn't a good time to go away because Daddy isn't well. How much he'll miss me at Christmas. Do I want to jeopardize his health by having him worry about me. That kind of stuff."

"I see. Not very nice, eh?"

"Emotional blackmail," Brenna grumbled.

She selected long wool leggings and a long-sleeved wool shirt as well as the camisole. The top garments had silk against her skin, soft combed wool on the outside. It was hard to imagine, here in a Virginia suburban mall, that she'd soon be somewhere cold enough to really need them.

"Coffee?" Brenna asked after she finished at the cash register. They strolled toward a nearby cafe. "I've never been away at Christmas before, but if I don't do this, I'll spend the rest of my life wondering what I missed. Whether I missed anything. And if there isn't anything, then, well, I'll have had a trip to Scotland. My grandmother's family was from Aberdeen, a long time ago. It won't be a totally wasted trip. I've always wanted to see the Highlands."

As they walked out of the store, Brenna wondered if she was trying to convince herself or Marina more. Even if she considered the idea folly, a driving sense of urgency possessed her. She had to go to Scotland, or miss him forever.

That was as far as she would let herself think, as much as she would let herself believe.

"What is it you expect to get out of this trip, Brenna?" her mother asked, setting her three timers so that each would go off corresponding to a different food being cooked. The timers were color-coded to the pots. Her father appeared to have forgotten that he had designed the system himself. He sat, staring out the window at the birds where they clustered at the feeder he supplied each day with food.

"I've always wanted to see Scotland," Brenna offered, knowing they were about to go over the same ground they'd covered before.

"You could go in the summer. Why are you rushing off now? You didn't discuss this at Thanksgiving." Brenna reminded herself not to clench her teeth, even though she had to restrain herself from saying that, at her advanced age, she hardly needed to check out her travel plans with her parents.

The doorbell rang. Her father rose to answer it. "I'll get it," her mother said, wiping her hands on her apron.

"No, no. You keep fixing dinner." Her father disappeared down the front hallway. Brenna heard the door open, felt a chill wash of air blow into the kitchen. Her dad must have left the door open again, which always irritated her mother no end.

Brenna cast a look at her mother, whose expression was beginning to take on that long-suffering look that always presaged a difficult evening, when she heard her father call.

"There's somebody here to see you, Brenna. He says he knows you." Peggy Sirin started, brushed her hand against a hot frying pan, and swore.
"Mom, are you all right?"

"Fine, fine," her mother muttered, turning back to the onions she was browning.

The proper military wife, swearing? How unlike her mother, Brenna reflected as she exited the kitchen. She flipped on the hallway light as she went. If it was someone her father didn't know, no wonder George didn't invite him in. She couldn't really fault him for standing there with the door open under the circumstances, even if the early December air was frigid.

"Daddy, why don't you . . ." she began, then stopped dead about three feet behind her father.

"Jim?" she said. "What are you doing here?"

"You know him?" her father asked.

"Brenna, what's going on?" Jim appealed to her over her father's head.

"Daddy, this is Jim. You remember my friend Jim." She wasn't about to say fiancé, even if the word would help jog her father's memory.

"I don't," George Sirin responded testily, "but whatever you say. Did I meet him at your college the other week? It's fine with me if you want to invite your boyfriends home, honey, but you should give your mother some notice first."

Brenna saw Jim's puzzled expression lighten. When she realized he was about to speak, she put a finger to her lips and shook her head.

"Let's not stand here in the cold, OK, Daddy?" she said, drawing her father away from the door with a gentle arm on his elbow.

"Jim, would you shut the door please?" Brenna asked politely. She neither moved toward him nor offered him a smile in greeting. Interesting that her mother had not yet appeared, Brenna thought, smelling a plot afoot.

Her father stuck out his hand. "Let me take your coat, son. Pleasure to meet you. Name's Dick, did you say? Like our president, eh?"

Oh no, Brenna thought. Of all the nights for her father to be "off." Dinner was going to be awkward enough without this.

The doorbell rang again. "I'll get it," Brenna quickly said. "Why don't you take Jim in to see

153

Mother?" She glared at Jim when he looked as if he was about to speak again.

"Let me see who this is, then I'll be right there." Brenna pulled open the door, hoping her mother hadn't decided to make this a regular dinner party. She didn't think she could stand much more strain.

To her vast relief, Marina and Vincenzo stood on the doorstep. Vincenzo handed her a bottle of private-label wine from his family's restaurant. Marina had brought a bouquet of flowers in Christmas red and white.

Marina shot her a semi-apologetic look as she stepped in the door. "I saw him coming up the steps. I didn't know," she whispered.

"Come on in," Brenna said. "You weren't the only one in the dark."

George Sirin recognized neither Marina nor Vincenzo, both of whom he had met at least half a dozen times before. He was the jovial host, though, even if he asked and received replies to questions whose answers he had once known.

Marina looked worriedly at Brenna. "Just go along with him," she said to Marina in the living room when her father headed into the kitchen to open the wine.

By the time dinner was served, it was obvious that the tension level was not going to decline. Jim was puzzled by her father's behavior—and possibly Brenna's, since who knew what her mother had told Jim to get him to come. Both the Sirin women were anxious about George, and Peggy surely knew Brenna resented her mother's interference in her daughter's private life.

Brenna also begrudged Jim the time at her family's table when she was leaving so soon, although she was glad the presence of guests kept her from arguing with her mother about it.

She was going away, she reminded herself, softening her clenched jaw with an effort. *I won't spoil this last night,* she thought. *But why did you have to, Mother?*

Jim took her by the arm afterward as her mother served coffee. With a polite excuse to her father, he cornered her in the hallway leading to the basement. "What in hell is going on, Bren?" he demanded.

"Why don't you ask my mother? She invited you," Brenna snapped.

"No, I mean your dad. What's with him?"

"He's forgetting things." Brenna did not want to soften toward Jim after his recent behavior.

"I can see that. Is he all right?" Brenna scanned his face suspiciously, but all she saw was genuine concern.

She unbent a little, confessed her anxiety. "I don't know. Mom won't take him for tests."

"Jeez. I'm sorry, hon."

"I am too. When are you leaving for the Philippines?"

"After Christmas," he replied. "You're still pissed at me, aren't you?"

Brenna crossed her arms over her chest. Jim had no trouble picking up her body language.

He smiled rather sheepishly. "Hey, you can't blame a guy for trying, can you?"

"That's just it. You knew I didn't want that and still you . . ."

"Still I did what—wanted to spend some quality time with you? When did that get to be such a sin?"

"Give me a break, Jim. What a euphemism. You knew I wasn't ready for—"

He cut off her words with a gesture. "Cut the crap, Brenna. It would've been a lot better if you had just told me you met somebody else. You're too old for the anguished virgin routine."

She stared at him. "What do you mean, I met somebody else?"

"Your mother told me. You're going to spend Christmas with some guy in Scotland."

"I never told her any such thing."

"Yeah?" His laughter had a bitter edge to it. "Then what are you going for?"

"To see the Highlands."

"In winter? Even a dumb jet jockey like me knows that's no place to be in late December." Brenna realized that behind his bravado, there was genuine hurt.

"I never meant to insult you, Jim. Please believe me. I just don't think we were meant for each other. I don't want to follow a man around the world the way my mother did."

"It's all right," he said after a long moment. "I'm not really ready to settle down yet, I guess. So I pushed you, hoping your reaction would help me decide. I guess it did." He pulled her close, but only to brush a light kiss over her lips.

"Listen, I'm going to split, all right? Good luck with your dad. The Old Man's a good guy. And he's got a hell of a daughter. Thank your mom for me too. Bye, babe." After a last kiss dropped on the top of her head, Jim grabbed his leather jacket from the hall-way closet.

Brenna let him out the basement door, glad things had ended better this time. She wondered if she'd said good-bye too soon, then recalled the spiraling, intense sensations of her dreams of Cairn. She might never find anything like that in real life, but that didn't mean she had to settle for less.

Cairn determined to avoid frightening Brynna at all costs. He had learned that on Earth, the time they called the twentieth century was an age of disbelief. He was not certain whether this would help or hinder his cause. These people apparently did not believe in demons, but that probably meant they no longer believed in angels, either. In a way, it mattered little. If he had only one more chance, he had best use it wisely.

With Phanu-el and Gabri-elle beside him, he had seen Brynna's hand clutching the necklace tightly, caught a glimpse of dark-rimmed green eyes. But time had no meaning Above, only on Earth. He had seen a true moment in time, but did not know exactly *when* that moment was. He was in the right time frame generally, but he could be days—or worse, months—off. As before, the rules Gabri-elle had ex-plained gave him only seven days once he touched down and resumed his mortal form. He had to locate the *when* as well as *where* correctly.

He recognized, eventually, the city across the wa-ter as the nation's capital. As he flew restlessly over it, searching for Brenna, he helped out people when he could. He fished a drowning man out of the river, kept a woman from running off the road into a telephone pole by causing light to shine brightly around her, adjusted a fireman's net with a breath to catch a man jumping from a burning building. But though Cairn was certain he had found the city, never did he sense that she wore the necklace. He could not pinpoint where in this city she was.

Then fate smiled on him. The moment arrived in real time when Brynna held the necklace. Cairn immediately recognized the vision he had beheld from Above. Emotion poured through her, through the necklace that linked them, reaching toward him. He felt the yearning in her confused spirit.

Elation and concern filled his heart in equal measure. Would she believe him? Would she believe in him? Would she listen to the knowledge buried deep inside her? He sensed that she struggled with conflicting feelings.

She must have put the necklace away after that, because he felt its special vibrations no longer. But before he despaired, some time shortly after that, she linked the stones about her neck and deliberately turned her thoughts toward him.

Cairn was startled. *She sought him.* At last. He knew he had been right to wait, to gamble his precious mortal time on earth until the very end.

Whatever had transpired in that short span of mortal time since she had held the necklace and now, when she put it on, she was more knowledgeable than before. About him. About herself. About the two of them.

He had the *when*. It was now.

This time Brynna's soul had some inkling of what had gone before. He had no idea how much Knowledge she had, but he was heartened by the openness he now perceived, whereas before he had felt mostly challenge and disbelief. Brynna had been—or perhaps still was—wrestling with her beliefs, but she was not afraid.

I will find you, he sent silently toward her, reaching out with every extended sense he had for *where* she was now, knowing only that it was no longer in Washington, the city across the water.

The dim "answer" that came back to him could not have shocked him more. Flying.

She was flying? He reached again, sending the essence of himself out across the world in time to the sweep of his powerful wings.

A picture formed slowly in the dark night before him. She was in a silver machine with metal wings, ugly compared to the incomparable flying beings he knew. However, the machine was serviceable, and it was an invention humankind had built on its own.

An airplane.

Scotland. She was flying to Scotland.

Cairn smiled. He had the *where*. He would meet her near where it had all begun—and ended—for them.

Chapter Ten

Brenna fiddled with her hair, twisting the shorter ringlets near her temple around one finger. The airplane cabin was dark now, during the movie, but she had no desire either to watch it or to sleep. She thought of her session with Maud, her mother's story about the Graham girl and the necklace, her own wild dreams.

Was it possible there was a man somewhere who had waited for her to be born—to be born again—to recognize him? Was he an angel or a man? If he had waited for her so long, what kind of man was he now? Did he know anything about the modern world? Could he live in it?

She remembered one of her favorite books, a time-travel story by Jude Devereaux called *A Knight in Shining Armor*. The modern heroine had lost the hero, an Elizabethan knight, when they made love. He had faded back into his own time, beyond the ability of either of them to prevent. But she had rediscovered him, or rather his soul reincarnated, in a man she later met on an airplane.

Brenna looked around the cool, darkened cabin. Could that happen to her? How would she recognize him? Her seatmates in economy class were a mother and a five-year-old. The father and older child were in the row ahead. Across from her, an elderly couple sat watching the movie intently. No candidates for romance that she could see.

Brenna sighed, reaching for something to read in the seat pocket ahead of her. As luck would have it, it was her own magazine, the December issue. She resolutely avoided her own article, although the artist's depiction of the angel hovering in the air captured her attention for a minute.

The cover dramatically portrayed the moment when Maud's car had been about to career off the road. In the air above Maud, wings whirring, hovered the angel, hand outstretched to ward off the disaster. The angel had been depicted as an ethereal pre-Raphaelite being in the style of Dante Gabriel Rossetti. All long flowing hair, delicate features, and sentimental expression, with a white robe worthy of the Mormon Tabernacle Choir.

She was obscurely disappointed with the depiction. *That isn't at all what he looks like,* she thought. She stopped herself. What had made her think Maud's "angel" had anything to do with her?

Brenna turned determinedly to the *In Search Of* pages. It never failed to amuse her how so many apparently sexy, exciting, slim, non-smoking, dog-loving, opera-going, scuba-diving professionals of both sexes couldn't find dates in Washington.

An hour later, bored, she pulled out her carry-on bag. The necklace was there, wrapped in a blue velvet pouch that had held the pearls her father gave her on her twenty-first birthday, the year she'd graduated from college.

She sighed, holding the soft, heavy pouch. She had taken her mother aside before leaving that night and told her that if she didn't agree to take Daddy for tests after her return, Brenna would take him herself.

Was she really selfish to be away at a time like this, as her mother had said? It didn't matter anymore, because she had gone ahead on this crazy trip. Brenna reached up to clasp the stones around her neck. She wasn't sure whether the gesture was one of defiance or acceptance. If Fate was moving toward her, then she invited it. She lifted her hair up over the stones, feeling the heavy crystals settle about her neck with a weight and heft that were reassuringly real.

Marina and Vincenzo, who together drove her to the airport, disagreed with her mother's contention that she was selfish. Dark-haired, intense Vincenzo almost lost his grasp on the wheel when he gesticulated in typical Italian fashion to emphasize his point.

Marina backed him up. "There's nothing you can do, *cara*. Your mother is there with your father. She was probably scared by the accident with the jewelry box. I'm sure she'll keep a close eye on your father. He'll be fine."

"It's time you had a life, Brenna," Vincenzo added, giving her the wink that was part of his Italian charm.

"All right, now you've offended me." She laughed. "What do you mean, I don't have a life?"

Now, alone on the airplane, she knew Vincenzo was right, bless his extroverted Italian soul. She had spent her whole life guarding her heart so carefully, she'd let no one in.

Only with her dreams had she realized what she was missing. In loving Cairn in her dreams, she had come to realize that such powerful tenderness and passion could only occur when all barriers were down, when each person was completely open to the other. Loving someone that much came close to pain, the sensation was so exquisite. For the first time in her life, she longed for it nearly as much as she feared it.

But the jump to believing that some deep, ancient part of her was waiting for Mr. Right? That was too much. Brenna groaned quietly, tightening her hand on the cairngorm necklace. She let her mind drift, feeling her eyes grow heavy as she watched the flickering movie image without the headphones. Relaxing, she felt a part of herself flow into the night around her.

There was something exciting about flying through the night in a machine that defied the laws of time and space. Human beings careening through a space once reserved for the supernatural beings imagined to live up here. Now she was racing through that night in a long metal tube, stars sparkling in the black, cold air over the Atlantic as they gave off their cool, revelatory light.

Just before she fell asleep, she heard—felt?—a voice in her mind—faint, very faint, but distinct.

I will find you.

Brenna was too sleepy to fight the notion that she was flying toward Cairn. She merely smiled, sliding the stones against her palm like a caress. Then she slept, undisturbed and untroubled by dreams for the first time in months as the jet streaked across the night sky.

No contest on this point: Scotland was cold. Brenna snuggled deeper into her parka, adjusting the brim of the fedora over her curls as she emerged from the car. She had flown from London to Aberdeen, then rented a car to drive across the Grampian Highlands to Braemar, passing Balmoral Castle on the way. The queen would shortly be in residence there, she remembered reading as she passed it on the highway. She wondered if the troubled royal family would find any peace this Christmas season.

The hotel had her reservation in order. The porter showed her to an elegant room with a cozy sitting area and fireplace. A welcoming fire was already lit. Although she wanted to go for a walk in the bracing air, Brenna feared she wouldn't be able to resist the lure of an afternoon nap. If she went to bed now, she probably wouldn't wake up until midnight.

"You might want to take tea downstairs, miss," said the porter, whose lilting Scottish accent had probably been remarked upon too many times by foreign visitors. She held her tongue, although hearing the syllables slip from his tongue with an almost musical lilt certainly charmed her.

"We serve tea and scones from three to five, miss," he said. He was over fifty, with reddish hair going gray and high color in his cheeks. She almost wished he'd called her lass, even if she was a bit old to claim that status.

"Scahnns?" Brenna said, forcing her mind back to what he'd actually said. That wasn't how she'd heard it pronounced in America, where the word rhymed with "stones." But she wasn't about to argue with a Scotsman.

"Aye, miss," he said, unperturbed. She tipped him with a heavy, gold-colored, one-pound coin. He frowned briefly, and she remembered that the Scots had held on to their own one-pound banknote. Well, banks in London didn't give them out, and that was where she had changed her money.

"I believe I will take tea," she said. "Thanks." He smiled at her typically American shortening of "thank you." Brenna didn't mind. She felt an exhilarating sense of anticipation.

On the way downstairs, she remembered a line from a movie she'd seen years ago, *2010: The Year We Make Contact.* "Something wonderful is about to happen."

If the "something wonderful" was this creep next to her, the cosmos was having one big joke at her expense, Brenna thought, disgruntled. She'd been in the hotel's tearoom all of ten minutes and some guy was already trying to pick her up.

Brenna felt her incipient bubble of excitement burst. The currant scones, dusted with flour, were wonderful. The clotted cream and homemade straw-berry jam were exquisite. She was savoring her Darjeeling tea slowly, a welcome change from the strong coffee she usually drank. Then some jerk at the table next to hers in the comfortable tearoom tried to strike up a conversation.

"I'm going hiking tomorrow, yes," she said politely in response to his query. The fellow was nice-looking enough, she supposed, with his mustache and dark eyes. He had a British accent and seemed quite well educated. But there was something faintly sinister and repelling about him, and she did not want to encourage him.

"It's rather cold for that, isn't it?" he said.

"I suppose so, but this is my only chance at a Scottish holiday, so I have to make the most of it."

"Here all alone?" he asked in a voice that was not quite insinuating, but irritating enough that she turned her eyes away from him.

"That really isn't any of your business," she said coolly.

"Quite right," he said. "My apologies." He rose and looked as though he were about to offer her his hand. Brenna made sure she had both her hands fully occupied with straining tea leaves from the teapot.

After an awkward moment in which his hands finally dropped to his sides and she wished him to hell, he gave a little laugh.

"If only you knew," he said, and left.

How peculiar, Brenna thought, but she refused to have the rest of her afternoon spoiled. After the substantial tea, she thought she would just go up to her room and sleep, skipping dinner. Then she'd be fresh for hiking tomorrow morning. She only hoped it wouldn't snow.

A man checking in at the front desk captured her attention briefly as she went up the carpeted stairs after tea. There seemed to be something almost familiar about him as well.

But unlike the intruder, she did want to see *this* man. Brenna held her breath, willing him to turn around. As he turned to pick up his suitcase, she didn't recognize him at all.

He seemed almost nondescript, except for his strong physique. His hair was mostly covered by a wool hat, but she thought it was light brown, and so were his eyes, as best she could tell, for he did not look toward her. Not blond and blue-gray.

Brenna chided herself for foolish hopes and continued on upstairs.

Cairn sensed Brynna's nearness even before he saw her. She was wearing the necklace. The combination of the necklace around her slender throat and the essence of who she was called to him the moment he walked in the door of the Fife Arms Hotel.

Although his muscles shivered and tensed with the desire to turn, he kept to his resolve and did not stare at her, much less approach her. He did not want to frighten her or risk her disbelief. Although he knew how little time he had, he did not want to rush, not when everything might depend on the outcome of their first encounter.

His skin tingled with awareness of her, with all the stored memories of the normal human body that was his again. He wanted to touch her, taste her lips, see her eyes light with welcome when she saw him. He wondered what her American accent would sound like. Would her voice be low and rich like Brynna's?

He tried to remind himself that she was her own person, not his Brynna come to life in a modern-day setting. Instead, all he saw, all he felt in his own skin and sinew, were memories of the night they'd been together, when she'd lain before him, her heart and body offered to him under a star-dappled sky in a Scottish glen.

He nearly groaned aloud as his body ran away with the memories. Cairn gritted his teeth and tried to focus on mundane details around him instead. The hotel still looked charming and comfortable, although he expected they no longer used gas lamps for light and the fireplace was no longer the only source of warmth.

Once in his room, Cairn continued to observe the changes he had found since the last century, paying close attention to still more new inventions—the telephone and TV. The latter he'd already heard called the "telly." He thought he should familiarize himself with it.

He spent a futile half-hour struggling with the incomprehensible dialogue and peculiar melodrama of a story called "Eastenders." Finally, he gave it up as a bad job—their efforts and his own.

Cairn snapped off the television. He couldn't stop thinking about her, the differences between her and the Scottish girl he'd met before. Though he'd had only a glimpse of her as he gathered up his luggage, he thought this woman was made of sterner stuff than young Brianna.

She wasn't nearly as young, which was a good thing. There was a sense of purpose about her that Brianna had lacked. Also, she displayed a slight aloofness, as if she weren't quite sure she trusted people, at least at first glance.

Cairn wondered if the centuries had changed her ability to trust. Certainly the girl Brianna had been more open, more vulnerable, or she wouldn't have fatally trusted the crofters to understand that she was no different for having seen him. If this modern woman was suspicious of strangers or, more specifically, of men, certainly he bore the responsibility for it.

But would he get to make it up to her? Cairn focused on the gemstones again, sensing them as they nestled against the warm skin at her throat. They vibrated softly.

Asleep. She was asleep. He was still attuned to the stones. But his only image of her now was the one his imagination supplied, his special vision having vanished with his angel form.

Cairn fought down the human urges that again swamped him relentlessly. He wanted to take this rediscovered body of his, which he realized now was tired in a perfectly normal human way, and slide under the down comforter with her. Cairn felt the urge to look into her eyes, to touch her fair skin and red-gold mane, with such intensity, it hurt.

Even as he contemplated that thought with pleasure, his body was not content with such a pure, chaste idea. He fought himself, intellect against heart—or a less noble part—struggling to be satisfied with the mere idea of holding her, healthy, beautiful, alive once more. The ache burgeoning in him was both wild and tender.

Obviously resuming his mortal form had increased physical sensations. He flexed his muscles, wished suddenly that this century had not declared fighting among gentlemen a less-than-civilized pursuit.

Practice with another skilled swordsman, wrestling, throwing javelins—any of these activities would have channeled his energy into the blissful forgetfulness of well-earned fatigue. But this was a more sophisticated, sedentary—and hypocritical—society, and the pity of it was, he had learned to channel his "barbarous" urges over the centuries too.

Yet his hard-earned patience was no match for the growing restlessness, the need for her to recognize him, accept him, believe him . . . love him. His body went one step further. He wanted to make love to her. Dear God, he wasn't accustomed to urgent desire or swift arousal any longer. Cairn paced from one end of the carpeted room to the other like a caged lion.

He needed an outlet for this surge of unconnected electricity that crackled through him. He was rather pleased he'd assimilated the twentieth-century concept so quickly, for the metaphor suited his current mood perfectly. Brynna wasn't ready for it, to be the glowing end of the loop that connected them. Not yet. He could not approach her until he had grounded some of this energy.

Cairn left the room in a rush, forgetting that his human body needed protection against the elements outside. All he knew was that he had to get outside, away from the walls that suddenly closed in on him, away from the demands of a body he had not yet brought under the control of his will.

He strode into the dark night, heading for the mountains that rose like a beacon welcoming him home. He forgot there might be other things in the darkness waiting for him as well.

The next morning after a refreshing sleep and an enormous breakfast of eggs and sausage, broiled tomatoes, and good Scottish porridge, Brenna walked out to her rented car. She drove along the road to the picturesque bridge at the Linn of Dee, a few minutes from Braemar. This was as close as she could get by car to the Cairngorm range. As she looked over the bridge spanning the small rocky gorge through which the waterfall—the Linn—tumbled, she reviewed her plans.

Although initially she had been drawn to the peak called Cairn Gorm—thinking of her necklace—her heart had practically stopped when she consulted the more detailed map of the region downstairs in the hotel. The Scots name had meant nothing to her, but the hair on the back of her neck rose when she peered at the English translation beneath.

Sgor an Lochain Uaine. The Angel's Peak. Had he stood there, on that cliff, grieving for the soul of the young Scottish woman? Brenna knew then that she had to find the cliff she had seen from her vision, where Cairn had shed tears that turned into cairngorm stones. Although she noted it on the map, she paid no particular attention to another peak called The Devil's Point.

She had the conviction that if she found anything—anyone—this area was where she would find
it. Maud Barrett would surely approve this fuzzy reasoning, telling Brenna she was listening to her intuition at last.

Brenna usually went hiking several times a year in
the Blue Ridge mountains a couple of hours from
Washington. These slopes were much the same
height, but they were stonier and carpeted more with
scrub than trees. The Blue Ridge was old and un-
dulating, its peaks, except for Old Rag, covered with
evergreens and forest.

These Scottish hills were not much higher, but
they had the forbidding beauty that made the Highlands so romantic, at least in the imagination of
those who had never had to live off its sparse bounty.
One other thing. They were cold as a witch's nose on
Halloween Eve. She hadn't hiked much in winter at
home.

Brenna decided to make camp beyond The Devil's
Point, south of Cairn Toul tonight. She should be
able to reach The Angel's Peak the next day. The
peaks were dusted with snow, but the weather promised to hold fair.

Despite the craziness of this sudden "vacation,"
Brenna remained practical. She'd made sure the hotel knew where she was headed and when she expected to be back. She knew quite well how suddenly
mountain storms could whip up, and the danger they
posed to the unprepared. She had no intention of
disappearing into the Highlands in late December
without a trace.

She stood at the Linn of Dee, watching from the

bridge as the water tumbled through the deep chasms it had forged in the unyielding rock over the centuries. From here, she could not see the specific peaks she sought, but she knew a few minutes' walk would take her over the next ridge and into the glen. Brenna wished she could see this area in summer when the vegetation would be green, the hills carpeted with purple and white heather.

Brenna saw the man a few hours later. As she climbed down a ridge, descending into the valley in the afternoon, she caught sight of someone several hundred yards ahead of her. What kind of idiot went out in weather like this without a coat? she thought as she moved closer.

Maybe he was a local and had just popped out of a cabin, although from the sluggish way he was moving, she doubted it. Besides, she hadn't seen anything resembling a cabin or a croft for hours.

The low winter sun was already falling from the sky, and he appeared to have on only a wool sweater for a coat. No parka, no gloves, no hat. The only reason she had spotted him from a distance was because the bright yellow wool of his Shetland sweater made him visible from a distance.

She picked up her pace when she saw him stagger and fall. Too much whiskey at the pub? No, they were pretty far from civilization for someone drunk to have wandered out so far. Of course, he might be a shepherd with too much fondness for his pocket flask. But she hadn't seen any sheep as she'd climbed higher, and in winter, they would be unable to forage here anyway. They would have gone to lower winter pastures.

Her questions were about to be answered, Brenna thought, or would be as soon as she revived the fellow.

But when she reached him, she realized the situation was more serious than she'd thought. He was face-down, and as she turned him over, she saw that he had passed out. His face and hands were cold and stiff. Dressed for indoor weather, he was obviously unprepared for a climb in the freezing Scottish mountains.

The man's skin was pale and tinged faintly blue beneath an even tan. He didn't open his eyes when she spoke to him. He probably had hypothermia, maybe frostbite too. Night had begun to fall, and this man might very well die within the next few hours. Certainly she had no time to hike back to her car or even to see if there were any shelters or way stations where she could take him.

She had to do something now and pray it would work.

Brenna pulled off her heavy backpack, retrieving first the hand-warming packs that heated when the ingredient inside broke under squeezing. There was no smell of alcohol on him, although he looked as if he'd clawed his way through dense underbrush with his bare hands.

His hands were scratched and battered. His face bore what looked like claw marks on one side. A bear? A wildcat? Brenna wasn't terribly knowledgeable about Scottish mountain wildlife, but she did not think either animal lived in this area.

Still, though his scratches looked painful, if she didn't get his core body temperature up quickly, it wouldn't matter what had bitten him. He would die of the cold first.

Crossing his arms on his chest and placing the handwarmers under them, she pulled out her tent and cooking gear. The butane stove she carried would heat water to warm him.

While she got the pot over the flame, she set up her turquoise-blue geodesic tent. It looked a little incongruous out here, as if she should be blending into the Highland scenery rather than calling attention to herself, but she had no time to worry about something so trivial.

He was well and solidly built, probably around her age. He mumbled something unintelligible when she pulled him into the tent, but didn't revive. She quickly unzipped her sleeping bag, pulling and twisting until she got it under his body. She would never get him into it, not without his cooperation, but the warm down would keep him away from the major source of cold to which he was still exposed, the ground.

Even without Marina's dire warnings, Brenna had known enough to bring all the cold-weather equipment she could find. She had a light foil blanket, the kind carried in cars for snow emergencies, and she wrapped that around his torso next.

"Warm . . . let me sleep," he muttered. She couldn't distinguish an accent, just that he spoke English. She was alarmed. This was the surest sign that he had hypothermia, although he might also have frostbite on the tip of his slightly crooked nose, and possibly his fingertips.

A little frostbite on an extremity was far less serious than the hypothermia. Brenna knew that hypothermia victims often died when they lay down in a blanket of snow, sinking into an illusion of warmth and peaceful sleep.

Most of them never woke up.

Chapter Eleven

She would not let him die. "No, you don't," Brenna
said aloud, although she doubted he heard her. "You
aren't dying on me," she said in a fierce, low voice.

The water in her cooking pot had warmed now.
She tossed bouillon cubes into a thermos, pouring
part of the water in after it, then screwed the top
tightly closed. She let the rest of the water cool
slightly before starting to gently dip his fingers, then
his hands, into the warm liquid.

Her own hands were shaking. She had never tried
to help somebody in this condition before. It just
didn't get this cold in Virginia. She would need to
warm his feet the same way, she realized, and bent
to unlace his shoes.

He wore comfortable walking shoes, but they
weren't hiking boots. What on earth had possessed

this man to go out into the Highlands so woefully unprepared? Brenna wondered again, oddly angry that he hadn't taken better care of himself. His feet felt like ice, but she didn't think he had gotten frostbite on his toes.

It was a damned good thing he was young and apparently hearty, Brenna thought. She rooted around in her backpack until she found her extra wool socks and thermal liners. They weren't going to fit him, of course, but at least she could probably get them onto his feet. She found her spare heavy wool cardigan and wrapped that around his feet once she had put the socks on him.

Taking a peek out of the tent, Brenna observed that dark had completely fallen. The temperature had dropped ten degrees since she had dragged the man in here, but the atmosphere inside the tent was fairly comfortable. The lantern didn't provide any real warmth, but the butane stove did.

The man hadn't stirred again after he'd muttered about being warm. She had expected he might come around by this time. She wasn't especially keen on pouring hot liquid down an unconscious man's throat, but it was the only way to get warmth into him internally.

Holding the thermos in one hand, she lifted his head up by placing a hand behind his neck. His wool cap fell off, and Brenna realized for the first time that he was the man who had checked into the hotel yesterday.

What an odd coincidence. If he'd come here for some exploring, he certainly wasn't going about it the right way.

178

His hair was blond, she noticed. It seemed to be very short, or else pulled back. It was bright, thick, and wavy. Why had she thought his hair brown yesterday?

She looked at his chin stubble as she uncapped the thermos. Definitely blond. His skin was a healthy golden color too, as if he spent a good deal of time outdoors. He seemed vaguely familiar. . . . Her heart tripped double-time. Could it be . . . ?

No, she'd entertained that fantasy briefly yesterday. *Get a grip, Brenna,* she told herself. Every man she looked at was not a possible candidate for the man she sought. A man who probably didn't even exist, except in her dreams.

She forced her attention back to the more immediate problem of his survival. If he was at home in the outdoors, then why had he done something so stupid? Brenna resigned herself to not knowing the answer to that until she brought him around. She refused to think in terms of anything but *when.*

Opening the thermos spout, Brenna tipped his head back so the liquid would flow into his throat whether he swallowed on his own or not.

She tried a few cautious sips at first, fearing to choke him. It seemed to be working. Then she tried again. A slight motion caught her eye. She looked down at the strong column of his throat. He was swallowing.

"Good job," she muttered aloud to him. "Keep it up." The more she encouraged him with softly uttered words, the more liquid he took in. Soon she had half the contents of the thermos down him.

She touched his cheek, his head wedged into her

lap so she could get the bouillon down his throat. He didn't feel as cold anymore. With his golden complexion it was difficult to tell, but she thought the bluish color had faded. She wondered if there wasn't just the faintest flush along his strong, sharply defined cheekbones.

This was quite a good-looking man she had in her tent, she thought self-consciously. If only Marina could see her now. Then she sobered. The man hadn't even regained consciousness yet, and she was surveying him like a prize bull at market.

He jerked a little. Brenna realized that she hadn't regulated the stream from the thermos well enough, and he had taken in a bit too much. He coughed forcefully, trying to sit up to clear his airway.

Brenna put an arm behind his back to help him, feeling the rippling muscles through his sweater with a kind of wonder. As a fighter pilot, Jim had been careful to keep his body in top form, but this man had muscles she'd never even suspected existed. The supple strength of his body reassured her that if he was in such good shape, he was probably going to make it through this crisis.

As he pulled himself up reflexively to cough, Brenna lowered the thermos bottle to the ground, patting him on the back. It hardly seemed necessary, given how hard he was coughing, but she wasn't eager to let him go. She felt deeply invested in this rescue mission, in an intense and personal way that was very odd, given that she didn't even know the man.

"Enough," came his strangled voice. She dropped her hand from his back, the other from his shoulder.

"You're OK," she said.

"So it seems," he said in a deep voice with just enough burr in it to make her think he was a Scotsman by descent or one who perhaps hadn't lived here in a long time. She looked at him curiously, but he looked away, as if he didn't want to make eye contact with her.

Perhaps he was ashamed to be rescued by a woman. Or maybe he was just disoriented. He looked around, at the thermal blanket that had fallen into his lap, the cardigan wrapped around his feet, anywhere but at her.

Brenna suddenly felt just as awkward. "Well, uh, um," she started. *Oh good job, Brenna,* she thought. *What did you say to a man you'd dragged inside your tent and who was wearing your socks—"pleased to meet you"?*

"I found you outside," she said finally when he made no move to rescue her from her awkward bumbling. "You got hypothermia from spending the day in the cold and . . ."

"The night, too," he interrupted absentmindedly.

"And the night? You're lucky you're alive," she exclaimed.

He choked again and she thumped him on the back, although she would have sworn that this time it was laughter and not liquid in his throat.

"Alive. That's a matter of opinion," he said. "But thank you very much for your efforts."

"You're welcome," she said after a moment, nonplussed.

He said nothing more. She put a hand up to his forehead. "Listen, do you feel all right? Maybe you should lie down. I don't think you should worry about making conversation for a while."

He took her hand, gently returning it to her lap, where he held it between his long, cool fingers. At least they weren't cold anymore, she thought, wondering why a sense of dreamy contentment was creeping up on her suddenly. A reaction to seeing her patient sit up and live after worrying about him, she told herself.

"You're probably right. Conversation would only be . . . confusing," he said. He hadn't let go of her hand, so when he shifted back onto his elbows, she found herself going down with him.

"Hold on a minute, buddy," she said as she started to fall against him. He continued to stretch out his long length, still tugging gently at her hand until she nearly fell into his shoulder. A moment later she found herself tucked against his side, her head on his shoulder. She was even more surprised at how good it felt.

Remembering the other stranger she'd met yesterday, the one she'd mistrusted, she started to protest. "Hush, Brynna," he said. "You are tired as well. It cannot hurt either of us to rest."

After the day's long walk and the responsibility of helping someone in distress, he was right. It wasn't until she was about to drift asleep that she realized what he'd said.

"How did you know my name?" she said, struggling to sit up. He pulled her gently down with an arm he slipped around her shoulders as she tried to lift herself up on one elbow.

"I'm certain you told me," he said. She was too tired to resist and there was the strangest sense of rightness about being held by him. *The patient's turned the tables on the doctor,* she thought fuzzily. *Now he's taking care of me.*

"As I should have before now," she thought she heard him say. But that wouldn't make any sense because she hadn't spoken aloud. Had she?

Brenna wasn't sure how long she slept, but the dark and cold outside had not diminished. In fact, full night was upon them. The temperature had dropped, too. Brenna had been lying on top of the sleeping bag with him. It was now far too cold for that.

As if he knew what she was thinking, his voice came quietly in the darkness. The lamp had gone out. "We need to be inside this thing of yours for the night," he said.

"Sleeping bag," she muttered, not in a particularly good mood at the prospect. "It's a sleeping bag. You're right, we'll both freeze if we don't. But it's going to be a tight squeeze."

"Then I will just take this, shall I?" he asked, sounding oddly formal. From the rustling sound she knew he held the thermal blanket.

"That isn't nearly enough, and you know it," she said irritably. "After I rescued you from your own folly, I'm certainly not going to let you compound it. Why don't you unzip it while I step outside?"

"Where are you going?" he asked, in a voice that sounded alarmed. She couldn't imagine why unless . . .

"Were you attacked by a wild animal last night?" she asked abruptly, her heart pounding.

"You could say that," he said slowly.

"Is that why you don't want me to go outside?"

"I hardly want my rescuer to freeze," he said, affecting a light tone. Yet Brenna had the strangest conviction that he was suppressing some deep and powerful emotion.

"Relax," she said more breezily than she felt. "I just have to answer a call of nature."

He was silent. "I have to ask you to explain that," he said finally.

"Not a Scottish expression, huh?" she said. "I have to go to the bathroom. I'll be right back. Is, uh, the creature nearby?" she asked, wondering why he hadn't told her what the animal was.

"Yes, I am afraid so."

"Will carrying the light help?" Most wild animals feared the light. She had a small can of pepper spray, too. She assumed it would work as well on animals as on people.

"No," he said. "No, no lights. Here we are further north than I was last night, and I believe they have gone to ground, but I would not go far, were I you. Let me go with you," he said, standing.

Were I you? He sounded like a knight from a heroic book. The impression was dispelled when he bumped into the roof of the tent with his full height, swearing quite creatively. Brenna felt the whole structure shiver.

"Don't knock the tent down, please," she said. "Or we'll both be in the shape you were when I found you." She started to unzip the flap.

"Don't come out," she added. "I'd be too embarrassed to . . . well, you know. I mean, it would be like

a bashful kidney thing, if you know what I mean."
She was babbling again.

"No, I really do not know." He sighed. "But I can tell you want privacy. Do not wander too far. I will be listening for you."

"Oh, great," she muttered. She understood the reason, but it wouldn't help her bashful kidney problem anyway if she imagined him in here, straining his ears to be sure she was safe.

"Tell you what," she said, grabbing her small, powerful flashlight. "I'll leave the lamp here. You get out a tin of stew"—she rummaged around in her pack until she found one— "and make us a midnight supper, OK?"

"It is not that late," he said in a serious voice. Oh, great, Brenna thought. Another expression they didn't have in Scotland.

She slipped out the tent flap, zipping it closed behind her. "I'll be right back."

Cairn's heart was pumping blood through his veins at a remarkable rate, heating his body and his blood in a way that had little to do with his survival and almost everything to do with her nearness. He was not sure what to say, what to do. The fact that she thought he was an idiot did not help either. If he said any more, she'd be certain he was crazy.

He had the stew bubbling in the pot when she slipped back inside. She shivered. "It's unbelievably cold," Brenna said. "But I didn't hear anything."

He stirred the beef stew. "Good," was the only thing he said.

"That reminds me. What attacked you? I need to get out some ointment for those scratches."

Trapped in a truth that he feared would send her screaming from the tent and into the arms of the Adversary searching for him, he could not even think what to invent.

"Or maybe you just ran into some trees," she said. "Here, turn around. I have some Neosporin."

"Some what?"

"Do you live here? Maybe they call antibiotic cream something different here."

"You are American," he said.

"That's right. Are you British?"

"Yes."

"But you're not from here?"

"Why do you say that?"

Her irritation finally erupted. Maybe the hypothermia had scrambled his wits, or maybe he was a stereotypical dour Scot, but he was going to get a piece of her mind whether he wanted it or not. "Because I can't imagine anyone familiar with this area going out on a cold night without one single piece of cold-weather clothing on!"

He laughed then, a full-bodied masculine sound that filled the tiny tent and made her want to respond to its warmth. "I forgot," he confessed. "I am not usually . . . so susceptible to weather," he said.

"There's nothing funny about it. You could have been killed!" She was angry, but it was more than that, Cairn saw, as her color rose. Their proximity, her fatigue, her concern for him, the fact that she didn't know why there was attraction sparking between them when she so obviously thought him half-witted—all these worried her.

Her emotions were reaching a fevered pitch that

attracted the Dark as surely as a wounded animal drew predators.

"Calm down," he said, catching her hands. "I know I was foolish to go outside without protection, but I was not thinking clearly last night."

Brenna looked down at his strong, brown hands holding her chilly ones. She hardly knew this man, didn't even know his name. Then what was this strange sense of attraction, of rightness, about being cramped in a small tent with him in the dark of a Scottish night?

She tugged her hands away, grabbing the ointment. She twisted the top off. It was the night, the adventure, feeling attached to him because she'd rescued him, she told herself. So what if she was attracted to him? They were hardly going to make love in a tent. She hadn't waited almost thirty years only to meet some stranger on a mountain in the middle of nowhere and suddenly hand him her virginity on a plate.

She giggled. She was getting punchy. Too much exertion, too much worrying. And she was ravenous. Dinnertime had passed hours ago.

"Is that stew ready yet?" she demanded. "I'm sorry to change the topic," she said, apologizing for her abrupt tone. "I'm starving."

"So am I," he said. The smell of the stew filled the little tent. Brenna's stomach growled in response.

"Then let's get this stuff smeared on you and we can eat," she said. She brought the lamp closer, holding it up in one hand with cream on the finger of her other hand. The scratches raked down one side of his face. They looked just like claw marks.

She touched his cheek lightly, smoothing on the cream, unprepared for his gasp. She felt strange herself, as if a spark had arced between them when she touched him.

"Does that hurt?" she asked, fighting the shiver that wanted to dance down her spine from her fingertips. "The scratches don't look that deep."

"It . . . isn't that," he said, taking her arm to move it away from his face. "I will be fine."

But she had felt it, too, the sense of a current running between them. Now that she was no longer touching his face, the feeling had diminished somewhat, but she had the curious desire to touch him again.

And not let go.

He dropped her wrist before the connection sizzled between them again, taking hold of the lantern and moving it back toward the pot. "This is bubbling," he said in a strained voice. "Let's eat."

Brenna hadn't counted on company when she'd packed her hiking gear, so she used the tin plate, giving him the bowl. They had to share her lone cup, though. She poured water into it and passed it to him without comment. When he finished, she held out her hand.

"I only have one cup," she said. Their fingers did not meet on the rim of the cup as she'd seen in romantic movies, but there was something very intimate about drinking from the cup, knowing her lips touched where his had been.

She shook her head. This was really ridiculous. She was about to climb into her sleeping bag with this guy and she was practically trembling from the brief physical encounters they'd had so far. She wasn't the abandoned, sensuous type, she reminded herself.

Thank goodness she had an old-fashioned sleeping bag made in a straight rectangular shape. With the newer "mummy bags," the two of them would never fit. His legs, encased in brown corduroy pants, looked long and fit. This was going to be an extremely tight squeeze.

He looked down where they were sitting on it, unzipped between them, and frowned as if he knew what she was thinking. "We could avoid this, if you wish," he said.

"*Au contraire,*" Brenna said with more assurance than she felt. "We don't have any choice. My sweater isn't going to fit you, much less my parka, and you don't have any other way to keep warm." She ate the last bite of stew on her plate.

He didn't respond.

"What is your name anyway?" she asked after a minute. "After all, if we're going to spend the night together, we should at least introduce ourselves," she said self-consciously.

Then she remembered that he knew her name. "Well, what's your name?" she prompted, when he didn't answer.

He hesitated.

"What, it's some kind of secret? Oh wait, you're not some secret agent running around out here on a mission, are you?"

The thought disconcerted her. Maybe this was some kind of survival exercise or something. She certainly had respect for the physical ordeal Rangers and SEALs and other special forces were put through. Yet the idea that he might be in military intelligence, that all the way out here, she'd met yet another handsome, shallow military officer, rang chimes of disappointment deeply within her.

She was imagining all sorts of wild things, Cairn realized, watching her mobile face change expression in the dim light. He had to tell her now. They were shortly going to be sharing a few tiny feet of sleeping space, and he knew he could not contain his dreams—and probably not his body—once she lay in his arms.

And even if by revealing who he was, he earned her scorn and disbelief, he also had to tell her what was out there looking for him. Although he had escaped Devil's Point last night, he knew he had met only with local representatives, hill-demons of no great power. He had not fared well in that encounter, mostly because they had overwhelmed him with sheer numbers.

Tonight he expected more powerful demons. There was not much time. He had hoped for better circumstances. But Fate had dealt him this hand and he had to play it.

"Brynna." He looked up, finally meeting the wary expression in her eyes with his own direct gaze. One hand lightly cupped her chin, just the merest hold, to make certain he had her full attention. To help him use the power of the physical connection he already knew ran between them.

"My name is Cairn."

Chapter Twelve

At first, Brenna wasn't sure she'd heard him correctly. The touch of his fingers was enormously distracting. Then she met his gaze and knew she had been wrong yet again. His eyes were not light brown, any more than his hair had been brown.

His eyes were blue-gray, his lashes long and dark, turning gold most unusually at the tips. His brows were golden, like his skin.

She raised one hand, and he blinked reflexively but did not move. Did he think she meant to slap him, that she would be angry with him? Her hands moved of their own volition, as if she knew what she was looking for. She reached instinctively for something she had felt when she lifted his head to make him drink from the thermos.

Something held back his hair. His hair was long

191

and had looked short only because it had been pulled back. Her fingers trembled as she pulled the band from it. Golden, thick, tumbled.

Cairn continued to regard her steadily, without moving, but she saw a pulse beating strongly in his throat. Pulling his hair free of the constraint, her hand trailed over his shoulder, sliding over his sweater as if her fingers wanted to linger on him. Lightly she traced the outline of the scar at his shoulder.

Brenna withdrew her hand. His dropped away from her chin. Suddenly Cairn could not stand it any longer, could not bear the confusion in her wide green eyes, the explosive feelings held so tightly within him. He leaned forward, imprisoning both her hands within his and drawing her toward him. He did not put his arms around her.

As he leaned toward her, her eyes closed. He closed his. Cairn found her mouth without error, without hesitation, and as she trembled, he kissed her, covering her lips gently. He pulled back to scan her face, but her eyes were still closed and their breaths mingled in the chill air.

Did she know him? Recognize him? He was afraid to speak, hoping the silent communion of their bodies would tell her what, somewhere deep inside, she must already know.

Cairn drew her up against him, his arms going around her to hold her at last, and he could not prevent himself from kissing her again. Soft, gentle kisses at first that turned to slanting, deeper ones as her lips warmed and swelled under his.

He covered her face with kisses, her closed eyes,

Thrill to the most sensual, adventure-filled Historical Romances on the market today...

FROM 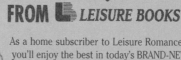 LEISURE BOOKS

As a home subscriber to Leisure Romance Book Club, you'll enjoy the best in today's BRAND-NEW Historical Romance fiction. For over twenty-five years, Leisure Books has brought you the award-winning, high-quality authors you know and love to read. Each Leisure Historical Romance will sweep you away to a world of high adventure...and intimate romance. Discover for yourself all the passion and excitement millions of readers thrill to each and every month.

Save $5.⁰⁰ Each Time You Buy!

Each month, the Leisure Romance Book Club brings you four brand-new titles from Leisure Books, America's foremost publisher of Historical Romances. EACH PACKAGE WILL SAVE YOU $5.00 FROM THE BOOKSTORE PRICE! And you'll never miss a new title with our convenient home delivery service.

Here's how we do it. Each package will carry a FREE 10-DAY EXAMINATION privilege. At the end of that time, if you decide to keep your books, simply pay the low invoice price of $16.96, no shipping or handling charges added. HOME DELIVERY IS ALWAYS FREE. With today's top Historical Romance novels selling for $5.99 and higher, our price SAVES YOU $5.00 with each shipment.

AND YOUR FIRST FOUR-BOOK SHIPMENT IS TOTALLY FREE!
IT'S A BARGAIN YOU CAN'T BEAT! A Super $21.96 Value!

LEISURE BOOKS A Division of Dorchester Publishing Co., Inc.

Get Four Books Totally FREE – A $21.96 Value!

PLEASE RUSH
MY FOUR FREE
BOOKS TO ME
RIGHT AWAY!

Leisure Romance Book Club
P.O. Box 6613
Edison, NJ 08818-6613

AFFIX
STAMP
HERE

her small nose, the freckles he could just barely see on her fair skin in the lamplight. When he urged her closer to him, tugging her onto his lap, his love and need for her swelled into an overwhelming torrent.

Plunging his hands into the thick richness of her bright hair, Cairn kissed her cheeks, her jaw, her earlobes. He explored the white column of her neck until her turtleneck stopped his questing lips and gently nipping teeth. Then he drove upward again, half-mad with need and desire, until he had her soft, pliant lips beneath his again.

He plundered her mouth, his tongue sweeping past her teeth to discover the sweet, moist warmth inside. She moaned deep in her throat, and he thought he would die from not having enough of her to taste. Her hands crept up to his shoulders as he kissed her, his arms bringing her in close to press her against his chest.

His used his thumbs to trace the smooth contour of her cheekbones, caress her delicate skin, while he ravished her mouth again and again. Then the spark burst into flame, and instead of accepting, instead of merely yielding to the tender onslaught with tentative curiosity, she came to blazing, vivid life.

Her hands went to his hair, running through the thick strands in a caress that made him groan. Her tongue boldly swept into the cavern of his mouth, seeking to learn him, to arouse him, as he had done to her.

There came a moment finally when they could no longer breathe, when they could get no closer to each other through all the layers of the garments they wore, when they had to pause or begin again in a wild frenzy of haste that part of him demanded, even as another part of him insisted he stop.

Brenna drew back as he did, although the retreat was a very short one since they had their arms around each other's necks. Her mouth was sweetly bruised. He stared at it, longing to taste her again already.

Drunk with the giddiness of desire, filled with wildness, Brenna felt a sense of frantic haste—to join with him again and not stop until they were together in every place that could be touched, every way that a man and woman could be together.

She shook her head slightly to clear it, feeling his fingers rubbing against her scalp. Not soothingly. No, they had left the tamer emotions behind what seemed like hours ago. His fingers were in her hair, separating, lifting, stroking. He would do all these things and more to her body with his clever hands, she knew with a shiver of desire.

Then there was his hair, which she held between her own exploring fingers. That was where this had started, she realized slowly.

She opened her eyes. Tousled now and fallen forward from her ministrations, his thick, golden hair fell to his shoulders. His blue-gray eyes regarded her intently, the wildness just barely contained beneath the surface.

Cairn. The man in her dreams and visions. The angel. The man whose kiss awoke unknown desires, unwanted memories of a time and place she knew, but could not, would not, claim as her own.

"My God. It's you. It can't be. Who are you?"

Brenna quickly put a finger to his lips. "No, I mean *what* are you?"

"A man, Brynna. Just a man," he said, his gaze holding hers, letting her see the anguish, the need, the desire, the love.

You don't know him, some part of her mind screamed. *He called you Brynna. You are not Brynna. Never were.*

"You know me," he said with soft insistence. "Look closer." She did, peering into his eyes until she saw a reflection of herself, although she would have sworn there was not enough light in the tent to make that possible.

As he continued to look at her steadily, she saw the faint echoes of the other times, the other places, the other people she wanted to deny. The girl Brianna, the warrior woman Brynna on the battlefield. Through it all, she saw him: waiting, searching, defying his own fate over and over again, all to find her.

No! It was too much. She dropped her gaze and made a movement away from him, but he anticipated her. He gently pressed her head down onto his shoulder, turning her until she sat comfortably sideways in his arms. He inhaled the scent of her hair, kissing the top of her head as she settled against him.

"It's not possible," she whispered, burying her face against his neck. Whatever was or was not between them, she could not deny the rightness of this moment. But this was the present, and she was willing to accept only the possibility of instant attraction. The rest, the past, the knowing—she could not bring herself to believe in that.

She willed herself to ignore the impossible way he

knew what she thought, the familiarity of his features. The way their bodies fit together without awkwardness. Her dreams.

"Anything is possible," he said in a low voice. "I learned that the hard way," he said with a trace of humor. "I believed no more than you do now, Brynna, but I learned. Lived, waited, learned." He was no longer just a crude soldier, he realized, as she had predicted so long ago. Perhaps, he even dared to think, perhaps he was worthy of her now. If so, the long crucible of pain and despair were all worth it.

"You act as if you know me," she said, her twentieth-century skepticism rising to the fore. "But I'm not Brynna," she said in an irritated voice.

Cairn felt exasperation. After so long, even after the kiss they had just shared, how could she say such a thing? "But you do know me," he said.

"No," she said in a voice suddenly strong.

"How can you say that?" he asked, stung. She had felt it, the connection that ran between them. He was sure of it.

"I'm Brenna," she said stiffly. "I'll admit we're attracted to each other, and part of me feels like I know you, but that's impossible."

He had forgotten that she was not as familiar with their situation as he. As she talked, his joy vanished. He realized how very difficult this was for her to accept. Much harder than in his dreams. In them, she looked into his eyes and remembered, drank the knowledge from his eyes, delighting in it, that he had remembered for both of them.

"I've even seen you in my dreams. But that doesn't mean I know you," Brenna continued uneasily. She remembered the gold-trimmed robe, the brown-and-gold wings, the grief on his rugged, magnificent face. It seemed impossible that the angel she had seen behind her eyes could be the very same man who was here holding her in his very human arms.

It was impossible. She had conjured up a lover and found him. Somehow it was all a product of her imagination. Or his.

All she had found today was a man, hurt and unconscious. He had been ill, his face cut. Blond whiskers had scratched her gently when they kissed. The way he looked now could not have been further from the winged being of majesty that she had seen. And yet they were the same, her intuition told her. It was her practical head that wouldn't cooperate.

"But that was just a dream," she said, injecting a dismissive note into her voice with effort. "We've never met before."

In the silence, Cairn continued to regard her, disbelieving, not sure what to say in the face of her determination not to know him, to acknowledge their past. For it was only that which made the present possible, believable. Unless this age was so promiscuous that women kissed men they had just met, with all the abandon and passion in their shallow souls.

No, he would not believe that of her, could not.

Cairn became aware of her thoughts as he pushed his own back, fighting for control. He saw the two images of him that she had and would not acknowledge, the angel and the man, blurring and overlapping. At least she accepted the reality of him in the here and now, even if she would not admit to

197

what he was and had been.

It wasn't much of a basis to go on, but he had survived for centuries on much less than that. "You do know me, but you do not want to admit it," he stated, determinedly keeping his voice neutral. His hand stroked lazy circles on her back, seeking nothing more from her than she was willing to give.

Had she spoken aloud or could he read her mind? Brenna thought with a start.

Although she had been parted from him for so long, she had not spent every second of her existence waiting for him. The thought cut Cairn like a knife, bringing almost tangible pain in its wake. It took all the strength of will at his command to continue to treat her as if they had just met, were just casual strangers sharing an attraction, his touches by necessity light, unthreatening. Insisting on any kind of intimacy, presuming even that he had the right to kiss her again, would be useless now.

But his heart twisted inside him, futility waiting to swamp him with cold remorse.

Cairn heard a sound outside the tent. How foolish. He had no right to relax, to enjoy even the light caress that was all Brynna would accept. Danger lurked out there; evil sought him. It would engulf her too, if he did not take care. It came slouching toward them now.

Grabbing her hand, Cairn rose swiftly to his feet, dragging Brynna with him. He grazed the top of the tent again. "We have to go out," he said.

"What? Are you crazy? It's cold out there," she began to splutter.

"Do you have another lantern?" he asked, his face a mask of urgency.

Brenna felt wariness seize her mind again. Maybe he was a madman. Or maybe she was the one who was nuts and he knew it.

"No, no, no," he said impatiently, but could not smile around the strain on his face. "You are not mad and neither am I. But the Dark is coming and we have few weapons to defeat it. Oh, for a sword," he muttered, looking at her eating knife with disdain.

"Of course it's dark out there, that's my whole point," she began. He saw the Swiss Army knife attached to the loop of her blue jeans.

"May I use that?" he said politely.

"What? Of course."

"Thank you." Before she could unhook it, he tugged at it with his strong fingers, tearing her belt loop. Her eyes widened at his temerity. He flicked the blade out expertly but eyed it as if he thought it, too, was small and pathetic.

Which was how she was beginning to feel. She had given him a weapon. The thought flitted through her head as she watched him turn the knife over in his palm. He put it down beside him for an instant, stooping to pull his socks and shoes back on.

Before she could decide to move toward the knife and retrieve it, he was standing again, the knife in his palm, his head ducked to avoid bumping the roof of the tent.

He tossed her parka to her. "Put it on," he said, the tender man completely buried beneath a powerful, muscular stranger who made her idea of a military officer look like a first-year cadet. "I would tell you to go, to keep you safe, but it is too late. You are safer with me than alone," he said in crisp tones.

"Danger? What danger?" Brenna asked, bewildered. She was talking to his back. He was leaving the tent. Oh, this was getting crazier and crazier!

She followed as Cairn strode outside. He carefully tilted the lantern to pour some of its oil over a small bush near the tent. He moved to douse another nearby scrubby bush. "Light these," he requested.

She would humor him because she knew from his tense shoulders and stern expression that whatever he thought was going to happen, it was serious. Even if she thought the idea of this mystical bond between them too overwhelming, she could not deny the qualities of leadership and command that emanated from him like a lighthouse beacon blazing across the sea.

"Why do you want to start a fire?" she asked.

"If we keep the light going, we may have a chance."

"The beast won't attack in the dark?" Brenna asked, remembering the gouges on his cheek, wondering what kind of animal it was.

"That I do not know. But light always favors the Light, while Evil is strongest in the dark." She had no idea what he meant, but she dug matches out of her waist pack and handed them to him. He looked at them blankly for a moment.

"What were you expecting, a flint?" she asked, sarcasm born of his strange behavior and the fear settling in her. "Never mind," she said, brushing past him to the first oil-wet bush.

"You'll explain all this later, I hope," she said as she tossed a lit match onto the first bush. It caught fire, and the flare of light sent a burst of heat through the immediate area where they stood.

"If you are willing to listen," he answered her sarcasm in an even voice. Cairn watched her strike a second match. He took the book from her without a word after seeing how her hands trembled when she tried to light the second bush.

"Are you all right?" he asked, bending to set the second bush ablaze.

"You do have a way of sweeping a girl off her feet," she began. She heard a sound like a wild beast roaring somewhere in the dark. Goosebumps dotted her skin.

"What is that?"

"It comes," Cairn said grimly.

"It? A monster attacked you last night?"

"Of a sort. I cannot explain now. You must trust me." He turned back to her after lighting bushes around them in a circle. Strangely enough, the bushes did not send sparks from one to the other. She and Cairn were in the center, but instead of being in a suicidal position, she saw that this was what he had intended.

Cairn seized her hands, pulling off her gloves for a minute to fit his palms under hers. A warmth that was not physical flowed through her at his touch. "I will explain when this is over, but you must promise me one thing."

"What?" His eyes and the touch of his hands were filling her with a flood of strange emotion. Beneath his pulse, his blood beat in time to the message he wanted her to hear: Trust me. But if she heard it and acknowledged it, then all this would be . . .

"Real," her fickle mind whispered. Her heart was no use at all, because she feared it was already half his, but her intellect should not be listening to the persuasive rhythm of his blood.

Not real. Not possible. That was *her* refrain.

Cairn squeezed her hands impatiently, forcing her to look up. "Set aside your doubt for now," he urged. "Do not believe anything the Enemy says. Do not trust the way he looks, what he says, the sound of his voice." Cairn's eyes were deep pools of charcoal blue. Wisdom and knowledge lay somberly in their depths.

"Do not leave the circle of light, no matter what you see, or what happens to me. Promise," he said, squeezing her hands until they hurt.

"I . . . I promise," she said. "But Cairn . . ."

He bent to kiss her quickly, the hard pressure a promise, a warning, a message. He slipped her hands back into her gloves.

"Do not forget," he said. Brenna reached up to touch his forehead where a lock of thick bright hair fell across it.

"I won't," she said simply. She had nothing else to give him, although she knew "I believe you" would be what he most wanted to hear.

Then the night roared black and angry around them; the darkness became palpable. Between one second and the next, Brenna found herself looking into a pair of coal-black eyes.

She jerked back. The man who had been trying to pick her up yesterday in the hotel stood within the circle of light with her, his dark mustache twitching with amusement.

Cairn had disappeared.

Brenna took one step, two, toward the darkness outside the burning circle, preparing to flee.

"No!" Cairn's voice cried from within the dark man. But then she saw Cairn appear beyond the circle of fire, reaching toward her. She moved toward him.

The dark man grabbed her arm. "No!" she screamed at him. "Let me go."

Cairn's words, Cairn's voice, issued from the dark man's mouth. "Do not believe in this illusion. He has no power to harm you inside this circle."

"But you're . . . you're out there."

"I am not," came Cairn's voice insistently. But it was still contained within the dark, insidious man beside her. Cairn, in all his golden glory, stood in the darkness outside, beckoning with one arm outstretched.

"Calm down," his voice said. *Look within,* sounded his voice in her mind. She forced herself to look at the man she now recognized from her dreams. He was the image of the devil on the road, the one who had flown around the earth with leathery wings and tail. Swallowing down a surge of revulsion, she turned toward him.

He was not so tall as Cairn. She was able to look directly into the night-black pupils without any difficulty. As she turned toward him, the figure of Cairn outside the firelight stepped closer.

She turned back toward the image that attracted her. "Why aren't you in here?" she said to him. He remained mute, while Cairn's deep voice came to her from the mouth of the man who revolted her.

"Look at me," the dark man said. "This is a trick," he said in Cairn's voice.

"I know," she cried. "I don't know whose."

"Look at me," he repeated, gently seizing her shoulders and spinning her to face him. She almost threw him off to run through the burning bushes, but something held her back, something she felt through his touch.

Forcing herself to meet his eyes, she looked into the dark eyes where iris met pupil with no separation, and saw.

She saw herself in the circle of light. She saw the dark man next to her. But faintly superimposed over his image was the outline of Cairn's frame, taller, broader, filled with light.

With the image of him inside her eyes, she turned toward the figure standing at the perimeter. Brenna saw an outline that was Cairn's body reaching for her, but within it lurked a dark presence, smaller, denser. Inside that darkness where no light shone, she also saw bat-like wings and a tail.

She turned back to the dark man who was really Cairn. "What do I do now?" she asked.

"It cannot last if you do not believe," came his voice. Brenna closed her eyes tightly, willing the false images to be gone. When she opened them again, she heard the roaring in the darkness, but Cairn stood beside her.

The dark man was nowhere to be seen.

"That can't be it?" she said, although relief flooded her in a tide so potent, she had to catch Cairn's arm to keep her wobbly knees from collapsing under her.

"No, it is not over. The battle is barely joined," he said in a grim voice. He stepped between two bushes quickly to cut off branches from trees that were outside the circle. "We have to keep the fire going."

Brenna helped Cairn distribute the branches in the gaps between the bushes, although as best she could tell, the bushes remained alight without burning up. The light glowed more brightly after their latest effort, but she found herself at the edge of the circle, peering fearfully into the night.

"Brynna," Cairn said from behind her, turning her to face him, "can you remember anything you used to know?"

"Remember what?" she asked, annoyed again that he had used the name that was not hers.

"Once, you knew where the Enemy was, when they would strike. We could use that Knowledge again, against this Enemy. You might be able to tell when and how the next strike will come."

Still touching her, he felt her disbelief even before she spoke. It rocked him like a physical blow. He stepped back, shaken.

"Cairn, I'm sorry. This has all been too much, too soon."

"You do not believe me," he said in a flat voice.

"I believe you are sincere," she cried. "But I can't believe in the impossible. I'm not the woman you loved. I am Brenna, not Brynna. Just Brenna."

"Then we are lost," he said.

"Isn't what we have enough?" she asked.

His look seared her where she stood, although there was no contempt in it. But it was contempt she deserved, she thought, not understanding.

"You cannot love if you do not believe in us, in yourself . . ." His voice dropped to a husk of sound. ". . . in what we were. Because if you do not, then I am a stranger. You cannot love a stranger, and all that has passed between us tonight is only lust."

In her century, if people had even that, they were lucky. He caught the thought and smiled sadly, his hard-won knowledge a painful weight, heavier than time. "Even though we all to some extent reflect our era, you can be more than that, Brenna. That is what you once told me. You do not have to settle for lust."

She heard the voices of the couple she had seen on the long-ago battlefield while she sat in Maud Barrett's McLean mansion.

The Power, the Knowledge of the Light are yours. I am only a crude man.

"No. You are much more than that. You will be much more than that," the woman said, her voice weak but confident.

"We will be much more than that," he returned.

The echoes died away inside her, faltering inside the cavern of her disbelief. Paralyzed with fear, indecision, uncertainty, Brenna did not know how to reach out to him. She wanted more time.

There was no time. She heard the roaring again. Still she could not meet his eyes.

When she would not look at him, Cairn seized a burning branch and strode out of the circle of light. "Fight with me!" he shouted, inviting the Dark in a deadly voice that was strong, powerful, and yet utterly without hope.

He raised the burning brand. "Complete your victory, Dark Lord."

Chapter Thirteen

In response, Brenna heard the voice of evil ripping through the fabric of the night, exulting. She saw a host of dark creatures launch themselves from the blacker mound of Devil's Point to the south. They flew towards Cairn, avid jaws open, claws extended.

Cairn blazed like a beacon in the night, light flaring around him, through him, over him, but she knew he could not withstand all of them. Not alone.

Brenna ran from the circle of light in the opposite direction from Cairn. She escaped the protection he had set around her. There was nothing she could do for him here.

"George," Peggy said from the top of the steps leading into the basement of the Sirin townhouse. "I'm going out for a little while. I have to get a few more things at the store. All right?"

"Are Brenna and Jim coming?" he said eagerly, looking up from the wooden figure he was carving. "It's Christmas Eve tomorrow, isn't it?"

Peggy gave him her best long-suffering sigh. "No, dear, they're not coming. Brenna flew to Scotland for the holidays last week, remember? We're going to call her on Christmas."

"What about Jim?" George sounded irritable now.

"She broke off the engagement." Peggy wondered how many more times she was going to have to tell him.

"Good. Pompous young ass."

Peggy stared in surprise. This was the first time he'd expressed *that* thought. "I thought you liked Jim."

"Only as long as I thought Brenna wanted him. Wasn't so sure he'd make our little girl a good husband. She needs someone strong."

He blinked, his eyes wandering. "Strong, tough, but humble. Not somebody who thinks he's a big shot and she should recognize it."

"Then she was certainly looking in the wrong place," Peggy said tartly. "I haven't met an aviator yet who was humble. Almost as bad as you cavalrymen," she added teasingly.

"Hmmph," George replied, pretending to be miffed. "When I say humble, I don't mean some poor slob who doesn't know what he's doing. I mean someone who's been baptized in fire and learned from it. Been through the crucible."

Somehow Peggy doubted that her husband meant the recent conflicts in Somalia or the Persian Gulf.

In her husband's view, there hadn't been a "real" war since World War II, including Korea. "Baptized in fire. Do you mean a fireman?"

"Oh, go on." He waved her away. "You don't know what I'm talking about."

"No, and neither do you," she retorted fondly. "I'll be back by dinner."

"Fine, fine." He returned his attention to his work. Peggy wondered what he was carving, but she knew better than to ask. She locked the front door carefully behind her, lowering the garage door with her remote control as she backed the car out.

Brenna ran blindly north, not certain what she hoped to find—a supernatural host, an army? And then what? Cairn could not hold out against the creatures attacking him for long.

She didn't know how long she ran in the dark, stumbling over rocks and logs. The moon came out from behind clouds suddenly, and she realized she was at the foot of a cliff. Her small flashlight wouldn't show more than twenty-five feet up the surface, if that much. She slowed, panning the stony surface with her light, breathing hard.

Brenna moaned in frustration. She couldn't tell. There wasn't enough light to see by. She sank down, squatting, her head hanging over her knees, trying to recover her breath.

She had to do something to help Cairn. No matter how crazy it seemed, she had tasted the fear, smelled the evil. Something was out there, something malicious.

A memory kindled by Cairn's recent words rang in

her head. Seeing. She could *see*. They called it the Second Sight in Scotland. She had no need to see the Enemy, because they had already attacked. What could she do then, with this gift she supposedly had? She thought frantically.

"All right," she muttered, conceding the point to Cairn. "Let's try it your way." Disbelief hadn't gotten her anywhere. For just a moment, she would try to believe in what he had told her. Not for herself, for him. Because whether she had known him forever or just since this afternoon, she had to help him.

She focused on the cliff, remembering her dream, matching the contours in her mind to the ones before her. They came together, blurred, then froze, overlapping perfectly. She was in the right place.

The Angel's Peak. It had to be, she felt it deep within her.

Concentrating, letting things she had never known or wanted to know rise to the surface of her mind, Brenna focused intently, reaching out with her mind, seeking the stones Cairn had created in his grief. She knew instinctively that they held some kind of power. A strange kind of seeing layered itself over her normal vision. She saw into the cracks, crevices, and hollows that dotted the cliff face.

She moved back and forth, picking out the stones from the cliffside, able to tell from a certain glow which were his, which natural formations. As she gathered them, she clutched them tightly in her hands, calling on unnamed, unknown powers to help her, to help Cairn.

Help came to her as she bent, desperate and sobbing, mining the rough surfaces with her chapped, scraped hands. Visible at first only to her altered Sight, they came creeping out as her hands filled with the stones that glowed in her Sight.

Then they stood, shaking off their fey magic to become visible to normal eyes. Brenna gasped in wonder. Small and large, in all shapes and all manner of clothing, green and silver and blue, winged and will-o'-the-wisps—the Seelie Court, as the faery folk were called in Scotland, assembled around Brenna.

She recalled a legend she had once read that said faeries were fallen angels who were not quite bad enough to go to Hell. They regretted their misbehavior over the years. Some still worked mischief, of course; they had become creatures of earth, after all.

But she knew, according to folklore, that they prized talismans, jewelry, bright trinkets. They were also reputed to have a fascination with golden hair—some remnant of their earlier lives, no doubt.

Suddenly Brenna knew why she had been gathering Cairn's stones. She knew they would want them for treasure. But would they come with her? Something told her that she had to hold on to the cairngorms until they had helped her, something else she remembered from reading faery stories. Treasure and the promise of seeing an angel should keep them with her.

If Cairn's plight hadn't been so desperate, she would have felt like a fool. She was the fool, however, since she hadn't believed him. She threw her thoughts into the night around her, as commanding as she could make them. Power flowed in her, though her, streaming out into the night, invisible, intangible, yet weaving subtle threads of pleading.

The faeries were starting to grab at the stones now, dancing and trying to trip her. It was working! Brenna held the stones aloft, out of reach of their tiny, graceful, grasping hands.

Help me, said her mind. *Help him. Follow me.*

Find our weapons, added an authoritative mind-voice she barely recognized as her own. It must be Cairn's Brynna. Even as the thought flowed into the chill night air around her, she saw the picture of that battlefield, suddenly knew exactly where they were, the weapons of their last struggle.

As quick as thought, she found herself suddenly astride a gleaming faery steed, whose white mane flowed over the landscape as white hooves struck bright sparks into the night. The faery host flowed behind her, hundreds or thousands, she couldn't be sure. If she was mad, why not go out with a first-class fantasy? She threw her head back, laughing, as an ancient power throbbed in her veins.

They flew over the darkened landscape, faery wings flying, enchanted hooves galloping, past a dark mass shot through occasionally with golden light that she knew must be Cairn's battle that she had left behind.

The faery host was in control now, even if she still held the stones. Her hair whipped behind her as she turned her head to call out to Cairn, but the faery king beside her, crowned in silver, astride a silver horse, pointed ahead.

She realized where they had headed when she saw ghostly figures down below. Echoes of the past brought to light briefly by faery magic. She saw people she recognized as her own clan in a long-ago time when the Romans had invaded southern Scotland. She saw Cairn, strong, golden-haired, step forward to volunteer his services as war leader.

The Romans attacked. She saw the battle. She and Cairn defeated them in the end, fighting side-by-side, then back-to-back, as they fought farther and farther away from their people. Then they too were wounded, sinking down onto the bloody ground. Swords fell from their nerveless grasp as they held one another in their last moments together. Here was the glory she had denied.

But there was no time to consider that now. The ghostly tableau faded, and she saw a dark mound near the clearing where she and Cairn had fallen. Wordlessly, the faery king pushed her toward the barrow.

Brenna shivered. Would her bones and Cairn's be there? Or if she had died and Cairn hadn't, then . . . The speculation was beyond her. The faery horse she rode stamped impatiently, then plunged in on its own, ducking its head under the lintel.

Two swords lay side by side in the cold, stone-lined barrow. Carved symbols decorated the stones, Celtic patterns of intricate circles and interwoven runes, power sealed here against a future need. Vines twined the two gleaming swords together. They had never tarnished, never rotted.

The faery horse knelt, front hooves on the ground. Brenna slid off, falling to her knees as she approached the gleaming swords. One glowed golden, the other copper-bright, each with a property all its own. Yet she somehow knew they had to be wielded together or not at all.

"May I take them?" she asked the walls around her, the faery horse. The Seelie Court waited outside. Was there a propitiation, a rite, an incantation required?

She knew the answer. Her need, his need compelled her to raise these swords to help the forces of the Light. As she reached for them, the vines melted away. The swords leaped into her hands as if she had called them. She supposed she just had, although the power had come to her from nowhere, as before. With their weight in her hands giving her strength, not hindrance, she threw her leg over the horse's neck. Snorting wildly, the faery horse rose and charged the barrow walls.

Brenna thought they would run into the packed earth and stone lintel, but to her amazement, the barrow crumbled around them as the faery steed charged free. Then they were aloft, Brenna gripping a sword in each hand.

She felt stronger now, wilder, power flowing into her from the swords. Cairn's was in her right hand, her own sword in her left. She looked over at the faery king as they changed direction. His silver beard parted as he smiled approvingly.

Then he pulled his own sword from a scabbard at his side. It glowed an unearthly silver in the night. Wordless still, he seemed to grow in strength and power as they fled away down the hills, back to where Cairn wrestled with the dark host.

Cairn was on his knees, struggling to rise. His chest was covered with scratches, many of them deep and ugly. The sweater had been torn from him

214

long ago, his shirt soon after. There were wounds in
his scalp; his trousers were in ribbons. The burning
bushes had died to mere flickers of light. The flaming
brands he had used to ward off the Dark were de-
pleted.

He had no weapons left except his hands. He
would fight with those until the Enemy felled him,
but he knew he would not last much longer. Once
the demons were able to get closer to him, it would
be mere moments before they gouged out his eyes or
took whatever gory trophy of victory their Master
sought.

He knew he would not die, merely suffer. Gabrie-
elle had informed him thoroughly. The demons'
Master did not intend for him to meet such a clean
fate as death in battle.

Cairn had realized some time ago that Brenna had
fled. There had hardly been time to think about it,
although he knew an eternity was coming when he
would have all the time in the world to contemplate
her defection.

No, he did not believe that. Even if she had not
been able to accept the reality of who she was, he
could not believe she had abandoned him. She possessed too much courage for that. The demons'
voices screamed at him that she had done exactly
that, of course. He had expected nothing less.

Then horns blew, dozens of them, their clear silver
sound from a source that pierced the unnatural Dark
around him. The demons stopped shrieking, frightened or surprised into silence. They drew back mo-
mentarily, allowing Cairn to see into the night sky.
Across the glen, thundering between earth and sky,

215

came a host that he had seen before only in his imagination, conjured from the stories told him as a lad by his grandmother.

The Seelie Court rode toward them in full battle array, dressed in faery armor that could be neither pierced nor tarnished. They galloped toward him on the midnight air in unearthly shades of green and blue and silver, a flame-haired faery queen at their head, a silver-bearded king at her side. His friend, old Mrs. Graham, transformed into her true self?

Cairn blinked blood out of his eyes. The woman was too large, too human. Flame-haired. Brynna— my God, it was Brynna! His heart leaped within him at the sight of her.

Riding directly toward him, her eyes flashing green fire, she swung a sword in each hand that it took him only a moment to recognize. Brynna threw herself from the horse as the faery horde galloped into the demons, scattering them like garbage thrown upon the seashore before the surging tide washed it away.

She landed on her feet and tossed him the sword that had once been his. It gleamed golden in the dark night as hers glowed red-orange.

There was no time to wonder or question what she had achieved or how. They arranged themselves back-to-back, the fighting stance they had assumed when she had led the clan and he had been war leader.

The lesser demons had already been chased back to Devil's Point and interred in the hill there by the faeries with such devoted care that Cairn doubted they would ever emerge again.

But the monster directing them had been toying with Cairn, staying back, assuming he would not have to exert himself, since Cairn fought alone. With an angry roar, he moved out of the concealing darkness, calling on all the power received from his master in Hell.

The small, neatly dressed man Brenna had seen earlier had grown, his height, weight, strength now dark sources of deadly power. He launched himself at Cairn, a huge black sword wielded in each Herculean hand. Brenna did not know his name, but she recognized the demon who had taunted her earlier. Circling, feinting, he had the speed of three men and the strength of ten. Although she could not see any extra arms and legs, it seemed to her that he was three, four, five men at once.

Cairn and Brenna fought with one thought, one mind, neither speaking. Cairn was certain Brynna had allowed the Knowledge in her to take over, that she drew on the strength and wisdom of all her previous lives. The surge of hope lent new strength to his arms and legs. Yet, despite it all, they were giving way slowly before the deadly double swords, when the Seelie Court returned.

It was the edge they needed. Distracted for a moment by the hundreds of tiny clawed hands stabbing at him, the demon slowed, twisting to escape the new attackers. As Brenna reached with the flat of her sword to harry him, Cairn leaped forward into the dark swords' path, turning and slashing in blindingly swift motions that knocked both weapons from the Dark Lord's hands.

Then Cairn lunged in a final thrust.

The night sky shook with the explosion as the man split into a thousand tiny pieces. A putrid-smelling smoke hung in the air, scattered quickly by hundreds of faery wings. The Seelie Court cleansed the air until the night sky was clear and star-strewn once more.

Soon they reformed in a buzzing circle around the two humans. As Cairn and Brenna sank to their knees, breathing heavily, dozens of tiny outstretched hands began patting Cairn.

"What the . . . ?" he said.

"I . . . think I promised . . . them . . . something . . . if they helped," Brenna said between gasps.

"What did you promise them, me?" he asked.

She didn't have enough breath to laugh. "No, the cairngorms . . . And they wanted . . . to see your hair." Brenna heard little cries of disappointment in the no-longer-silent crowd around them. When she looked up, the faery king still had not said a word. He shook his fist at her.

"They expect to see an angel," Cairn translated, trying to sort out the hundreds of tiny voices.

"This is the angel," Brenna said, pointing to Cairn. She had to cover her head when they buzzed angrily around her.

"They don't believe you," he said.

"Can . . . can you prove it?" she said weakly, caught somewhere between hysteria and exhaustion.

Cairn closed his eyes. Brenna saw for a moment, as if projected before them in silhouette, an image of himself in angel-form. The buzzing increased, then quieted. The faeries calmed down gradually, although they didn't stop touching him. This time, every place they touched or patted, his wounds began to heal.

For the first time, Brenna began to really think this was all true. The wild ride, the magic weapons, the instinctive knowledge of how to fight—nothing had the same impact as the quiet shadow she stared at, and the faeries' awe.

Cairn said something to them in a language she did not understand, but under the now-benign gaze of the faery king, soothing, silvery touches began to cascade over her hair and body. "What are they doing? I'm not like you," she said.

"I asked them to help heal you. Oh"—he smiled at her—"and they most definitely believe you should give them their reward now." Their tattered clothes repaired and rewove themselves, wrapping gently around them as the cuts and wounds ebbed and faded.

Meanwhile Cairn regarded the fey creatures with amusement. They chattered back at him, smiling, singing, laughing. A couple of the faery women were caressing Cairn's head and shoulders in ways that did not seem at all designed to promote healing.

"I don't think you have any more cuts there," Brenna observed.

"Jealous?" asked Cairn in a quiet voice.

"Mmm," Brenna murmured noncommittally, unwilling to admit she was.

It was the best thing Cairn had heard all evening. He detached the clinging arms of one sylph from around his neck, while discouraging another from running her silvery fingers through his hair. They were getting rather bold.

"The reward, my love?" he said.

Brenna envied him his easy ability to utter such an important word. She was far from ready to think about her own feelings for him, although tonight's bizarre adventures had certainly forged some kind of bond between them.

Perhaps we'll be put in the same asylum, she thought with a flash of humor. Hallucinations or not, the little creatures were pushy, so she fished the stones she had found out of her pockets, then looked at them, dismayed. There were not enough to go around, and the faeries were crowding her, abandoning Cairn in droves as they saw the quartz stones.

Brenna shook her head back to get her hair out of her way as her hands rapidly emptied. One of the dryads who had been nuzzling Cairn spotted the bright sheen of the polished stones on the necklace around Brenna's neck and set up a wail instantly.

The whole Seelie Court started lamenting. Brenna didn't need a translation to know what they wanted. She looked at Cairn, who sat next to her against a rock that was only just now beginning to seem cold after their frenzied labors.

He raised a golden eyebrow, offering to translate.

Brenna laughed. "Oh yes, I can figure out what they want." She sobered quickly. "But this is yours. Do you really want me to give it to them?"

"That necklace is yours. It was made for you."

"Before I was born? Then it wasn't made for me." Here she was, smack up against her disbelief again. Yet with faeries flowing over them in a multicolored stream, what was so fantastic about having been loved by Cairn in another life? She wasn't ever going to get used to this, Brenna thought with something like despair.

"You will," he said, responding to her thoughts once again. "And yes, the necklace was made, actually before your grandmother would have been born." Brenna's eyes widened at that idea, then she felt a very unsubtle tug from behind her.

She turned to glare at an unabashed pixie who stared at her with eyes greener than Brenna's, greener than any emerald's. "You wicked thing!" she exclaimed.

Cairn reached around Brenna to unclasp the necklace as the noise around them grew to a high pitch. He brought his mouth close to her ear while he was unfastening it and for one glorious moment Brenna imagined his lips and tongue there. . . .

"Not the best choice of words, love," he whispered instead. Remembering the origin of faeries, Brenna clapped one hand over her mouth in dismay.

Brushing a light kiss against her ear, Cairn slipped the necklace gently off. "I think they will take this as an apology." He cradled the necklace between his hands. "Are you certain you do not mind parting with it?" he asked.

Seeing him hold the stones so gently, so carefully, Brenna longed for the moment when she would feel those hands on her. He looked up sharply then, and she lamented his ability to sense her thoughts. Until she met his eyes.

The glow in his blue-gray eyes, darkened now almost to indigo, took her breath away. The sensual promise implied there, the images that suddenly formed in her mind, were both raw and exquisite. As if he—they—hovered between a hunger so elemental that it admitted no finesse, and a centuries-long love that demanded tenderness and the slowest savoring.

"You're not helping," she accused him, realizing where her thoughts were coming from, at least in part. She was perfectly willing to admit to some fantasies of her own.

"I believe I am not alone in this," he said with a smile that crooked one side of his full mouth slightly higher than the other. Brenna opened her mouth to deny the images were hers, too, then abruptly closed it.

"You're right," she admitted, dropping her eyes. Cairn laughed, then lifted her chin with one hand. The Seelie Court had fallen mostly silent, although there was a sort of collective crooning sound emanating from them that enhanced the intimacy between Brenna and Cairn. She had a feeling they would applaud and urge them on if she and Cairn started to kiss.

"This is embarrassing," she moaned. His smile broadened shamelessly, and his thumb stroked gently along the curve of her jaw.

"The necklace, just give them the necklace," Brenna said, unable to bear another moment of his touch without responding. But she'd be damned if she was going to perform for them. Cairn never took his eyes off her as he lifted the necklace, tossing it into the air with a flick of his wrist.

The necklace never touched the ground. The faery king reached out his arm to grasp the shining object spinning through the air. In less time than it took to blink, the necklace, the king, and the entire Seelie Court vanished.

As soon as they disappeared, Brenna reached for Cairn. She wrapped her arms around his neck and fitted her mouth to his as if she were a beggar at the feast.

Chapter Fourteen

They were lost to everything but each other for a few blissful moments. Brenna's doubts were silenced, at least while she no longer had to think. She was happy to give herself up to complete sensation, to the unfamiliar twinning of arousal and utter security that she found in Cairn's arms.

She entwined her fingers in his hair, outlining his lips with her tongue, darting into the recesses of his mouth teasingly, lightly. She allowed him to deepen the kiss when the initial playfulness passed and both needed something stronger, deeper.

Cairn tensed and pulled away while Brenna still poured herself into the kiss. She felt his distaste before she knew the reason for it, and felt a sudden stab of shame. Was she failing at this too? she wondered grimly, before withdrawing to face the disapproval she expected to see in his eyes.

Instead Cairn looked at a point past her shoulder, out into the darkness. Brenna heard nothing this time. She realized quickly that his revulsion had nothing to do with her. He pulled her to her feet and into the circle of his embrace, his chest warm and solid behind her. She remembered the wings that had enfolded the girl Brianna and suddenly wished for that protection now.

"You feel it too, do you?" he asked.

"What is it?"

Suddenly a large pebble bounced onto Brenna's face as she twisted to look beyond the circle of Cairn's arms.

"Ouch," she cried. "What was that?" She looked at the ground to see what had hit her. As she bent to pick up what appeared to be a glowing reddish-yellow stone, Cairn jerked her upright beside him.

"Do not touch it," he said sharply.

"But it looks like a cairngorm." It was, a faceted one that looked as if it had come from her necklace.

"Anything can be made to serve Evil." Cairn's voice was low and grim.

He had not finished the sentence before a falling star streaked into the little circle around them, still aglow from the rush-lights left behind by the faeries.

Brenna was about to exclaim over its beauty, wondering what trick the faeries were pulling now, when a second stone struck Cairn on the cheek and a cloud of red smoke obscured her vision.

The red haze cleared, leaving at its heart a tall, dark being who made the demon they had defeated look like a child. Powerful, with strongly sculpted arms, legs, and torso, the creature looked like a Greek statue dipped in onyx.

But the twitching tail and hideous bat-like wings protruding from his back undercut the dark perfection. He bowed to her mockingly, and as he straightened, Brenna saw his face.

Half-beautiful, half-hideous, the demon's face made her gasp. One side was achingly beautiful, a glowing golden coral, like polished copper dipped in gold. Curly copper locks sprang from the lovely side.

But the rest of the face and head was a nightmare. Brenna shrank back against Cairn, whose body had gone as rigid as tempered steel. His arms gripped her shoulders so tightly, she wanted to ask him to relax his grip.

Gazing into the blackest eyes she had ever seen, she changed her mind. A few bruises were nothing compared to this—this vision from Hell.

"Very good, my dear," the creature said in a surprisingly mellifluous voice. "A creature straight from Hell!" he shouted. A pitchfork suddenly appeared in his hand. He stabbed it at the ground point-first.

A huge chasm opened up at Brenna's feet, so close that she feared she would fall into it. She heard wailing and moaning. Leaping flames alternated with writhing darkness as the Pit sought to devour her. But although he did not relax his grip, Cairn did not try to pull her back, so she assumed it was another illusion and held her ground.

"How disappointing," the creature said. "That's one of my better ones. But such a cliché, I will admit."

The Pit closed as suddenly as it had opened. The

demon stood before them now without wings or tails. He was elegantly dressed in a red cashmere turtleneck, tailored black wool pants, and black Italian tasseled loafers. He looked quite modern, but his devastated face had not changed.

"You are not allowed that transformation," Cairn said in a menacing voice Brenna barely recognized.

"And you are, you mutant?" the demon sneered, its mellow voice giving way to a raspy growl that frightened Brenna. "If the servants of the Li . . . from up there are not to walk on earth, then what are you doing here?"

Cairn remained silent. Lucifer crowed. "Ha! Do not plead ignorance, or did that witch Gabri-elle really think she could sneak you past me? Well, my minions spend more time on earth than those from up there." He examined his fingernails. "Such a shame, really. They should have told you the cost of breaking the rules."

Lucifer? Brenna thought. *This can't be happening. It just can't be.* She pulled herself together. After all, this was no stranger than anything else that had happened tonight.

"I was given seven days," Cairn replied.

"It is not for you to question my limits, mutant," Lucifer snarled. "Besides, your precious Gabri-elle forgot to tell you that you could not display *their* powers down here, didn't she? I suppose she thought you would be safe, that you would not disturb the balance between that realm and mine. But when you killed Beloth, you alerted me to both your presence and your power."

He appealed to Brenna then, showing her only his

beautiful side. "Surely you do not wish to couple with such an unnatural creature, my dear lady?" he said in courteous tones.

Cairn pulled Brenna behind him. "Answer him not," he said curtly. "No one wins an argument with him."

"Fine, let's just get right to the bottom line then, as it were," Lucifer said in tones befitting a stockbroker, chuckling a little at his own humor. "You interfered in my area, buried my servants under a heap of dirt and faery dust, and destroyed one of my most senior minions. Is that succinct enough for you?"

"War between Good and Evil is a constant of the universe," Cairn pointed out in a calm voice.

"So it is," Lucifer agreed jovially. The pitchfork appeared in his hand again, this time a half-inch from Cairn's chest.

Red light flared up around the Lord of Darkness in a virulent glow. "But by whose authority do *you* wage it?" he thundered.

Cairn did not answer. Lucifer appeared to grow tired of waiting for a reply. The pitchfork vanished once again as he thrust his hand forward. The stones that had struck Cairn and Brenna sprang from the ground into his hand, where they joined with the necklace already there.

"Recognize this?" he asked. "Your friends protected you well, mutant, until your vanity gave you away. But once you decided to create a charming monument to yourself and your lady love, Beloth placed these altered stones within your necklace. I might not have discovered Beloth's death for many days, or even who killed him, since my legions are so vast. But with these lovely little stones set to tell me when you and your lady came together"—He fluttered his eyelashes at Brenna in the twisted semblance of a lovelorn swain—"why, I just had to visit."

"How did you get that?" Brenna dared to ask. She moved to stand beside Cairn. If he could face the creature, so could she. She would not hide behind him. "We gave the necklace to the faeries."

Lucifer smiled, waving his arm to reveal something hidden in the background of the landscape. Interred a thousand feet away, deep in an underground barrow, the faery host howled in frustration, screaming to be let out and to retrieve their reward.

"Can't kill the pesky damned things," Lucifer said. "They're worse than mosquitoes. Can't even keep them there forever. Most unfortunate."

He smiled in the direction of the underground barrow. He waved his arm, and the transparent screen that had displayed the inside of the barrow blackened and faded from view. "But the several hundred years it will take them to break out should take the twinkles out of their cheesy little wings." His voice had turned vicious again.

"Oh, the poor things," Brenna said. "I hope they don't think we tricked them."

Cairn had been staring at the gems and didn't appear to have heard her last statement. "Those give you no power over me," he said, looking at the glowing cairngorms in Lucifer's callused palm.

"Quite right. They only enabled me to find you in time. Oh, it's possible there's a way out," Lucifer said, juggling the gems in one hand, one up, one down, one up, one down. "But you don't know what it is.

229

You've only got another couple of days. Your ang . . . friends up there can't help you while you're in this form, mutant. Not a faery in Scotland will get within a league of you now. Which leaves you with your own limited human resources."

He turned his back for a moment. Brenna wanted to break and run, so strong was her sense of horror, but Cairn seemed to be expecting something more. He held her firmly, carefully.

Lucifer turned around suddenly, transformed into the awesomely evil creature he had been at his first appearance. A many-caped red greatcoat swirled from his massive shoulders, while black breeches and riding boots hugged his muscular legs. Only his ruined face and the twitching tail spoiled the effect of sinister beauty.

"If you return to the form they gave you up there, mutant," he continued in the same jovial voice, "you lose the little lady forever. So enjoy the next few days, because they are your last."

"What about my lady?" Cairn seemed to revert to archaic language when under a lot of strain, Brenna noticed. "She is innocent in all this."

"Tsk, tsk, tsk. I never take one when I can have twice the fun." He fixed the gaze of his baleful eye on Brenna, who couldn't help cringing.

"Your lady friend's stake is this: If she takes you as a man, she shares your fate. And you certainly can't take her any other way!" He laughed hugely at his own disgusting joke.

"Your cohorts may have terrific wings, but you are all lacking, if you know what I mean, in certain areas." He swirled the cape around himself dramatically. "So, to sum up: Return to the form they gave you Above by the end of the week and you can escape me, but you lose the lady."

When Cairn would have spoken again, he waved a hand in warning. "Listen now, this is the part that makes my job worthwhile: Give in to those urges you two are feeling, and she's still mine, even if you fly back up there."

"How can you exact that price?" Cairn demanded, while Brenna listened with numb horror.

"Because, my future tenant, you broke the rules. You can't be two things, man and . . . and one of them, Above. Choose upstairs and you live alone for eternity. Choose love and I'll personally check you out of your hotel and carry your baggage all the way down. It's a long way down to my residence hotel." He laughed immoderately at his jest.

"And if I do neither, and send her home?"

"You're still mine, my friend, because you shouldn't have gotten caught in that mortal body you're assuming. It simply isn't allowed. How do you think I got half my recruits from your ranks? Taking mortal form is just too tempting for the lower orders from Up There. Once they get down here, they invariably fall apart.

"Temptation is such a marvelous thing." Lucifer sighed, his fluent, mellow voice a sickening contrast to his evil words. "Sometimes I wonder if they aren't on my side upstairs. Why hand me a tool so marvelously easy to use otherwise? Sternness, morality, good behavior. It's boring. Positively stultifying. No wonder you humans fall all the time."

His speech finished, Lucifer began to spin in a circle, rapidly boring a hole into the ground. "You see how things stand, mutant," he called out. "Damned if you do, damned if you don't." Still chuckling at his own play on words, the red cape spinning around him faster and faster until only a black puff of smoke floated up out of the hole, Lucifer vanished.

Brenna turned around and buried her face in Cairn's sweater. "Poison," muttered Cairn.

"What?" said Brenna, alarmed, raising her head to look at Cairn. "He hasn't poisoned you, has he?"

"No, he has poisoned the well, made the situation impossible. I cannot abandon you. I will not."

"You will. You must!" Brenna cried. "You can't allow yourself to be taken by him, much less go willingly."

"I will not leave you."

Looking up at him, Brenna understood for the first time how he had carried out his defiance so many hundreds of years before. There was more than stubbornness in his face, in his stance. Fierce determination and an implacable will had made him the extraordinary man that he was.

Brenna felt touched, moved, and excited all at once that this man loved her that much. "Never, ever say you are nothing but a 'crude man'," she murmured, plucking at his shirtfront almost shyly, not quite able to meet his eyes.

"You remembered when I did not," she continued. "You looked for me when I did not know where or how to look. You believed in me, in us, when I did not. I won't let you face anything more alone." Even if she did not believe in the past, she knew she cared for this man as she had no one before.

Cairn wrapped his arms so tightly around her, she could scarcely breathe. Brenna didn't mind. For long moments they stood together in the cold, dark night, taking comfort in the simple act of holding one another.

She didn't know what would come next, and she was frightened even to think of the encounter with Lucifer. In saying what she had just said to Cairn, she had taken an important step. She had acknowledged his importance to her, if not admitted the reality of everything he had said. Perhaps it was all still some colossal dream or hallucination. But what she felt was very real.

But if they only had a few days, then she was determined to make the most of it. Even if she had to coerce Cairn's formidable spirit.

"Come," he said, dropping his arms reluctantly. "We must get back to the hotel." Amazingly, after everything they had endured, her domed turquoise tent still poked its rounded contours bravely above the rocks and brush nearby.

"Yes," Brenna agreed, not bothering to tell Cairn that he wasn't about to pack her off on the next plane. He'd find that out soon enough, she figured.

Cairn helped her strike the tent and gather up her belongings, moving slowly, as if his body ached. Which, despite the faeries' ministrations, didn't surprise her. The faery host had healed the wounds, but nothing could undo the effects of everything they had experienced in the last several hours. She had no idea how much strength or power he had in mortal form.

233

She ached too. It would be dawn before they hiked back to her car parked near the Linn of Dee.

Cairn fell deeply asleep as soon as she put the car in gear. Maybe he knew they wouldn't be disturbed again until after Christmas. After all, Lucifer wanted them to fall into his lap. Or perhaps Cairn was simply exhausted. He had a right to be, if he'd fought off local demons the night before she found him, nearly died of exposure, then had to fight again.

Could he have died of exposure, she wondered? That was one of the many things she didn't know about Cairn. How had he gotten to be what he was? Why wasn't he immortal if he had lived so long? He wasn't any older than she was—to look at—that was for certain.

Filled with questions and still reeling from the aftermath of their bizarre experiences, Brenna was much too keyed up to even think about falling asleep. Which was a good thing, since Cairn didn't even stir when she pulled into the hotel's parking area.

She left him there while she went inside, covering her green tunic with her parka. "Good morning," she said to a sleepy young night clerk. "I found another guest when I was hiking yesterday. He . . . he wasn't well equipped for the weather, and he's not feeling well. Could you get someone to help carry him inside?"

"Who is it, mum?" the clerk asked.

"The blond man who checked in day before yesterday. He's—uh, Scottish. Do you know who I mean?"

"Yes, mum."

Brenna had never thought about Cairn having a last name. But he must have, to check into the hotel. The night clerk didn't seem to find it necessary, however.

The older man who had been her porter the day she checked in was just coming on duty. He went out to the car with Brenna and the three of them got Cairn upstairs and into his room. He did not stir.

This was more than sleep, Brenna supposed. Maybe he couldn't keep his mortal form very long, or maybe the wounds and exertion had caused some injury to his system. She was afraid to call for a doctor. Would a doctor find Cairn to be fully human?

She refused the hotel staff's suggestion that she call for a doctor, putting them off with the excuse that it was only seven A.M. and the doctor surely wouldn't be in his office yet.

The hotel staff did give her Cairn's key, however, and acceded to her request to move her belongings into an adjoining room. She had noticed the door when they brought Cairn in, and she was sure the hotel was not full this close to Christmas.

Unlocking the door between their rooms, first from his side, then from hers, Brenna went in to use the bathroom in her new room. She examined herself. Other than looking haggard and pale, her cuts and bruises were gone. But her body still had some idea of what it had been through. A hot, fragrant bath appealed to her far more strongly than breakfast right now.

She called and asked room service to send up breakfast for both of them at ten o'clock. Then she went to pour the bath salts so thoughtfully provided by the hotel into a big tub of steaming hot water.

Cairn entered the bathroom like a zombie about a half-hour later. Brenna realized she'd left the door between their rooms open.

"Exit room, straight ahead, turn right," she said, to direct him back to his own bathroom.

"Yes, thanks," he said absently. Then his head swiveled up and his blue-gray eyes grew bright. "Brynna?" he said.

Brenna felt her heart contract at the tone of joyful amazement she heard in his voice. She couldn't even begrudge him using the different name this time, because he'd been used to it for so long now.

Would it be like this every morning, waking up with him, this sense of wonder and discovery? Discovery. Now that gave her ideas. . . . She was glad the steam was responsible for her high color and that Cairn's state of exhaustion apparently reduced his ability to read her mind. Because if he had read her thoughts, he'd probably have her bolted in here with a reservation on the next plane out of Aberdeen.

Instead, she smiled at him and watched his tired features respond to her like water falling on a withering plant. Next, he realized where he was and what Brenna was doing. Embarrassment colored his golden complexion.

"My apologies, my lady." He started to close the door behind him, trying carefully not to look at her again.

"Wait," Brenna said, laughter trembling in her voice. "I thought people were considerably less modest where you came from."

"Originally, that was true." He paused. "However, I was on earth last during the era when Queen Victoria ruled," he said, his golden brows drawing together thoughtfully. "I believe this situation would have been considered quite . . . shocking. Is that the word?"

Brenna laughed, feeling some of her own lingering tension subside. "Oh, sugar," she said. "Customs have changed drastically since then. Men and women can share the same bathroom, even the same bedroom today, without being married. Sometimes without even knowing each other very well," she said.

"Still . . ." he began.

She waved an arm covered in bubbles at him. "But they don't generally share the bathroom at the same time." He looked profoundly relieved.

"Go on now," she said. "Lie down again. I'll call you when breakfast arrives."

"Then we have to find you a way home," Cairn said slowly, his eyes irresistibly drawn to the point where the water and bubbles covered her, just above her breasts. She could tell from his expression that he didn't feel much like lying down again.

Not alone anyway.

Like a soap bubble detached from a cluster to drift in the air, one thought hovered between them. *"So little time."*

Lambent sensuality lit Cairn's eyes, his gaze speculative, appraising. Memories lingered there that were meant to be shared.

Brenna suddenly felt much warmer than the water

temperature. "Mmm," she said noncommittally, knowing she had no intention of going home. "We'll talk about it at breakfast."

"All right," he agreed absently, his gaze shifting to the red curls that drifted down her shoulders and back to trail into the water. Damnation wasn't beginning to seem like such an awful prospect, if it meant a few moments of bliss with Brenna. As his blood heated, he watch her breath catch and her green eyes go wide with understanding when her gaze met his.

He doubted she could be innocent in this day and age, especially not after what she'd said about today's customs. And he knew her body, loved it almost as much as he did the woman inside.

Cairn's body tightened with anticipation even as his mind railed at the thought of someone before him. Of her sharing with someone else the joy and love they had so briefly shared, and never would again.

She was not Brynna. She was Brenna. No matter what he thought, what he felt, for her it would be a new experience.

His mind cleared. What had gone before did not matter. What did matter was that he refused to drag her down with him. No matter how willing he might be to brave the Pit, he would never risk her. Never.

Cairn closed the door resolutely behind him.

Watching determination finally edge out the desire on his handsome, expressive face, Brenna sighed as the door shut behind him. She threw the washcloth at the closed door. It hit the wall with a wet plop, then slid slowly to the floor. Was she frustrated or relieved?

Frustrated, she decided. Definitely frustrated.

Chapter Fifteen

There was no possible way to hold a conversation about what would happen next, Brenna thought over their breakfast of grilled tomatoes, sausage, eggs, tea, and toast. Everything that had happened was just too strange, and the idea that it might all have been a hallucination crossed her mind.

One thing was normal, at least. Cairn, she was relieved to see, ate like any healthy man.

"I came to like this sort of breakfast when I was here before," he told her, eyes glinting, as he tucked into his second round of sausage and toast. Brenna was already full and had passed him her sausage.

"Good. Didn't they feed you—uh, up there?"

"There was no need to eat."

"Oh." Her next line of conversation proved even more difficult.

"Cairn, I want to stay with you," she said.

The answer to that came immediately. "No," he said.

"But after all this time . . . I mean, if we've been supposed to find each other for so long, well, I mean, how can you?" she asked incoherently.

Cairn reached out to cover her hand with his. "I will not damn you. If I am doomed anyway, then I will not take you with me."

"If you're already a goner, then what difference does it make if I want to be with you?" she said, frustrated again beyond all bearing. The familiar normalcy of the hotel, the food, a bath, and clean clothes had made the preceding night's horror fade somewhat. Brenna toyed with the tempting notion that the threat wasn't real.

Cairn communicated a distracting warmth to her through his touch. She could believe in this, the man before her, his affection for her. Couldn't she do without the rest?

Cairn divined her thoughts again, although she could see it took him a minute to work out what 'goner' meant. "What happened was indeed a nightmare but not the kind you mean. It was real. And even if this age you live in no longer thinks there is a Hell, your people are wrong."

She started to protest. "Think a minute," he urged, withdrawing his hand to gesture in the air.

Brenna focused on Cairn's intent face. "What need would there be for agents of the Light if there were no Darkness?" he asked.

"Are you saying it's all right that there is such a place?" Research for her article had turned up polls showing that Americans believed in Heaven, but most no longer thought there was a Hell.

"All right?" He frowned a moment. "Evil is never 'all right.' But if there were no Evil, there would be no Good. Every coin has two sides, does it not? Without that other face, it would be one-dimensional. And so would the world. If we had no choices, what would it matter what we did?"

"I give up," Brenna said, brushing her hair back from her face, consigning intellectual debate to the farthest reaches of her consciousness. Something else surged in her veins now, and she wanted to abandon herself to it. "We don't have time for philosophy anyway. I'm supposed to go back to the U.S. in a few days. Can't we just enjoy the time and see what happens later?"

"I won't leave you alone to face *that* again." She shuddered. The memories were vivid in her mind. No matter how much she tried to focus on rationality and convince herself they'd been in some shared nightmare, the horror of it lingered far too strongly. In the end, she admitted to herself that they had encountered something. Something very evil.

"I do not want to leave you," Cairn said. "There is nothing I want less than for you to go. But I was warned that this might happen. If anyone suffers, I should be the one, for I am the one responsible for all this."

"What did *he* mean when he said there might be a way out?" She couldn't bring herself to say the ugly name.

"I do not really know," Cairn admitted, pouring himself another cup of tea. "Perhaps just what I already knew, that remaining in this form requires a bargain with the Devil. I did not and so broke one of the rules."

"What?"

"My entire existence has been an anomaly. There has been no one before me, mixing earthly and angelic form. I should not be what I am."

"And what are you?" Brenna held her breath for the answer.

"A man who has lived too long." Cairn took her hand in his, turning her hand over, palm up. "It may be that I could not have survived anyway. I never thought about what would happen once I found you. They told me seven days only in this form, and that is all I had last time."

He stroked her palm tenderly. "Three are gone. Four now remain—three, since a new day has already arrived. Next week, the millennium arrives and the guardian angels told me in no uncertain terms that it was the outer limit of my strange existence."

"I can't believe you found me with no reason to hope we can be together," Brenna said vehemently.

His eyes brightened a little. "Thank you, love. We can try, as you have suggested, to spend the day enjoyably, but I . . . doubt it."

"Why?" Brenna said.

He brought her hand to his lips, kissing the palm that still lay, face up, within his. "I cannot be with you chastely," he said.

Oh boy, archaic language again. Brenna colored as she realized what he meant, understanding now that she had waded into deep waters.

"You want to sleep with me," she stated neutrally. Inside, his kiss and his words sent sparks flying through every part of her body, fire licking along her veins in their aftermath.

He winced. "This century has a gift for ruining speech. Yes, I want to love you, to be with you."

He paused. Her hand still in his, he lightly flicked her palm with the tip of his tongue. Heat sizzled through Brenna.

"I want to be inside you."

The simple statement devastated her. Brenna felt her entire body melt like wax. From someone else, some other time, the bald assertion might have angered or insulted her. But from Cairn, after what he had been through . . . His words resonated with sincerity, with truth. With love.

She pulled her hand away, remembering that he knew more about her when there was that link. "Yes," he continued. "I want to love you. In all the senses of that word."

Then his inner flame faltered, and she saw briefly the anguish he had been holding at bay. "Do you see why you cannot stay? I love you beyond life, but I am still human. Being human, the highest expression of love is that between the bodies of a man and woman."

He dropped his eyes as if the sight of her burned him. "What Lucifer asks is beyond me and he knows it. I have failed. Failed you and failed myself. But I will not be sorry for it."

He raised a hot gaze to her, and Brenna knew she was the one being burned now. The intensity, the sensuality, of his gaze were nearly more than she could bear.

"I will not regret that I want to love you in this way." A tiny smile crooked one corner of his mouth. "I will regret the lack of opportunity, however."

Brenna could not contain her tears. Or her love. As Cairn rose from his seat in concern, Brenna stood too. She moved toward him and fitted herself against his body. His arms came around her automatically, as she had hoped they would.

Brenna willed him to feel what she felt, to understand that she loved him. To understand also that the gift she had for him had never been given to another. And never would.

She couldn't say any of it aloud, but she held him around the waist as his head bent over hers to inhale the scent of her clean hair, to hold her close while their hearts broke together.

"It isn't fair," she whispered. "There must be a way."

"I will not risk you," he said.

"Damn it. Don't be so unselfish."

"Unselfish?" He put her away from him gently. "Selfish is all I have ever been. Never have I stopped to consider the implications of this, of what would happen. My own life I was willing to gamble. But not yours. In this selfish quest of mine, I have now put you in danger."

"Oh, Cairn, don't you realize?" Brenna cupped his cheek with her palm, feeling the power of her love flood her. No matter how strange their history had been, she believed this. "I love you. I can't let you go either. Don't do this to us."

"Brenna, I must. I could not stand the thought that I had put you within the reach of Evil."

"But at least we would be together . . ." she said wistfully.

He shook her shoulders lightly. "Never think that! It may be possible for souls to be reunited Above, but never Below. He would take you for a lover first, because he desires you, but mostly to torment me. Then we would probably be placed somewhere where we could eternally see each other but never touch."

"Is that so much worse than my returning to my life alone, knowing I will never see you again?"

"Yes," he said fiercely. "A thousand times yes. If you stay as you are, you could find someone else, have some semblance of a normal life."

This time Brenna was incredulous. She reached up to take his face between her hands. "Have you heard the expression 'hell on earth'? That's what it will be for me. That's what it is now!" She buried her face against his chest, sobs she could not hold back wracking her.

Brenna felt Cairn lift her into his arms and carry her to his bed, but the action had no effect on her tears. He settled his back against the headboard, placing her on his lap. Letting her cry without offering another word—for what could either of them say at this point?—he stroked her back, sliding his hand under her wool sweater to smooth down the soft cotton of her turtleneck. Trusting him completely, Brenna found his touch comforting. Her hands rested on his chest, convulsively clutching, then releasing, handfuls of his thick, soft chamois shirt.

She fell asleep finally against his chest. She was vaguely aware of Cairn easing her off his lap to lay her gently down on the bed. When the cooler air around her told her he was moving away, she reached out sleepily, encountering his arm.

"No," she murmured in sleepy protest. "Not one minute lost."

Cairn sighed raggedly, but lay down beside her, gathering her into his arms. He tucked her head under his chin. Brenna felt herself falling into sleep again, relaxed yet strangely empty after her crying jag.

The pain would come again, she knew, tearing at them both. But as long as they were together like this, as long as she could touch him . . .

"As long as I can keep you within sight," came the thought in her mind that had to be from him.

"We can have at least this . . ." was her answering thought.

Aware of the bitter irony of physical denial when they were already so intertwined in their thoughts and in their hearts, Brenna and Cairn fell asleep.

An hour later, when no one answered the knock, the room service steward removed the table quietly and drew the drapes to darken the room.

"I'm going for a walk," George announced to the silent workshop when he finished the carving he'd been working on. It was Christmas Eve, and it just didn't feel right without Brenna and some of her friends here. She had always invited friends from school who couldn't go home for Christmas, or others far from home for one reason or another. Like that Italian friend of hers . . . what was her name? Maria?

Not being able to remember irritated him. It had been happening a lot lately. He hated it, hated it with all a soldier's irritation at being denied a simple, clean fate. There was a reason men died at younger ages in past centuries, he thought. They generally died in battle. The Vikings thought it shameful to die in bed, as he recalled. Nowadays it was supposed to be a sign of a good life. Still, better that than dying in a hospital.

But in today's technology-driven culture, older folk didn't get to die with dignity. Oh, he didn't doubt there were many who wanted to hold on to life any way they could for every last second. God bless 'em if that was what they wanted. But not George Sirin.

He'd seen too much death to be afraid of it. For the young, death in battle was the worst way to die because a 19-year-old had yet to really live. But someone his age, seventy. Hell, the body hadn't been built to last this long.

He remembered a story about Henry Ford. The legendary carmaker would send his people out to the junk heaps to examine old Ford chassis. He considered the parts that were still in working order after other parts of the automobile had broken down to be over-engineered. Ford would tell them to lower standards on those parts, while raising them on the parts that failed early. No point having a carburetor good for fifteen years if the clutch only lasted five.

It was the same with medicine today, he thought. Doctors with all their fiddling were over-engineering the human body. More parts of it than ever before lived longer and longer. But the brain—nobody had yet figured out reliably what to fix up there. When it went haywire, it didn't matter how many miles you exercised on your bike, how long ago you'd quit smoking. Some things just weren't susceptible to tinkering.

The tinkering wasn't worthwhile. The last thing he wanted to be was some damned vegetable, body running, brain useless.

George finished lining up his tools, glad he'd decided on a walk. Fresh air was what he needed. They'd all go to the late service tonight. He was sure Brenna would be home from college by then.

Tomorrow he could sleep in, on Christmas. Too many years of rising with the dawn at reveille had ingrained in him a sense that weekends and holidays were for sleeping until he could smell the coffee brewing and the bacon frying. For thirty-five years, he'd fixed his own breakfast five days a week. The other two were Peggy's province.

"Peg?" he called. Maybe she was taking a nap so she could stay up tonight for the service. He'd probably be back before she woke up anyway, he thought. No need to leave a note. He had on his jacket and was out the door before he realized he'd forgotten his keys. They were in the pocket of his winter parka along with his gloves.

Oh, hell. It wasn't that cold anyway. At this time of year, it didn't freeze during the day. It frightened him for a moment that he couldn't remember what season it was.

Cold. That was the only word he remembered. Cold. He groped for the words that wouldn't come.

There, he had one. White. Another: wet.

Then he remembered. Snow. This was winter. Hell, he'd put on a spring jacket.

He remembered a day back on his family's farm in Iowa. It had snowed for days. The war was on. He was seventeen and determined to enlist as soon as . . . as soon as . . . He'd forgotten. His train of thought had derailed completely.

George started off at a brisk pace. No sense getting upset over a few little slips. A good, solid walk would give him a bit of fresh air, get the blood moving. He stopped after ten minutes. He didn't recognize this part of town. He didn't recognize this street.

Where the hell was he?

When Brenna awoke, she was disoriented, but not unpleasantly so. She was in a hotel room, but not hers. The man . . . She almost jerked upright, but caught herself just in time as memory flooded in on her.

The day before yesterday, finding him. Last night, the battle. Then the encounter with Lucifer. She thought briefly of Maud Barrett. Brenna could probably write a book to top Maud's now, if she wanted. Not that she ever would.

She was having enough trouble accepting what had happened herself. The thought of sharing it with anyone other than Cairn was utterly impossible.

Cairn. Her heart turned over at his name, the realization that it was his strong body she nestled against, his hair that brushed her cheek. She lay completely still, not wanting him to wake and tell her they should not be lying here together.

Did she believe everything that had happened? Did she have to? Wasn't it enough that she had found someone with whom every movement, every gesture, seemed utterly right? She felt connected to him as she had to no one else ever, in a deep, powerful way that went far beyond their one-day acquaintance.

An apt phrase drifted into her mind. "I know you, I walked with you once upon a dream. . . ."

Where had that come from? A melody joined the words, floating through her head. She remembered now. Tchaikovksy's beautiful *Sleeping Beauty* waltz. Paired with words in the Walt Disney film version. In her mind's eye, Brenna saw Princess Aurora dancing with Prince Philip in the woods, neither of them knowing the other's identity.

Unaware that she'd begun to hum the tune softly, Brenna was surprised to see deep, blue-gray eyes upon her, intent, assessing.

"Hello," she said, her lips curving in a smile. "Did I wake you?"

"Only from a dream of you," he said, smiling in return. He brought her hand up to his chest, where she heard his heart beating. He placed his hand just below her collarbone, his fingertips resting lightly against her throat.

"Would you sing that?" he asked.

"Me?" said Brenna, embarrassed. "I can't sing."

His smile deepened. "Wrong. I remember you singing beautifully at . . ." The smile faded. "Forgive me. I had forgotten that you . . ."

"You forgot who I was? I'm not the same person, Cairn. I am not Brynna."

"But you are," he said. "Yes, you are things she

250

never was, but in so many ways you are—"

"I know it's complicated," Brenna interrupted, wondering if he loved her or the woman he remembered.

"I know. Why don't you sing?" he suggested softly.

"I'll hum," she countered. "I refuse to embarrass myself otherwise." Even though his warm look told her otherwise, Brenna preferred to keep her modest singing voice to herself. She tried not to dwell on the fact that she was being compared with herself . . . or a version of herself . . . or . . .

This wasn't getting her anywhere. She closed her eyes gratefully, letting the soft hum emerge from her throat. She felt his fingers on the sensitive skin there and wondered if he saw the picture that formed behind her lids, that lovely moment in the woods. . . .

He was, because as she "watched," the lovers dissolved slowly, then re-formed. Prince Philip's golden-brown hair turned bright. Aurora's hair was now red, swinging down her back as they waltzed under the trees. And her eyes were green, not blue.

"That's very flattering, but my waist isn't that small, and I'm not that graceful," Brenna murmured when she finished and the delightful picture still remained. She didn't dare open her eyes, knowing it would vanish.

"You are to me," he said, kissing first her eyelids, then the place over her windpipe where his fingers had been. The soft kisses burned like fire. Brenna made a sound in the back of her throat. Cairn obligingly pressed another kiss to her throat, then another. Her turtleneck stopped him, as it had yesterday.

Yesterday. She wouldn't think about yesterday. This was the here and now.

"Why do you wear these things?" he said in a low voice that was a frustrated, sexy growl.

"They keep me warm," Brenna retorted, but she sat up and in one motion pulled off her sweater and turtleneck. She snuggled back within his embrace before she got cold—or got cold feet—and kissed him to distract him from the objection she expected.

After an initial, brief hesitation, Cairn responded with enthusiasm to her kiss. He lowered his mouth soon after to his previous destination, kissing his way down her throat, his lips lingering in the space between her collarbones.

"Much better," he murmured, widening his field of exploration, moving along her collarbone until he had covered one shoulder. Then he came back to the half-circle of her collarbones and kissed his way along the other shoulder.

His hands were stroking her back. Brenna found her own fingers slipping through the buttons of his chamois shirt. When she found he hadn't worn an undershirt after his shower, she grew bold. Sliding her hands inside his unbuttoned shirt, she tugged it from the waistband of his trousers, spreading the edges open to reveal his strong, muscled chest.

She murmured inarticulate appreciation while pressing greedy kisses of her own on his warm, golden skin. Cairn's kisses had moved down to the area below her collarbone, closer and closer to the upper slopes of her breasts.

His hands caressed her back above the wool and silk camisole that covered her bra. He then caressed his way to the front where the camisole covered her. Cairn gently tugged the thin straps of the camisole down, then found himself confronting her peach lace bra.

He lifted his mouth from her skin a moment, staring down at it. "How does this come off?" he asked finally.

When had she ever known a man who didn't know how a bra fastened, she thought, charmed. "In the back," she answered, reluctant to leave off exploring his flat male nipples, which were responding to her attentions. As she took one into her mouth to see if it would harden further, his fingers gently probed her back.

She smiled to herself, wondering if this was going to be awkward. It wasn't. He passed the universal male test for Foundation Garments 101 with flying colors, but she found herself moved by his obvious appreciation of her breasts and their covering. It made her feel sexy and loved and special.

Cairn palmed the lacy pale cups, running his long fingers over the eyelet-trimmed edges with a rumbling sound that had to be approval.

"I probably shouldn't ask this," Brenna said, "but have you ever . . . ah, do you have experience with these?"

"None," he assured her solemnly, his attention now focused entirely on uncovering her breasts. Maybe it was his nature, maybe it was the novelty, but Brenna had never known that the simple act of removing a bra could be so erotic.

He peeled off the cups as slowly and tenderly as if she were a rare and valuable object that could be damaged by rough handling. Next he slid the bra straps carefully down her arms, stroking her from shoulders to wrists as he did so. Only once he had removed the garment completely did he return his attention to her breasts.

Sliding his palms slowly upward from her ribcage, Cairn stroked her as he removed the camisole completely. Then he filled his hands with her breasts, watching with an intensity that sent exquisitely painful tingles to the place between her legs that no man had ever touched. Her nipples were already hard, her own hands still on his chest, when he bent his head to them.

Cairn had never beheld Brenna naked, and he nearly trembled with the sensation of seeing her lithe body partially revealed to him. The pale coral aureoles of her breasts were already puckered with anticipation by the time he pulled her erotic chest-covering away from her.

He thought he would die right there and then if he could not taste her. He flicked his tongue across one nipple for the sheer pleasure of seeing if it would tighten further, aware of Brenna's indrawn breath as he did so. Running his palm, the most sensitive part of his hand, across both tips brought sighs of pleasure from them both. When he lowered his head to take the nipple full into his mouth, she twined her hands in his hair, urging him closer. Cairn obliged her, pulling the nipple in with gentle, moist suction.

Cairn put one arm behind her back, urging her up against him to feel her frame pressed to his. His erection strained his corduroy trousers. He knew she felt it even through her jeans, because her hips rubbed him there. He arched her back against the arm encircling her to give him better access to her firm breasts. He suckled both, moving from one to the other, his hair brushing the soft white valley between until she twined her legs with his, restless, moaning.

Cairn was so inflamed, it was all he could do not to reach for his waistband, then unzip her jeans. Instead he dragged his mouth away from her breasts, moving with moist deliberation up through the shadowed valley, past her throat and over her chin until he found her mouth.

He took it as he wanted to take her body, thrusting his tongue into her heated, welcoming mouth in a rhythm that tortured both of them. Open-mouthed, hot, wet, erotic.

Their lower bodies were pressed together, nothing but cloth restraining them. He cupped her through the denim, pressing against the yielding flesh beneath, knowing she wanted him.

Sweet Heaven, what was he doing? There could be no more of this. "No," he whispered, dragging his mouth away from hers. "We must not."

"We can," she said softly. "Please, Cairn."

Groaning, he lifted his head from her mouth, but his head remained lowered, his thick hair brushing against her sensitized lips.

"No," Brenna said, knowing she had lost him. She raised her hands to his hair, but he shook off her touch gently, like a proud animal unwilling to be cosseted.

Cairn drew a deep breath as if girding himself for something unpleasant. He pushed himself from his elbows to his hands, sitting up and turning his back to her in one smooth motion. But not before a small, hot splash touched Brenna's throat.

She couldn't look at him as she retrieved her clothes and dressed, her own eyes filling with tears, unreasoning disappointment raking her with sharp claws. Cairn stared off toward the windows, his hair endearingly tousled.

Brenna craved his touch again desperately. She understood for the first time the smallest fraction of what he had endured, what it was like now to be here, to be together, and not to touch. Knowing what he had suffered, she could not be angry with him, even though her frustrated sexual tension screamed for an outlet.

Cairn opened the drapes, watching the display of gray and white clouds scudding across the landscape. Brenna approached him as he buttoned his shirt. He turned to see her come to stand beside him but did not lift his arm to bring her to his side.

She did anyway. "Cairn," she began hesitantly.

He turned to face her. His eyes were bleakly gray but clear. "Yes, love?"

"Have we ever . . . I mean did we . . . in the past?"

His lips crooked slightly. "Yes. The night before our last battle."

Brenna's eyes went wide. "I dreamed about it," she said. She touched her hand to his cheek, remembering her dreams. His tender sensuality flooded her, her dreams of him mingling with the very real caresses he had just lavished on her.

"You said . . . 'so little time,' " she murmured. He turned his head sideways to lean into her touch, to kiss her palm.

256

"Yes." he said, hardly daring to breathe. "Then you remember?" Was she ready to reclaim the past?

She ignored his last statement. "I . . . I never have," she said.

His eyes widened. "I thought after what you told me about these times that surely you had . . ."

"No. Although there was no reason for you not to think that, I guess. It isn't all that usual these days. In fact, it's quite unusual, if you believe what you read in the newspapers, but no, I haven't. I never met anyone before that I wanted to . . . to . . ."

"To share yourself with?" he said, his eyes suddenly very blue. "But you did . . . with me."

"According to you. But not in this life, in my life," she pursued. "Maybe I was . . . waiting for you." That much was certainly true. Why couldn't it be enough?

It was, somehow. "Then you did remember, somewhere deep inside. You said it yourself, you waited for me." That wasn't what she meant, but when his face blazed with fierce joy, she could not bring herself to contradict him. She believed in the threat against him, could not doubt that they had encountered Evil. Why couldn't she accept the rest of it?

Cairn stepped away with hands fisted tightly at his sides, the struggle not to touch her plain on his face. Brenna backed away, too, knowing the battle he fought now was not one in which she could help. Because the battle against desire was suddenly hers as well.

257

Chapter Sixteen

A short time later, they were walking down Braemar's deserted High Street, watching the shops shut one by one. Brenna remembered for the first time that today was Christmas Eve. Cold air skittered down the street, snow on the peaks ringing the Highland town. It must have snowed after they returned to the hotel and slept away yesterday.

Although it was not yet late afternoon, the sky was darkening already. Brenna looked forward to afternoon tea at the hotel, but confusingly, she both anticipated and dreaded being alone again with Cairn after that.

He had suggested the walk. Brenna figured Cairn wanted to put some physical and emotional distance between them after what had happened between them after breakfast. God knew they both needed it.

What had she told herself the other night—that she wasn't about to hand her virginity to some strange man on a platter? Now she knew she would refuse him nothing. That for the first time she longed, *ached,* to give herself to a man. Not just anyone, but this extraordinary man.

Who, if she believed it, had defied every rule of human existence to find her. The thought of being that important to someone warmed her, made her feel cherished in a way she had never known. The knowledge that he would not ask it of her was a bitter pill stuck in her throat.

Since there was no agreement on how to proceed, they walked mostly in silence, their arms loosely linked. Brenna tried to focus her thoughts on the present. She hoped Cairn was doing the same.

Cairn stopped in front of a shop window. "This is it, I am certain of it," he said, "although the sign is different."

"Certain of what?" asked Brenna, secretly enjoying the way he talked, which was still occasionally, unconsciously formal in the way of times past.

"You will see." Peering at the window more closely, Brenna saw the velvet backdrops that were the accouterments of a jeweler's shop. Looking up, she read a lighted sign that said "Braemar Jewelers." The backdrops were bare, suggesting the store had already closed. Cairn tried the door and found it locked.

"It's all right," Brenna said. "We can come back here after Christmas . . ." Her words died in her throat. She looked at the sidewalk, the shop window, anywhere but at him. She hoped she hadn't ruined the tacit agreement that existed tenuously between them. He hadn't raised the issue of her departure and she hadn't made any advances towards him.

Advances. How odd, Brenna thought. After so many years of saying no to men, here she was trying desperately to get this man to sleep with her. And he was the one saying no!

Cairn graciously ignored her words, pretending not to hear them. He found a small bell and rang it. After a minute, he rang it again. A light snapped on at the back of the store. Brenna peered around Cairn. A fiftyish man, heavyset, came to the door with a long-suffering expression on his face.

He shook his head at them through the door. Cairn tried to dissuade him. "May we come in?"

The fellow pointed at a sign on the glass front that said, "Christmas Eve closing 3:00 P.M." It was 3:15.

"I regret that we are late," Cairn said loudly. "Look sad, my love," he muttered to her in an aside. Brenna looked at him in amazement, enjoying the sight of his determination in a more playful light. She couldn't fake sadness, not over something small like this, not when their relationship was doomed. But she did try to appear hopeful.

Something worked, because with a sigh they could almost hear through the thick reinforced glass, the heavyset man began to open the door's various locks. His cheeks were pink with the high color so typical of the Scots. Then again, perhaps he was merely annoyed.

"The shop is closed," he said gruffly. "Can ye not see?"

"Aye," said Cairn, the faint trace of burr in his accent strengthening. "Aye, and we are sorry to disturb you so late."

"It's all right, I suppose. My da always said never to turn away a customer for ye'd never know what next might be waiting for you."

"I was here once long ago," Cairn said. "I might have met your . . . ah, father." Brenna watched him recover from his almost-slip of the tongue. He smiled ruefully at her. Thinking quickly, she realized that if he had been here in Victorian times, the proprietor would have been this man's great-grandfather.

"Aye, ye might have been here. We've been in this spot for more than one hundred years," the man said proudly, flipping on light switches. He closed the door carefully behind them, then moved to the counter where he started pulling out trays of glittering gemstones.

"But you'll not have seen my father, I think, since I've run the shop on my own for twenty years now, and you'd not be more than thirty."

Cairn didn't answer. "Is it diamonds you're after, a Christmas engagement, that sort of thing?" the man said shrewdly, assessing them, their linked hands.

Brenna didn't know what to say, since she had no idea why they were here.

"No," Cairn said, looking around as if expecting to see something familiar. Brenna remembered her dream, the dark man entering this store in some past time.

"He was here," she said to Cairn in a low voice.

"Who?" Cairn asked.

"The man . . . the one that night."

"Lucifer?" he said in the lowest possible voice.

"No, the other one. The one who tricked me, whom we fought later when he turned into a . . ."

She let her voice trail away, embarrassed. "He was at the hotel the day after I arrived—before you got here."

"You know it was the same creature?" Cairn asked.

"Well, yes. Wasn't I supposed to?"

"I was not certain you would recognize him when he changed form. That was Beloth. He was once an angel."

Pieces of her dreams were coming together for Brenna. "In my dream, I saw him come in here," she continued, feeling less silly since it was obvious that Cairn understood what she was talking about. "He had those stones in his hand, the two that glowed red."

"Ah, that explains how Lucifer tracked the necklace. But it was not a dream, Bryn—Brenna. You saw him," Cairn said.

Cairn drew her farther away from the counter as they talked in soft voices. "Remember what I said to you last night? That you had the Sight? It is there in your eyes. Anyone can tell if they know what they are looking for. A darker ring around the irises. Yours are rimmed in dark green-gray, darker than the centers."

The jeweler cleared his throat discreetly, reminding them that they were keeping his shop open on Christmas Eve, and that he had other things to do.

"Did you see me here?" Cairn asked intently.

"No."

"This is where I had the necklace made."

"What year was it?" Brenna asked, startled.

"Eighteen-eighty," he said. "At the suggestion of a Mrs. Graham."

"Graham . . ." Brenna said. "The girl who gave the necklace to my grandmother was named Graham. She told my grandmother the necklace came from her aunt."

"I saw her. The girl who had it," Cairn said. "I saw Mrs. Graham give her the necklace. Then suddenly I saw *you* holding it. I sensed your emotion about it, but I didn't know what time period it was or where you were."

This was incredible. Between the things that he had experienced and the things she had seen, the shards of her disbelief were being slowly chipped away. "You must have . . . felt what I was feeling. I was moved by the story my mother told me, about the girl dying in childbirth."

Then she remembered what else he had said. "Wait, you said you saw me?" Brenna asked in surprise.

"I knew it was you, but the time and place were not clear. Not even your face was clear. But I recognized your eyes."

Her heart tripped into double speed at the look in his eyes. The jeweler broke into their conversation with a polite cough. He had laid out several diamond rings and a few pearl rings against a black velvet cloth.

"Now if you'd care to try on a ring, we can set whichever stone you choose in it," he began.

"I'm sorry," Brenna said. "I don't think we're looking for a ring today. Are we?" She looked at Cairn.

She supposed he had come in here because he remembered the necklace he had commissioned. The idea of discussing marriage seemed absurd given what loomed before them.

Cairn did not answer. His eyes had lit on a row of boxes in a glass case across the room. "What are those?" he asked, walking over to the display case.

The jeweler left the rings on the counter and moved to where Cairn stood. "Ye've a good eye. This is fine-quality, sterling-silver jewelry from the Orkney Islands. Traditional Celtic design."

Cairn held out his hand to call Brenna to his side. If it had been Jim, she would have found the gesture arrogant and been annoyed. But Cairn did not act out of arrogance; rather his gesture sprang from the deepening emotional bond between them. Or renewed bond? she wondered briefly before the dizzying idea of centuries past made her head spin.

She put her gloved hand in his, allowing him to draw her to his side. "Do you like these?" Cairn asked quietly.

Brenna looked at the pieces in their lovely brown velvet boxes, stamped in gold with the name "Ortak." "Handmade in the Orkney Islands," a piece of paper inside the box read.

Then she bent to examine the jewelry more closely. The designs were intricate and beautifully worked. Intertwined lines, crossing, criss-crossing knotwork, winding around in a never-ending circle. The basket-weave appearance of the work fascinated her. There was also something very familiar about it.

"The Wheel, Brynna," he said as she looked at a circular brooch. She didn't correct his use of her name this time, but she wondered how much of his affection was for her, just her. Not for his Brynna and the past. Yet, how could she doubt the fierce sincerity in his eyes?

The jeweler, overhearing, smiled approvingly. "The wheel, quite right. The interwoven lines of the knotwork symbolize destiny, the thread of life. The circle or wheel shape means infinity. Patterns combining, recombining, the same yet always different, always new."

He could have been talking about them. Brenna felt her hand grow warm within Cairn's, felt the link vibrate between them with a resonance so loud she wondered that the whole shop hadn't started humming.

Cairn lifted up a box containing a circular brooch about two inches in diameter. It was formed entirely of interwoven sinuous lines, and it was impossible to tell where one line ended and the next came in. Brenna took off her gloves to stroke a finger over the fine detailing. "It's beautiful," she said.

"Aye," he said absently. He found pierced drop earrings next. From a silver post with delicate links hung smaller representations of the circle motif. Brenna had never particularly favored dangling earrings since they sometimes tangled in her hair, but she loved these. Finally, Cairn picked up a ring in sterling, a circle engraved into its center, from which a three-pointed shape spiraled out.

"The elements of life," the jeweler said. "Air, fire, water. The Celtic trilogy."

Cairn turned to Brenna. "Will you take off your gloves?" he asked formally. When she complied, he slipped the ring on. It fit her ring finger perfectly.

"Perfect on the lady, sir," the man said. "It's a delicate ring, that one, and suits her hand. Will that be all?"

"No, wait a minute, please," she interrupted as Cairn started to say yes. She searched among the brown boxes until she found a ring like hers for a man. It had a round, dark center, onyx perhaps, with silver inlay. It was a handsome ring, not effeminate, not too bulky.

"Fire, air, water," she said in a soft voice, slipping the ring onto Cairn's ring finger. It fit perfectly. "Set in a circle. Unity. Life."

Her hand lingered on his. She had no idea where her words were coming from, but they seemed right, so she let herself continue. "Love binds everything together."

They might have stood looking at each other that way, discovering a thousand shades of depth and meaning in each other's eyes, even, perhaps, remembering a time long ago. But the jeweler was already putting away the diamonds and pearls, eager to move along now that he had made the sale.

"That will be all, madam, sir?" he asked.

"Yes," Cairn said absently, never taking his eyes off Brenna.

"Yes," she echoed. They paid and, hand in hand, left the store, thanking the proprietor profusely for opening up for them.

They set off back in the direction of the hotel. "I didn't even look for cairngorms," Brenna said.

"They are not so valuable today," Cairn said. "There are so many other types of quartz now."

266

"But the sentimental value," she began.

"These mean just as much to me," Cairn said, touching her swaying earrings with one hand, rubbing his thumb over her ring with the other.

"I'm glad I was able to give you something," she said, feeling the smooth, silver shape of the ring beneath her fingertips, where their ungloved hands were clasped tightly together. She was unconscious of the double entendre until the words were out. Cairn made nothing of it, though, merely squeezing her hand. Feeling the chill in her fingers, he suggested that she put her gloves back on.

They entered the hotel still hand in hand, the silence companionable, a sense of peace surrounding them. At least Brenna felt that way. After a glance at Cairn's handsome profile, she thought he felt the same.

I have given him something of me, she thought, *even if he will not take the rest.* He "heard" her then, because he tucked her hand under his arm, smiling down at her with his lips curved in that slightly crooked way she enjoyed so much. Her heart turned over at the sight of him smiling at her with the fierceness of leashed desire in his eyes.

Brenna told herself to concentrate on the forthcoming afternoon tea, not on ways to break down his formidable will regarding their physical relationship.

The shops closed early on Christmas Eve in Washington. Peggy Sirin hated shopping in a crowd, but she had forgotten George's last present in her upset at Brenna's departure. She held the wrapped package carefully, opening the garage door into the house quietly. George had been down in his workshop when she went out earlier.

He was like a child about presents, so she walked past the stairs to his workshop silently. That was why she'd had the package wrapped at the department store, even though she much preferred to do it herself. If George had seen her with the gift in a shopping bag, he would have badgered and teased her about it.

She placed the package under the tree with the others, including Brenna's. Since she had left before Christmas and was returning after New Year's, Brenna had asked to wait on opening her presents until she came back.

Peggy hadn't minded. There wasn't much for Brenna this year, since Peggy had been so miffed that she was leaving. Some wool socks and a pair of gloves Peggy had intended for her to take on the trip, a calendar, a few other small items.

Peggy hadn't told her the gloves and socks were for Scotland. After everything Brenna had put her through with her thoughtlessness about this trip, Brenna would just have to see her presents when she got back.

It wasn't until dinnertime that Peggy started to wonder about George. The smells of cooking usually drew him upstairs. One of his favorite stunts was to tease her when she was cooking, sneaking tastes of food whenever her back was turned. It annoyed her sense of order, which was why he did it. George took great delight in keeping her slightly off-balance with his boyish charm, a trait she found endearing because it had contrasted so much with his austere military demeanor when he was in uniform.

When she was a few minutes away from serving, she went to the basement steps to call down. "George, five minutes," she said. Tomorrow would be turkey and the trimmings. On Christmas Eve she always roasted a leg of lamb. In a concession to Brenna's absence, Peggy had not bothered to fix the roasted lamb with rosemary that Brenna so loved. With just herself and George this year, she had deemed lamb chops appropriate.

George didn't answer, but that didn't particularly alarm her either. He often was so engrossed in his workshop that he didn't notice when he was being summoned.

At a quarter to five, she went downstairs to call him personally. Peggy wanted to go to the ten o'clock service, and knew they would both need naps, so she'd elected to eat early.

"George," she called on her way down the steps. No answer. *That man,* she thought with affectionate exasperation. Sometimes he could be so aggravating.

At the door to the workshop, she halted. George wasn't in there. His tools were lined up on the workbench with military precision, a sure sign that he had finished for the day.

"George?" she called. No answer. There was another door out to the back yard down here, but it was properly locked, including the chain over the bolt that couldn't be worked from the outside. The chain would not have been on had George gone outside from this door.

She went upstairs to see if he had indulged in a

nap on the couch in the family room, although she knew she would have seen him from the kitchen. When she did not find him there, she went to look in their bedroom. He wasn't there either. With a growing sense of alarm, she checked his study, the guest bedroom, and Brenna's room, just in case.

Peggy bit her lip, standing in the center of the living room. His car had still been in the garage when she came home, so he could not have gone far. She searched every room in the house this time, including both bathrooms and the powder room.

She walked back into the kitchen to look for a note telling her that he had gone out. There was none. On the verge of panic, Peggy finally remembered to check the hall closet. His parka was still there, but his lightweight spring jacket was missing. His house keys, hat, and gloves were in the pocket of his winter coat.

Peggy started calling the neighbors.

After a late Christmas Eve service, Brenna and Cairn walked back to the hotel, their breaths blowing clouds in the frosty air. Once inside and up the stairs, they halted at the door to Brenna's room. Cairn bent to brush a kiss across Brenna's brow, not trusting himself to do any more.

Brenna stood on tiptoe to reach his mouth, her arms reaching for his shoulders. Cairn was wary, for he knew all too well the utter sweetness of her kiss. He had not kissed her since she'd told him she had never been with a man, and he must not think of it now.

In truth, he had thought of little else since she had

told him. The admission meant far more to him than he could say. It told him that some part of her had remembered and searched, blindly perhaps, but she had known something was missing from her life.

Cairn willed himself not to respond to her innocent seduction, not to encourage her kiss by letting her lips part his own, or allow her hands in his hair to urge him to plunge his fingers into the glorious wealth of hers.

His will was for naught. For nothing, he repeated to himself, hoping rational thought would keep at bay the wild feelings she roused in him.

What a foolish idea.

Cairn was unable to form another coherent thought. His arms went around Brenna when he felt her press her lovely, lithe body against him, seeking and finding the fit that foretold how it would be together between them in the most intimate of ways.

No. They could not be together that way. Cairn pulled back from her tantalizing, arousing kiss. Brenna closed her eyes in defeat or despair; he didn't know which.

"Good night, love," he said, taking the key she held limply in her hand. He opened the door and pushed her through it gently, closing it before he pulled out his own key to the room next door.

Brenna dreamed. Alone and lonely, the man she loved next door and apparently forever out of her reach, the nightmares came back in force.

But they didn't start as nightmares.

She flew, unafraid and unhindered. She could fly because he was with her, because the two of them were together and the part of her soul that had been weighted down for so long was free. Brenna saw as if through a camera lens, swooping up and down with great, vast panoramic spans. She was not aware of her own body, nor could she see Cairn. But she felt his touch inside her mind and knew that he was there.

She flew up and up and in a dizzying blue sky, cloudless, warm, filled with sunlight. She laughed, happier, freer, than she had ever been. He shared her joy, fed it from a deeper, quieter wellspring than her own, but there was no mistaking his own joy.

She knew he was not so delirious as she, not so giddy. But then, he had never been afraid of heights, wary of the intentions of strangers, bewildered by echoes and sounds of a past she did not remember. She understood that Cairn had given her a great gift, his love helping her to strip away her fears and anxieties. With a huge surge that pushed the old inhibitions from her, a force rippled through her body, her mind, freeing her to pulse ever upward in the sky.

The blue sky faded and turned to night. Stars flared in the dark, cold vault of space. But Brenna wasn't cold. She felt free, wild, elated.

Then abruptly she found herself trapped, unable to move. She had been flying toward the golden warmth of the sun, knowing somehow that she flew toward a union with Cairn. Her body trembled with awareness, with the keen sensation of arousal, passion, fire, love. But now she looked through the barren eyes of the moon, its cold fingers holding her still while the fire and passion leached away.

The sun and moon. In some mythologies, ancient

peoples had described their rise and fall as the dance of two doomed lovers. The moon, delicate, ethereal, cold, longed to be the lover of the sun. The sun burned for her by day, sometimes seeing his beloved pale and far away in the bowl of the sky.

But inexorably, he sank into the abyss of night while she rose to reign over it. Should they ever unite, the sun would burn through the moon's coldness, warming her for a span of time perhaps, but ultimately his heat would bring about her death. As the moon would snuff out the sun were he to fall into the cold, lightless orbit that kept her frozen and forever out of reach.

Out of reach. A darkness fell over the sun, covering its fire with a terrible shadow too heavy to pierce. The shadow fell over her, too, dousing her light, her sight. She could no longer see the sun, no longer feel its heat. She sank into an unnatural darkness where only terror lived.

"Brenna!" a voice cried as she closed her eyes in defeat. "Help me, Brenna," came the voice, fainter now as the darkness closed over the earth too.

The voice was not Cairn's. It was familiar, so familiar. Whose was it? The darkness across the sky was almost complete. Stars were winking out, expiring in the dread new darkness like voices of hope unraveled, ravaged.

The darkness roared.

Brenna knew then whose was the voice and whose the darkness.

Chapter Seventeen

The phone rang shrilly. Brenna sat up, not sure whether she dreamed still. "Brenna?" came her mother's voice over the long-distance line, quavery, less sure than she had ever heard it. "Brenna, are you there?"

"Y . . . yes. Mother?"

"Brenna, your father's gone. Disappeared."

"What?" Brenna was fully awake now, with a surge of adrenaline that was pure fear sweeping through her.

"He went out for a walk, I think. He only has on a jacket. He didn't take his winter coat. But I found his house keys. They're here. The Harts saw him around three P.M. They came out to say 'Merry Christmas.' He waved, they said, but didn't look like he knew who they were since he didn't stop to talk. You know how he and Arthur love to trade stories. None of the other neighbors saw him."

"What time is it there? What time did he go out?"

"It's . . . it's nine P.M. I came back from Christmas shopping around four. We were going to eat dinner around five. What time is it there?" her mother asked, belatedly remembering the time difference.

"It's—umm, two in the morning." Brenna brushed off her mother's apology. "It's fine, don't worry about it," she said tersely.

Fear clutched her heart more tightly. "Mother," she asked urgently, "have you called the police?"

"No, I thought he'd be back by . . ."

"Why not? Mother, it's been five hours. Isn't it cold there?"

"Of course it's cold," her mother replied, sounding offended.

"Then he could be wandering around out there in the dark."

"I thought . . . I thought maybe he'd gone somewhere to see friends. But I called everyone nearby, since he didn't take the car. Then I thought he would surely remember dinner. And the Christmas Eve service is at ten o'clock. Maybe he'll be there."

"Mother, Daddy may not even remember *who* he is, let alone *where* he is. You can't count on that."

"But it's so embarrassing. Your father, a retired general. He'd be mortified if the police had to go after him like some runaway teenager."

Brenna unclenched her teeth, striving mightily to keep her voice from rising. "Mother, if he's wandering around in the dark somewhere, I don't think his dignity is the first thing we have to worry about. You have to call the police, tell them he has Alzheimer's. I'm sure they're familiar with it. Remember that lady in Maryland a couple of years ago who was gone for three days? They finally found her in a department store stairwell. She'd forgotten who she was and how to get home, but she was OK."

"Your father does not have a diagnosis of Alzheimer's," her mother said stiffly.

"I know, Mother, but you have to give the police a reason why it's significant that Daddy's missing and what kind of state he may be in."

"He doesn't have Alzheimer's."

"We don't know that!"

"Don't you shout at me, miss. You're the one over there on vacation, leaving us and never thinking about us once."

"Mother, there isn't time for this. Please, get on the phone and call the police. Call the Harts back, and the Andersons, and the Thompsons. Ask them to start looking. Get someone to come over and stay with you. I'll get the first flight out."

"Do you think he's all right?" her mother said in a small voice.

Remembering her dream, Brenna felt a frisson of fear lift the hair on her arms. "I hope so, Mom," she said. "I hope so."

Something woke him from a restless sleep. Cairn lay still for a moment, enjoying the feel of his muscles stretching, even though they ached and he was heartsore. Odd, the small things he missed. The feel of the sword in his hand—now that had been satisfying. If only he could take a sword to this situation and cleave through the rottenness cleanly and finally.

Interrupting his thoughts came a sudden stab of anguish—the reason he had awoken. The pain struck close to home, to him, but it was not the same pain he had experienced before in his human form. Shaking his head in an attempt to clear it as the pain lanced through him, Cairn sat up in bed.

He sought the source. Brenna. It had something to do with Brenna.

Cairn threw on the terrycloth robe the hotel provided, since he slept without clothes, then walked over to the door separating their rooms.

He knocked. There was no answer, but he saw the light under the door. Pushing it experimentally, he discovered it was not locked. He pushed it all the way open, stepping into her room. Clad in a long flannel nightgown, with her back turned to him, Brenna was packing her things in a gray tweed-covered suitcase. Her blazing hair was in wild disarray. She did not even look up at him as he entered the room.

"Brenna?" he asked. "What's wrong?"

"I have to leave, Cairn." She turned around and he saw her pale, ravaged face. Her elbows hugged her sides almost defensively, as if she did not want him to touch her.

"I understand," he said, although disappointment knifed through him. It was what he had wanted, surely? It was safer for her. It would keep her out of the Adversary's reach.

He would return to his previous form. At least he might be able to escape, to go into the Light, even if he would never again know who he was, no longer search to find the part of himself that had been missing for so long. Self-preservation warred with a part of him so stubborn that he would endure the torments of demons just to remember her each day.

No, something else was going on here. Why would she leave in the middle of the night? From Aberdeen, she had to fly to London and then back to Washington, but he doubted there were any planes before mid-morning. Had she just now realized she could not tolerate their situation any longer?

Cairn reached out toward her with his senses, but she blocked him—unintentionally, he was sure, because she was so overwhelmed with bleak emotion.

He sensed only that he was not the object of it. Something else was motivating her to leave. Something had happened to Brenna, hurt her. He moved toward her.

She held up a hand. "Please, Cairn, don't."

It was true then; she did not want him to touch her. Another pain lanced into his heart.

"What is wrong?" he asked again.

"You wanted me to leave, didn't you?" Brenna didn't want Cairn to touch her, didn't want to make eye contact with him because she wouldn't be able to keep the truth from him. She didn't want to burden him with her problems. He had enough of his own; why should he have to worry more about hers?

She could tell from his expression that he thought she was abandoning him. Maybe she should leave it that way. Perhaps then, he wouldn't try to dissuade her or help her.

"I did want you to leave for your safety," he said in a deep, slow voice. He took another step toward her, even though she had already warned him away. Brenna hoped he did not move any closer. She did not have the heart to be so cold again.

He came up behind her as she bent determinedly over the suitcase again. "This is probably . . . best, your leaving. For myself, I confess I wanted to keep you with me forever," he said. She knew the words sprang from the deepest well of his heart.

"Oh, Cairn," Brenna said, straightening. His arms circled her from behind, but she could not turn to face him. One more minute and all her defenses would crumble. No, she couldn't let that happen. Why have him worry about something he could do nothing about?

"Brenna, if you have to go, I understand," he said thickly, as if he struggled with himself. Just as she struggled to keep her turmoil over her father from him.

"I don't want to leave you," she said, turning suddenly. "I want you to know that at least." Fiercely, she kissed him. He mustn't go to whatever fate awaited him without knowing she loved him.

She tried to pull away, but it was too late. She had admitted too much in her passionate kiss.

Cairn's heart wanted to burst from its cage. Something was tearing her apart. He had assumed it was the situation between them, the wanting and not having, the inexorable fate that would descend the day after tomorrow.

Yet despite all that, her kiss told him that his emotions were fully reciprocated. She longed for him, to complete physically the bond that had already lashed their hearts and souls one to another.

Cairn arrived at a swift decision. He could not let her go completely untouched. He realized he could love her, yet leave her safe within the terms of Lucifer's dictate: by making love to her without possessing her, without being inside her. Cairn did not care whether his decision was profoundly selfish or self-sacrificing. He had no time for subtleties. Besides, he would have an eternity to contemplate his actions.

"When do you have to leave?" he asked, leaning his forehead against hers. His hands were at her back, shaping her waist in urgent strokes.

"At nine," she said, her tone indicating she did not understand the reason for his question.

"In seven hours. There is time," he said, then crushed his mouth over hers in a hard kiss that took her completely by surprise. This time there was no gentle mating, no long, slow exploration. He parted her lips with his tongue, sweeping in to find hers with devastating swiftness.

"I have to love you, Brenna, before you go." His arms brought her in even tighter against him, his hands reaching down to caress her buttocks. Briefly shocked, Brenna felt her body respond like a flower to the sun. Liquid heat flowed through her. Her body, naked under the nightgown, suddenly craved his touch in every secret part of her.

The swiftness of his approach and her own arousal startled her. She could not guess his reasons for changing his mind. She didn't care.

She did not know what Cairn intended, but she wanted to forget their troubles for a little while. Her own impending sense of loss left her feeling no less urgent than he.

She doubted Cairn had fully capitulated. She also knew there was farewell in his passion, as much as love. Brenna welcomed the forgetfulness his loving would bring, whatever he allowed them, allowed himself.

He kissed her as if he intended to devour her. She was as eager as he. In moments she found herself on the bed, the suitcase pushed to the floor with a heavy thud. Cairn took her face between his hands, renewing his sensual assault on her mouth as his body covered hers. His hands moved upward, caressing her face, moving to her hair and stroking it between his strong fingers.

The weight of his body on hers was so real, so welcome after all her dreams, that Brenna cried out. She responded ardently to his kiss, one hand twining in his hair, the other slipping beneath his robe to roam the hard curve of his shoulder.

Cairn plunged into her mouth, losing sight of his goal of restraint as her sweetness enclosed him and he felt her touch on him. He used the same rhythm he would seek if he could enter her body. His hips moved involuntarily against her. Then she took up the rhythm, until the two of them were engaged in as close an approximation of lovemaking as possible while clothed.

She parted her legs so his erection could press more deeply into her hips, her tongue receiving, then parrying in time to his own. Her hands pushed the robe off his shoulders, before she moved them to his back. She slipped one hand inside the belt of his robe.

Feeling her caress at the base of his spine undid Cairn's precarious control completely. He unbuttoned the top of her gown, freeing her breasts, which were uncovered under the nightgown.

He spread her flannel-covered legs further apart with his knees, his hands plucking at her taut nipples, his tongue thrusting in time with his hips and hers. He suckled her breasts, harder now, until she moaned and shifted to better cradle him between her thighs.

With a groan, he realized he had lost this battle. One final thrust as his manhood rocked desperately against her, blocked by the thick robe and her flannel gown, unable to find the home it craved. His fingers were at her lips, feeling the moans vibrating from her throat. She drew one of his fingers into her mouth.

Knowing she would enclose him in her body just as hotly, as wetly, imagining her mouth on him, he climaxed. In defeat, in surrender, in ecstasy, ashamed yet shameless at a release he could not prevent but one which had saved her—and him—for at least a little while longer.

Despite his shattered senses, he knew she had not yet found fulfillment. While his own libido was temporarily satiated, hers was not. Before she lost the edge, he gently pushed her gown up her legs to expose the triangle at the junction of her thighs.

He kissed his way through the nest of red curls between her thighs. He knew from her sharp, immediate reaction that she was indeed very close to her own peak.

She was damp and hot. Her scent arousing him past bearing, he insinuated a finger into her heat. He pressed gently until a second finger joined the first, while finding and circling her bud with his tongue.

Brenna clutched handfuls of the blanket she lay atop, her head tossing from side to side. Deliberately, Cairn stroked his tongue around her sensitive nub in a circular motion. Her moans were coming high and fast.

She bucked. He found his mouth directly on her. He sucked the tiny bud carefully between his teeth, then rotated his fingers rhythmically inside her. She called out his name. Cairn lifted his head for the exquisite pleasure of watching her face as her release rippled through her.

She subsided slowly, the scent of her body's pleasure all around him, on his hands, his lips. He was hard again. She could not remain this way, open to him and so tempting.

He slid his hand out of her, pulling the nightgown down reluctantly, moving up her body until they were face-to-face once more. Cairn could not help looking at her breasts, flushed and rosy. He knew he must pull her gown closed. But first he had to taste her again.

The nipples were hard and extremely sensitive. When he bent to flick his tongue across them again, she moaned and pushed his head away.

"Does it hurt?" he asked.

"Oh no," she whispered. "It's too good. Feels too good. They're . . . sensitive."

"Oh," he murmured, gratified, allowing himself

one last tingling caress with his palm before buttoning up the gown again.

And still it was not yet dawn.

He had no desire to sleep, not when every minute that ticked by was closer to the last they would spend together. So he pressed her gently against his shoulder as she let exhaustion and the aftermath of ecstasy claim her. She slept while he tried to imprint the feel of her soft body, the feminine scent of her, the sight of her wildly tumbled hair, deeply enough into him to last through eternity.

When he saw the sky begin to lighten, he knew his time was up. His mood was as gray as the sky. He could delay no longer. He had to let her go.

Cairn extricated himself from her deeply sleeping form, bending to retrieve the suitcase. Moving it to a table, he finished packing for her, enjoying the touch and feel of her clothes with an appreciation of material things that he had lacked for hundreds of years. His heart contracted at the thought of waking up with her, seeing her in these inner and outer garments, watching her dress, undress for him.

He twisted the ring she had picked out for him on his finger, feeling a vise around his heart so tight that he could scarcely breathe. To have found her, been allowed this taste of what could have been, only to lose it all . . .

His black mood must have reached her, just as her anguish had woken him a few hours ago. He strained toward it, trying to learn why she had been so upset, knowing that while waking she would be less guarded.

An image drifted from her mind to his. A tall man,

blue eyes dulled with age, his face an older, masculine version of Brenna's. Cairn sensed Brenna's fear as misty tendrils wound around the dream-figure. Then the man was gone, fading from Brenna's sight even as he called her name plaintively.

Cairn strode back to the bedside, surprised and angry. Brenna struggled out of the hold of sleep to find Cairn looming over her. "You fear for your father's safety. Why would you keep this from me?" he said.

She had never seen him angry at her. And yet the intensity of his emotion only deepened his golden masculine beauty. She knew immediately that he had seen inside her dream.

"So much for 'I'll still respect you in the morning'," she muttered, seeing a frown crease his brows. He didn't understand the expression, of course. "I told you I was leaving," she said defensively.

"You did not tell me why!" he thundered, but his grip on her shoulders was achingly gentle. Brenna had absolutely no fear that he would hurt her.

"I didn't want you to have anything more to worry about," she said, inching herself up to her elbows.

"Foolish woman," he said, more in sorrow now than anger. "This, at least, is one thing I can help you with. I know your city and I can help you find your father."

"All right, so come with me. There's probably room on the flight." But in her heart, she wondered just what he thought he could do. He knew her city— what had he meant by that? How could he know anything about Washington?

No time to ask now. Cairn was dragging her from the bed none too gently, in the direction of the table that now held her suitcase.

It was packed, she noticed. "Get dressed. Warmly," he said in a voice that brooked no disobedience. The war leader again, she thought, surprised that her mind had not automatically rejected the association with the past.

Then his tone softened. "Let me help you, Brenna. Would you meet me outside of town in fifteen minutes, at the Linn of Dee?"

"Are we leaving?" she said.

"Yes. Do you trust me?"

"Of course. What's the hurry? It's only seven."

"I mean, do you genuinely trust me?" His eyes held hers, intent, challenging.

She dared to touch his cheek, although he looked so tautly sculpted he seemed more a breathtaking statue than a man. But as she looked into his granite-blue eyes, she saw that he was indeed a man. His emotions were on a tight leash, as if he balanced at the edge of something momentous.

"I trust you, Cairn," Brenna said softly. "Don't ever doubt that. I love you."

"Thank you," he said, turning his head to kiss her palm where it rested lightly against his cheek. "Please remember that, no matter what occurs. And that I love you."

He turned away, then stopped. "Can you check out of the hotel for me? Wait." He strode into his room, returning with money. "This should cover my share," he said, shoving the notes into her hand.

"Cairn, wait, what's going on? I appreciate that you want to help, but really, I don't know what you can do—"

"No, you do not know what I can do," he said evenly. "The quicker we get there, the better chance there is of finding him. Hurry, Brenna." He strode back into his own room, closing the door behind him.

Brenna stared after him, perplexed. One more bizarre event in their bizarre relationship. Yet she had nothing to lose by doing as he said. She had to drive to Aberdeen to catch the flight anyway. She put on her warm cardigan, a pair of wool pants, and her lightweight hiking boots.

Donning her parka and hat, she took her suitcase and backpack and made her way downstairs.

"I'm sorry," she apologized to the night clerk, the same fresh-faced boy who had yawned at her yesterday morning. "I do seem to be coming and going early a lot. I have to leave today, I'm afraid. I'm here to pay for both of us."

"Och, he's gone to meet you, I suppose," the clerk said. Brenna said nothing, since she did not know. Where was Cairn going and how was he going to meet her at the Linn on foot in such a short time?

Dawn was spreading across the landscape as she drove. Pink and orange streaked from the eastern sky, while to the west, the darkness had not yet been pierced. Remembering her dream, Brenna shifted gears uneasily.

Get a grip, girl, she admonished herself. The sun is going to rise today, just like any other day. Yet she faced the possibility of losing the two men she loved most in the world. *Daddy,* she prayed, *please be all right.*

For Cairn, she sent up another prayer, hoping that

the time he had spent searching was not in vain. That somehow there was a future for the two of them. She could not imagine what would happen to him otherwise. Or to her, without him.

Brenna drove up to the roadside near the overlook a few minutes later. He wasn't there. She sat for a couple of minutes, looking around. It would be light soon. Where was he?

How could he have gotten here on foot, anyway? the voice of reason intruded. *Trust me,* he had said. All right, she trusted him. Physics wasn't something that seemed to be a problem for him, so maybe logistics weren't difficult either.

Cairn, where are you? she thought. A feeling that she should look for him rose in her without conscious thought. Was she supposed to leave the car and the luggage?

Trust me.

She climbed out of the car, leaving the keys in the ignition, taking only her waistpack which held her wallet and passport.

Trust me. The feeling grew stronger that he was out there waiting for her. That she would find him there, as she had before. Not as far as Cairn Toul— that was an hours-long hike. But here in the climb up along Glen Dee.

Brenna stopped by a clump of pines. Here. It was here he would meet her, she knew. She turned toward the east, watching the sunrise spreading, when she heard a sound behind her. She turned slowly, her heart pounding.

The sound she had heard was the quiet, majestic noise of massive wings beating, swooping gently down to earth. The wings folded as he landed and walked toward her. Clad in a brown robe trimmed with gold, the huge wings beige and brown, gold-tinged at the tips, Cairn looked at her steadily. He would have looked unmoved, except for the pulse she could see beating erratically in his throat.

He stopped a few feet away. "Brenna?" he said uncertainly.

Her heart was in her throat for a moment. She could not speak. He was magnificent.

Oh God, it was all true. Everything she had dreamed, everything he had said. Their shared history. The epiphany burned into her while she struggled for words and found none.

Too late. Her understanding, her acceptance had come too late.

"Did . . . did you come to say good-bye?" she asked finally. Brenna was relieved, really, that he had chosen this after all. It was the only thing that could save him. After what had passed between them a few hours ago, she could never be with him again without completing the union that they were meant to share. She did not want him delivered to the Dark. So this was for the best.

Then why was her throat so tight, she thought she would cry if she drew one more breath?

"No, not good-bye," he said, his voice quiet yet strong in the cover of the trees. "I told you I would not leave you. Let me help you, Brenna. I can get you home more quickly than an airplane. I will help you search for your father."

"But you can't," Brenna cried. "Doesn't that break

these rules he mentioned? Won't that give you to *him?*"

"You heard Lucifer. I cannot use what small powers I possess again on Earth. I can only return Above. But I would never abandon you that way to save myself, especially not now."

"Oh, Cairn, you mustn't," Brenna said, running toward him. She stopped near him, uncertain whether she could embrace an angel.

"I can think of no better way to say good-bye to you than this. Are you ready?"

"Ready for what?"

"To fly." He did not smile.

She eyed him dubiously. "Won't I be too heavy for you?"

"I do not think so," he said. His face took on a grave expression. "Does it bother you, this form?"

Brenna remembered Brianna and knew that after the tragedy, he had feared to risk appearing in this form. She stepped into his embrace without a qualm, relieved when his arms came around her as they always had before.

Then his wings swept forward to enclose them, the way he had tried to shelter the girl Brianna. She remembered her longing in the dream, to feel those wings around her.

They were soft and warm, powerful and tender, steel and velvet. They cocooned her in a private world for two. Brenna wanted to stay enclosed in this special embrace forever, but knew they could not.

"You are still Cairn, aren't you?" she asked, seeing him nod his head and hearing his wings move slightly for emphasis.

"Then I love you. That won't change," she said.

"Thank you," he said hoarsely, finally able to get words past his dry throat. He hadn't realized until then how much he feared her reaction would be one of shock or rejection.

"Hadn't we better get going before *he* realizes what you've done?" Brenna asked. Cairn didn't tell her that Lucifer would know what he had done within the next five minutes. She was already afraid enough for her father.

"Are you ready?" he asked.

"I . . . I guess so," she said.

"Then let us go," he said, gathering her into his arms. "Oh, hold onto your hat," he added, springing upward with no more preparation than a bird.

It seemed like only a few wingbeats before he paused over a mound that looked ancient and moss-covered. Cairn closed his eyes, remaining aloft with a constant steady sweep of his wings. The light that Brenna had seen around him in her dreams grew, until it was brighter than the dawn.

The top of the mound below them burst open as the light radiating out from Cairn struck it. Rough, yellow-brown stones shot out, followed by a host of tumbled, weary shapes.

"The faeries," Brenna exclaimed, delighted that he had freed them.

"I could not allow them to be imprisoned on my account," Cairn said, peering down intently to see if they were reviving.

"It was really on mine. I gave them the necklace, making them Lucifer's target," Brenna said.

One of the dusty shapes looked up. The faery king,

trembling with exhaustion, climbed to his feet. He saluted them and said something in his language. Reaching into an invisible pocket, he withdrew the necklace.

Brenna caught it as he tossed it expertly, high into the air. "Don't they want it anymore?" she asked Cairn.

"They are as enamored of it as ever," Cairn replied. "But they will make a necklace from the rough stones you mined, and they wanted us to have this back. With their thanks."

"Thanks to you," Brenna said, reaching up to clasp the necklace around her neck. "Wait," she said, suddenly alarmed. "Won't this bring *him?*"

"He threw the altered stones at us, remember? Extracted them from the necklace when he wrested it from the Seelie Court. He cannot use those to find us."

Releasing the faeries, however, would get back to Lucifer quickly. Cairn did not intend to tell Brenna that.

More and more of the reviving figures began to look skyward, waving and cheering. Cairn glanced at Brenna wearing his necklace, his heart so filled with love and grief that he could scarcely speak.

"Are you ready?" he asked again, his voice hoarse.

"This is the big one, right?" Brenna asked, trying to lighten the mood.

"Across the pond," he agreed. "As we British say."

Brenna closed her eyes, one hand on her hat brim. "Then let's go."

Chapter Eighteen

How long it lasted, Brenna could never say afterward. She retained mostly impressions, sensations. The cold, the rushing wind, the star-splashed darkness. Her ears grew so cold, they turned numb, but her body remained warm as Cairn held her securely in his arms.

Later, she remembered there had been dark and the night and a thousand stars above, around, between them. Surely they had been still in the atmosphere or she would not have been able to breathe. Yet earth was far away and indistinct, the curve of its horizon just visible against the darker night.

Although it had been dawn when they left, it was night as they flew westward. Flying through time with a steady beat of great wings, Cairn kept on, surrounded by the light that emanated faintly from him.

Perhaps she even slept. Brenna wasn't sure. But she knew it could not have taken as long as the airplane flight, or dawn would have been spreading over the east coast as they arrived. Here it was still dark over the Potomac, still the middle of the night.

"Life is at its lowest ebb between midnight and sunrise," Cairn said cryptically as they moved lower and closer to earth.

" 'It is always darkest before the dawn,' " Brenna murmured the quotation. Cairn smiled briefly, but his face was set.

Brenna wondered what this was costing him. A drain on resources he would need to fight the Enemy, perhaps. Or had this sudden move forever canceled his chances of returning to live life as a man?

It was only her assumption, Brenna told herself, that he had wanted to remain a man. Cairn loved her—there was certainly no doubt about that—but back in Scotland, the future had been too much of an intrusion when their present was so wobbly.

Cairn had said something about souls being reunited. For all she knew, maybe he wanted her to accompany him, to become . . . what, an angel? But wouldn't she have to be dead first?

"Hush," Cairn said gently. "I can't hear when you're in this state."

"What state?" Brenna demanded, indignant. She thought she'd learned to shield her thoughts, but then he was touching her, holding her close. She had no defense against that.

"You're broadcasting your emotions all over the place, my love," he said. "Normally I'd have no objection, but since we need to find your father, it's better if I can have the area around me clear."

"Sorry," Brenna said. They flew on.

"This is the Washington Cathedral, isn't it?" Cairn asked after a while, indicating a tower with glowing lights atop it.

"What are those?" Brenna asked. She wasn't sure she recognized the Cathedral in the dark from up here. There were so many lights of one color or another—on telephone poles, streetlights, monuments. She saw Christmas lights nearer the ground, especially the multicolored ones. The profusion of color and the unfamiliar viewing angle made it hard for her to distinguish landmarks.

Cairn appeared to understand her confusion. "Those are navigation lights at the top of the bell tower. For airplanes and . . . other things with wings," he said, a trace of humor in his rich voice.

Cairn turned. A moment later, Brenna saw an incontrovertibly familiar shape. It, too, sported blinking red lights near the top. Funny how she had never noticed these things from the ground.

"I know that," she said. "It's the Washington Monument. "It looks so different from up here."

"If you have your bearings, do you think you can pick out the Cathedral now?" Cairn asked.

"Yes. Why there, though? I know I live near there, but my parents live in Georgetown."

"Perhaps because it is a cathedral, there is some concentration of forces there, an orientation toward the Light," he said thoughtfully. "I do know that I am stronger when I am near your cathedral."

"Oh," Brenna said lamely. She supposed it made sense, as much as any of this did.

"Think about your father," Cairn suggested. "The closer you can feel to him, the more it will help."

"I thought . . . In the dream I had, the one just before my mother called, I thought I heard his voice calling me."

Cairn knew then that her Gift was still with her, as he had suspected, even if she did not believe in it herself. It was up to him to encourage her.

"Close your eyes," he instructed. "Try to see through his eyes. Imagine you are calling to him."

Brenna did. It was dark, cold. A shadowed, wooded place. Somewhere safe by daylight but not necessarily so at night.

Brenna sighed. There were a lot of places like that in Washington. Rock Creek Park, the Chesapeake and Ohio Canal towpath, the gardens of Dumbarton Oaks, the Arboretum . . .

"Focus," Cairn urged, his voice a whisper amidst the sound of his wings.

Brenna tried. As places open to tourists at certain hours, access was controlled to Dumbarton Oaks and the Arboretum. Her father could not have gotten in there on Christmas Eve. Both places would be closed. Rock Creek Park was huge, running all the way from the Kennedy Center in the south up through the city, ending finally in Maryland.

No, George Sirin wouldn't have been able to walk as far as Maryland. But he could certainly be wandering around in the Washington, D.C., section of the park.

The towpath of the former C&O railroad canal. Brenna kept her eyes tightly closed. Something about the towpath drew her. The sand and gravel path running beside the canal began in Georgetown. Mule-drawn barges worked it for the benefit of tourists during the summer, just as they did in the old days, when goods were taken inland all the way up to Ohio.

The reproduction barges only went up as far as Maryland. The path once walked by mules had been converted years ago to a popular walking and cycling path that ran for miles.

The towpath frequently paralleled the Potomac River. It was popular among joggers, cyclists with mountain bikes able to negotiate the pebble-and-sand footing, walkers, and nature lovers. But it wasn't safe at night, especially the part that ran through Georgetown.

Drawn by the prevalence of students at nearby Georgetown University, and the nightlife flocking to the many taverns and discotheques, thieves emerged after dark. And not just purse-snatchers. A man had been found murdered along the towpath in Georgetown in recent years, a woman jogger raped.

Brenna's heart pounded so loudly that she could hear only the roaring of the blood in her ears. Cairn squeezed gently, then more strongly when she did not respond.

"Brenna," he said finally, then louder. "Calm down."

"Oh, Cairn, I'm so afraid. Daddy's been missing for hours, and I'm afraid he's there somewhere."

"I know you're afraid, love. Let me help you. Why do you think he's near the towpath?"

"I feel drawn here."

"Are you sure it isn't just the presence of Evil you feel?"

"This is a high crime area at night. Is that what you mean?"

"No, not exactly." Maybe he shouldn't tell her, Cairn mused. It would only frighten her more. But he had felt Evil here, residues of a time past, a child possessed by a demon, a priest's death on a long, steep flight of stairs.

The image that came to him with these thoughts astonished him. A film had been made about the event, of the exorcist's trials. Details were altered, but the story had been told. Yet the forces of Light had won out in the end; perhaps the struggle between Dark and Light was not wholly forgotten by these twentieth-century people.

Like Devil's Point in the Cairngorms, Cairn knew that there were places where Evil concentrated, where it flourished. And places like the cathedral, where the Light shone brightly.

Evil was drawn to Evil.

She should be warned.

"There is an old Evil here," he began slowly. "A tragedy that occurred a number of years ago. There are local demons in most places, just as there were in Scotland. They act like sinkholes for the Enemy, drawing down the Light, trying to douse it."

Brenna heard him out despite her anxiety, recognizing that he was describing the true story behind Peter Blatty's novel *The Exorcist*. How had Cairn known?

Surely that could no longer matter, since the demon had been driven out. Brenna forced herself to stay focused on her father. *Daddy, where are you?* Brenna tried to cast her thoughts wide, across the sleeping city. *I want to find you. Help me.*

Help me. The echoing thought she heard was as insubstantial as a cobweb, as tenuous as dust motes scattered in a ray of light. But it was there.

"He *is* here somewhere," Brenna cried. "Can you go lower?"

"Not without risking tangling with trees and power lines. Try to see him, Brenna."

"I don't have that Power you're talking about, Cairn. This is the twentieth century, remember, the age of disbelief and all that," she lashed out wildly in her frustration.

"But you still have Power," he said in an authoritative voice. "All of us do, to some extent. Some are able to access it more easily than others. Your gifts have been buried over the course of your lifetimes, under doubts and anxieties, but they remain. You would not have heard your father otherwise. Concentrate," Cairn urged.

Brenna felt like screaming, but she tried again, straining to extend her senses around her. To her amazement, it worked.

"There," she pointed. "Somewhere down there." It was the section of the canal near Georgetown, the part that ran parallel to Canal Road. It was probably about a forty-five-minute walk from her parents' house.

"Hurry, Cairn," Brenna said. Suddenly she felt as if she were with her father, looking out of his eyes. "It's cold. He's very cold." A violent shiver rocked her.

It had begun to snow. Cairn did not hesitate, even

though Brenna knew the snow would decrease his visibility substantially. But maybe he was tuned in to her, to her feelings, and they acted like a beacon. He swept down toward earth.

They landed. Brenna was on her feet for the first time in what seemed like hours—probably was. "Are you tired? Did I hurt you?" she asked as she turned to face Cairn.

"Yes and no," he said, stretching out his arms in front of him to loosen the kinks while his wings folded silently behind him. "Don't worry about me. Where do you think he is?"

"Where are we?" Brenna peered through the snow, which was wet and, for now, sticking only on the colder grassy areas. She looked for something to give her an idea of which part of the trail they were on. Looking behind her, she saw the bulky shape of Key Bridge.

"OK, now I know where I am. That way is Georgetown," she said, pointing. "There are homeless people who live under the bridge." Was her father among them, confused and lost?

She turned. "And up this way is the towpath, heading north, or really west, at this point."

"Hey, shweetheart," came a drunken voice. "Howsh about sharing a bottle . . ." The man, his face covered in gray stubble and clutching a brown bag shaped suspiciously like a wine bottle, stumbled toward them.

"Bug off, buddy," Brenna snapped, her city-dwelling instincts leaping to the fore. She felt Cairn's eyes on her. "Find somebody else to drink with."

"What a bitch. How 'bout your boyfriend there? He wanna buy me a drink?"

Cairn had stepped in front of Brenna. The light surrounding him grew until the drunk's eyes went wide with shock.

"Holy shit, what the hell are you?"

"Leave her alone." Cairn did not think "go and sin no more" would make much of an impression on this derelict, and besides, he did not have the right to say it.

"Shure, as shoon as you buy me a drink," the man leered.

Cairn took two steps toward the man. The drunk pulled a knife and rushed him. Cairn sidestepped neatly. As the drunk turned again to stagger toward Cairn, swinging wildly, Cairn slipped in under his arm and belted him in the jaw. He fell, limp and unconscious.

"Wow," Brenna said. "I didn't think you were allowed to do that."

"I do not suppose I am," Cairn said. He looked up at Brenna, a feral grin briefly transforming his face. He must have looked like this in battle, Brenna thought, impressed.

"But I have to say I rather enjoyed it." He knelt by the man's side, checking his pulse. It was strong and steady. Cairn dusted off his hands and straightened.

"I do not think it matters much now what other rules I break," he added as he moved to Brenna's side. "Whatever happens, this is the last time I will be able to assume this form."

That sounded ominous, but Brenna had no time to contemplate Cairn's words. A shiver shook her from head to toe, her whole body going cold in response.

"Daddy's outside somewhere, Cairn. I can feel it," she said, rubbing her hands together even though her fleece-lined gloves, which had protected her in Scotland, should have worked as well here.

"Make haste then—there is little time." He grabbed her hand and started off up the path, away from the lights and noise of Georgetown.

They rounded a curve. There was almost no lighting. Cairn's ambient light was very low, whether because he was fatigued or because he didn't want to draw attention to himself, Brenna didn't know.

"Daddy?" Brenna called. "Daddy, it's Brenna. It's Brenna. Can you hear me?" Nothing but the hushed sound of falling snow and the slow passage of water in the canal.

They moved up the towpath slowly, scanning the bushes and trees. Nothing. They kept walking, Brenna's sense of panic growing. Cairn gripped her hand reassuringly, but she was too upset to receive much comfort from him.

About the only good thing about the dark and the snow was that it should keep people from seeing what Cairn looked like, Brenna thought. The trees sheltering the towpath would keep passing cars on the road from seeing them.

They were halfway to Chain Bridge when Brenna experienced her strongest premonition yet. "Up ahead," she said, hurrying over the gravel which was getting slippery with the wet snow. "Up on the left is Fletcher's Boathouse. In summer you can rent bikes and rowboats and canoes."

Cairn looked up, his long-distance vision restored by his change of form. He saw through the trees to the river, recognizing some way off a bridge where he had rescued a fisherman from drowning, during his search for Brenna and the necklace. "I know this place. I have been here," he said.

"You have? When?"

"Not long ago. A man here fell in the river . . ."

"And you rescued him, didn't you? Cairn, I think I talked to the man for my article."

"Article?"

"I wrote an article for the magazine I work for. It was called 'Angels Around Us' and I interviewed local people who said they'd had experiences with . . ." She broke off as the old clapboard house that was the site of the rental complex came into sight.

"Listen," she said, coming to a complete stop. Cairn stopped. He thought he heard a faint sound that might be a voice, but it was difficult to distinguish over the other noises around them.

Remembering their first encounter by the canal, he had misgivings. "Could it be another person like the one we met?" he asked.

"You mean a drunk? No, I don't think so." But Brenna walked forward a little more slowly at his urging. The noise, whatever it was, had stopped.

Brenna wished she had thought to bring a flashlight. "Daddy?" she called softly. "Are you there? It's me. It's Brenna." There were no lights around the boathouse, nothing she could see.

Then an irritated voice rose. They heard the words clearly. "Damnation, the boat's too small. How do you expect to get across the Channel in that, Major?

Thousands of troops here. These landing craft aren't big enough."

"It's Daddy," Brenna said.

"What is he saying?" Cairn asked.

"He was in the Normandy invasion, in World War II." They heard a splashing sound through the trees. Brenna ran, not caring about anything now except reaching her father.

She came to the path that led down to the river and plunged down it. Cairn was right beside her. There was scarcely enough moon to see the rowboat bobbing on the water, but her father had put on a lifejacket stored in the boat. Its silver reflective tape glinted dully in the dim light.

"Daddy," she called. "Daddy, it's Brenna. Come back!"

"What's that? Who's there? Never mind, going to Europe." But he turned around to peer back toward shore.

"Daddy, do you have the oars out? Can you row back here?" called Brenna.

"Oars, she says. This is a D-day landing craft. I told you stories about these." Then his mind seemed to clear a bit. "Brennabear, is that you? You make up with that fellow Jim?"

As he talked, the boat was being carried out toward the center of the river. "No, you've got someone else there. Good. I think you did find the right one, sweetheart. Take good care of her, you hear?" he called to Cairn as if they were standing in the living room having drinks.

"Sir, we need you here. Can you get back?" Cairn

said in a respectful yet urgent voice. He would worry about who Jim was later.

"What? No, don't think I can. No fool like an old fool, eh?" George Sirin said, looking around him. He stood up. The boat wobbled alarmingly.

"Daddy, sit down."

"Thought you wanted me to come back."

"Yes, but you have to row. Hold on, Daddy, I'll come get you." Brenna threw off her coat and jacket before Cairn could stop her.

Cairn grabbed her arm at the water's edge. "What are you doing? You'll freeze out there."

"There isn't time to get a boat. I don't even know how he got the padlocks off to take that one. The boats are supposed to be locked up at night."

She struggled to pull away from Cairn. "Let me go. I've got to get him," she screamed at Cairn.

"No." Power poured through his touch. Staring at him, watching the pale nimbus around him grow, she realized that he intended to use the power of his angel form. "I will get him."

His huge wings lifted him above the ground. "Cairn," Brenna whispered, knowing his actions now would call the Enemy if releasing the faeries hadn't already done so. What had Lucifer said? *I won't let you interfere with mortal lives on earth. That's my province.*

She bit her lips as she saw Cairn approach the boat in which her father still stood, swaying alarmingly from side to side. Before Cairn caught up with her father, the boat reached the current that swirled from the nearby falls.

It seized the boat like an invisible hand, yanking it

strongly downriver. Her father lurched, then fell. The empty boat flipped over as her father spilled out of it.

The reflective tape gleamed, then disappeared. Her father had gone under. "No!" Brenna cried. She plunged into the freezing water.

The shock of the cold stopped her. She wasn't going to help anyone if she got herself drowned. She paused, water up to her knees. She was standing on a shallow ledge that dropped off to the river's full depth immediately. Cairn hovered over the water, searching.

He moved downstream, following the current. He knew there was no time to lose. Only a few minutes in this water could kill Brenna's father. Cairn risked drowning himself if his wings were soaked, but he could not afford to wait until the current coughed and spat up George Sirin. By then it might be too late.

He flew as close to the surface of the water as he dared, using his vision to search. Seeing distances was one thing. Seeing through night-dark water was another. Cairn willed the light around him to increase, hoping it would penetrate the river's black surface a little bit.

The boat popped up, overturned. Cairn made a quick grab in the vicinity of the boat. Nothing.

He heard Brenna shout and looked in her direction. She was standing knee-deep in water, gesturing toward the other shore, giving every indication of plunging in herself.

"Stay there," he called, "lest you drown."

Moving in that direction, he looked ahead. A dull

flash of something metallic caught his eye. The life-jacket.

Cairn did not have enough height in the air to swoop down. His wingtips were almost in the water already. He used the air current above the water to propel himself downstream. Brenna's father was going under again as Cairn drew even with him. He reached for the older man, but the current had already dragged the unconscious George Sirin under the surface again.

Cairn realized there was only one way he was going to be able to rescue Brenna's father, but it might kill them both.

He folded his wings, held his breath, and dove into the water, trying to follow the silver gleam. It faded, but if Cairn stretched, he might just reach George Sirin. He snagged Brenna's father by his vest, dragging him upward toward the surface.

George Sirin was unconscious but breathing. But Cairn's wings were now too wet to lift either one of them above the water. Cairn started swimming, one hand pulling George, the other stroking upstream against the inexorable current.

He called on every physical strength he'd ever had to aid in this impossible rescue. George Sirin was a dead weight. With his own wings sopping wet, they were useless. It was like bearing the weight of two men with him instead of only one.

Brenna saw the faint glow of light working its way upstream, bobbing and wavering. She was sure Cairn had found her father, but she didn't understand why they weren't moving faster. It should only be a matter of seconds for Cairn to bring her father here.

Then she realized what had happened. The light was too low to the water, its progress too slow. Cairn was swimming upstream with her father.

Swimming. The thought shocked her to her core. He had gone in, or fallen in, to retrieve her father, and his wings would now be dripping wet. Heavy and wet, they must be useless.

Brenna unlaced her boots as quickly as she could, then dove into the ice-cold water after them. She reached them quickly, since she was headed downstream and had no extra weight to carry.

"You . . . should not have risked this," Cairn panted as she reached him, following the trail of light.

"I have his right side," Brenna said. They could argue about heroics later. Sharing the burden lightened Cairn's load, although each of them could only stroke with one arm. The going was rough, but together they had enough strength to swim sideways across the current and out of it.

They headed toward shore, reaching the riverbank not far from where they had started. Brenna's arms were cramping and she could barely feel her numb legs. She stumbled twice trying to stagger up the riverbank. Cairn bent over, pulled her father's limp body from her weak hold, and carried him up the bank.

Then he came back for Brenna, helping her to stand with a hand under her arm. He was clearly laboring under the weight of his drenched wings. Brenna wanted to refuse his help, but she had no choice. Her legs were too numb to support her weight. Cairn helped her clear the riverbank. Then they both collapsed onto the ground on either side of her father's prostrate form.

Brenna pulled herself up, placing her head on her father's chest to listen to his heart. She couldn't hear anything.

"Is he alive?" she asked Cairn.

Chapter Nineteen

At her words, Cairn looked up to scan the sky. Brenna thought the response odd until she remembered the vision of the silver angel taking Brianna's soul aloft. Of course, angels came to take the souls of the dead to Heaven.

"Say he's not dying, Cairn—oh please, no," she pleaded, unzipping her father's jacket for better access to his chest.

"No, he isn't dead," Cairn said, his head almost on his knees. Brenna realized that he couldn't lie down, at least not on his back. The wings pulled at him too heavily.

Brenna began to push on her father's chest rhythmically. "I can't hear his heartbeat," she said.

"It beats," Cairn replied briefly, as if he had no breath or energy himself.

Suddenly her father coughed, and river water spewed out. He turned his head, then lay still, unmoving but definitely breathing. Brenna wasn't sure how much progress that was. Her father wore neither a hat nor gloves. She wondered how many hours he'd been out of doors. His hands were like blocks of ice. She started massaging his chill hands and face.

"Oh, God," she said to Cairn, "this is what you had. Hypothermia, only worse. He's older and he was in the water, too. We have to get him to a hospital." Guilt stabbed her suddenly. She hadn't even thanked Cairn.

"Are you all right?" she asked.

"I . . . will be," he said slowly. "Can . . . you get back to Georgetown by yourself to call help?"

"I won't need to. There's a hospital near here." Thank goodness Georgetown University Hospital was only minutes away. Brenna had been born there. "What about you?"

Cairn lifted his head a moment. "I can't go there, not in my condition."

"But that's exactly why you need attention too, and—" Brenna broke off. He hadn't meant his medical condition; he'd meant he couldn't go in a hospital looking the way he did.

"Are you subject to . . . I mean, is there any danger that you might . . ."

"Do you mean, can I die in this form?" he filled in for her. "I don't know. I can't say I feel exactly invincible at the moment."

"Cairn, I can't leave you here," Brenna said. George Sirin started to cough weakly. Brenna turned her attention back to her father. His lips were blue.

311

As she watched, he started to clutch weakly at his chest.

Brenna was in a momentary stupor. *Do something*, her mind screamed, but her body wasn't sure what to do. What was wrong with her father?

Then she realized, as his face became more ashen and he appeared to be having difficulty breathing.

"My God, I think he's having a heart attack." Having an inkling of what was wrong freed her from inaction. Brenna tried the CPR she had learned in a class when writing a story about paramedics. She pressed her father's chest rhythmically, blew air into his mouth.

To no avail. Her father's body shook spasmodically, then went still. Brenna looked up at Cairn, who was on his knees on the other side of her father's body. "Cairn, he's going to die."

Cairn put his fingers around George Sirin's wrist, his other hand at the older man's temple. "There is still life here," he said, so low Brenna scarcely heard him, "but it is weak."

He bent over George's body, holding back his sodden wings with all the strength he possessed in his shoulders and back. Cairn knew he didn't need physical strength for what he was going to try to do. But it wouldn't help to drip water all over a man already ill.

Brenna watched Cairn's intent face. The light around him gradually increased until it glowed clear and golden, enclosing the two men. Cairn said a few words, but mostly he seemed entirely focused inward, as if he called on some strength or power within him.

The light began to hurt her eyes and she had to avert them. Suddenly a terrible thought struck her. "Cairn, you're not . . . you're not taking him, are you?"

He looked at her briefly, his eyes seeing somewhere beyond her, above her. Then his gaze met hers, catching and holding it as if she were a lifeline to bring him back to Earth. Piercing the glare, his blue-gray eyes shone with an intense light.

"No time to explain," he said. "I won't take him, Brenna. I couldn't even if I wanted to. That is Their job. I . . ." Still on his knees, he swayed. Brenna saw the color draining rapidly from his complexion, the golden light around him graying at the edges. He looked terrible, drained of strength with the suddenness of a bolt of lightning striking a tree.

Amazingly, Cairn maintained his posture, his fingers firm around her father's wrist. The light around him glowed again, pulsed, then dimmed. Looking down, she saw her father's ashen tone fading, his normal skin tone returning.

Cairn was looking at her father, whose lips parted faintly. George took a breath. Although his eyes remained closed, his arms were at his sides, as if his chest no longer pained him.

Satisfaction in his face, Cairn looked at her for a long moment as the light around them faded. Brenna stared at her father, astonished. He looked now as if he were only sleeping, his cheeks their usual ruddy color once more.

She glanced back at Cairn, whose hands had dropped away from her father. He tried to stand, but succeeded in getting only one leg half-bent under

313

him. Even that looked tenuous. He swayed.

Cairn's other-worldly expression left him as the bubble of light around the two men vanished. Then Cairn collapsed, falling backwards onto his wings.

Quickly patting her father's face and hands to make sure he was warm and seemed healthy, Brenna moved around him to get to Cairn.

She reached for him. "Cairn," she said. He didn't move. She tried shaking him. Nothing.

Finally, she dragged his head into her lap, noting that his face was cold. "Cairn," she pleaded, rubbing his face, his cheeks, combing her fingers through his hair. "Cairn, look at me."

Finally he opened his eyes, but the effort was obvious. His blue-gray eyes were filled with love for her. But also with the dark sadness of imminent loss.

"Oh Cairn, what have you done?"

"Your father's all right now," he said in a low voice husky with pain. "Physically. Can't heal all ... couldn't touch what was in his mind. Surprised I could do what I did . . ." His voice trailed away. He smiled tiredly. "Finally did something more than what I was born to be."

She tried to think, but the fact of his dying was taking over her brain, paralyzing her. Born to be what? What had he been? A soldier, she remembered.

She remembered something else, felt the reality of it flood her suddenly. It wasn't just the pictures of herself and Cairn she had seen, together on that battlefield. She felt it, touched suddenly the person she had been so long ago. She had sensed the woman within who knew how to fight when she had handled the sword. Now she drew on another facet of the woman who had come before her, perhaps was a part of her—the woman who loved Cairn. As she loved him.

"You were never just a soldier, Cairn," she assured him, stroking his thick, damp hair off his brow. Her voice even sounded slightly different, deeper.

He knew the difference too, his eyes brightening as she bent over him. "Brynna?" he said.

"Brynna, Brenna. Some part of me is the same, has always been the same. The part that loves you," she said, willing her eyes not to fill with tears so her vision wouldn't be obscured. "Thank you. Thank you for saving my father."

His strength was running out. He could not answer, but one hand moved. She reached over to clasp it tightly. His hands were cold. She was losing him.

"No," she said. "No, don't leave me." His eyes held hers, steady, unwavering. She knew intuitively that he wanted her to be the last thing he saw.

"You can't die. Not when we've just found each other again. Not after everything you've been through," she said. His fingers tightened briefly over hers. His eyes closed, but he forced them open again slowly.

She could not keep him here, Brenna realized. No matter how much she wanted to, no matter that he didn't want to go.

Death was overtaking him. Her heart shattered at the knowledge.

Then something above attracted her attention. She tried to ignore it, but even Cairn finally shifted his gaze from hers, looking toward the sky. So she did as well.

Angels filled the sky above her. *So that's what they mean by a heavenly host,* she thought, in a kind of stupor. Silent, yet not silent, the beat of their wings and the light around them warmed her, restored her, gave her hope. Even though she knew her heart lay broken inside her, no one could fail to be uplifted in the face of such glory.

The golden angel, the most beautiful woman Brenna had ever seen, was at the forefront of the host. She was the angel who had stood beside Cairn on the cliff in long-ago Scotland. Gabri-elle.

An angel in silver hovered beside her. Brenna recognized him, too. Rapha-el. He had borne the Scottish girl Brianna's soul up to Heaven when she died.

Her arms tightened around Cairn. *I don't want you to take him.* The defiant words echoed in her mind. She knew they had heard her, although no words were spoken aloud. Their faces were sympathetic.

They were not human. Cairn was. Cairn belonged here. "He belongs here," she said aloud this time. "With me."

A voice spoke from behind her. "No, he belongs to *me.*" Cairn's eyes were closed, his chest rising and falling with each shallow breath he drew. His voice sounded in her mind, very faint, but it was there. *The Evil ones here called him. From the place we passed.*

She hadn't been listening when she was so desperate to find her father. Now Brenna remembered why Cairn had sensed Evil, recalling an article her magazine had run. The true story behind *The Exor-*

cist. The struggle for the soul of a child. One of the priests had been driven—or pushed—to throw himself from the long, steep flight of stairs that led from the street to upper Georgetown.

They had called their Master. He had come.

Lucifer stood in an angry glare of smoky red light, folding his leathery wings, while his tail twitched behind him. "I told you not to interfere, not to use *their* powers," he said. "Did you think I wouldn't find you?"

Beyond her father, coming from the towpath, dark shapes crawled in the night. The demons in this area had been emboldened, called by the presence of supreme Evil.

This was a dark host, with a dark lord at their head. He stood on a little rise, looking down at the group huddled on the ground. George Sirin, unconscious, but apparently healthy; Cairn, his face pinched and drained from the life force he had given to Brenna's father; Brenna, cold, wet, but defiant.

Satisfaction was written in the malevolent beauty of Lucifer's face. The Lord of Darkness had come in person to collect his prize. He tried to avoid looking at the host above them, but Brenna knew his words were not for her.

Squinting, as if the sight of the massed ranks above pained him, Lucifer planted his feet and called out, "He belongs to me!"

Never, came the weak voice in her mind. *Never.* Gabri-elle and Rapha-el stooped to earth, landing in front of Lucifer, blocking his view of Cairn.

"He is not yours to take," said Gabri-elle, the defender of humankind.

"He broke the rules," Lucifer thundered. "No ang . . . none of you can take mortal guise yet still use your powers."

"He is not an angel," said Rapha-el.

"No human may take the form of . . . your form." Lucifer tried a different tack, while his minions hissed and writhed.

"He is dying," Gabri-elle said calmly. "He will not remain one of us. Therefore he is beyond your reach." While she pronounced these terrible words, Rapha-el turned to look at Brenna.

A dull horror filled her mind with a darkness that had nothing to do with the presence of the Enemy. The angels in front of her were shielding her—and Cairn—from any such attacks.

Brenna reeled with the knowledge that Gabri-elle had just pronounced Cairn's death.

As comprehension of Gabri-elle's words set in, Brenna knew she would rather die than be separated from Cairn. But she followed Rapha-el's gaze and looked at her father. She could not leave her father here either.

"What do I do?" she whispered to the winged being who regarded her with compassion. Rapha-el held out his arms. "Give him to me."

"No!" Brenna cried, knowing what it meant.

"Do you want Cairn to go with *him?*" Rapha-el asked.

"Is there no other choice?"

"Not now. Let me take him. See to your father." Tears poured down Brenna's face as the angel gathered up Cairn.

Cairn opened his eyes. Brenna kissed him gently

on the mouth. When she touched his lips, a sense of longing but also reassurance flowed through her. She tried to shake it off. She didn't want comfort, whether it was Cairn's or Rapha-el's.

She would never see Cairn again. Even if he were to be reborn, as she had been, he would not remember. And she could not live as long as he had.

Trust. Believe. The words caressed her mind. They were Cairn's last gift to her. Then his eyes closed, his face a still mask of peace. His male beauty had never been more pronounced, more perfect. Brenna closed her eyes, unable to bear looking at him.

She staggered. As if a knife stroke had fallen between them, she no longer felt Cairn's presence, Cairn's love, in her heart, her mind, her soul. The connection between them was broken. She could no longer sense the link between them. He was dead.

Rapha-el flew upward swiftly, while Gabri-elle faced down Lucifer alone. Brenna no longer cared personally about the struggle in front of her. Her father was alive. Cairn was dead. The contest between Good and Evil would not be decided today. It would continue, as it had for centuries, each side winning and losing in its turn.

Gabri-elle stepped back, revealing Brenna on the ground, her father nearby. There was no trace of Cairn, nothing to indicate he had ever existed.

"He is free," Gabri-elle said to Lucifer, assurance ringing in her voice like a bell.

Lucifer roared. His creatures screamed and clawed. "He was mine. Mine by right. You broke the Bargain."

Gabri-elle's chiming golden voice contained a note

of steel. "No. In his last act, he gave his life to another, thus ending any claim you had on him. Such unselfishness does not go unrewarded. He is no longer on Earth. There never will be another like him. These are diminished times."

"My work," Lucifer smiled, bowing mockingly. "Thank you for the compliment."

Gabri-elle lifted her arms, throwing out streams of molten gold that flowed from the sleeves of her robe. The golden liquid—if that was what it was—coagulated and settled over the creatures behind Lucifer. They were instantly silenced. Then they vanished as if they had never existed.

Lucifer howled in agony, his face contorting. But he stood his ground.

"There is now a little less Evil in the world," Gabri-elle pronounced.

"And a little less Good," Lucifer snarled, recovering, his pitchfork appearing in his hand. "You may have won this round, my lady, but I take comfort in knowing that she"—he pointed the pitchfork directly at Brenna—"will be forever diminished by his absence." Striking the ground three times with his pitchfork, he disappeared in a puff of viscous black smoke.

Gabri-elle turned as Brenna moved to her father's side. Brenna looked up but saw nothing but the dark sky. The snow stopped. The host had disappeared. She assumed Rapha-el had, too, with his burden.

Brenna looked at the glowing being in front of her. She could not keep from searching the angel's countenance. Brenna was surprised that Gabri-elle was still there and that she could see the angel. She had thought a person couldn't see angels unless close to death or in great danger, like the people she had interviewed.

Unless her father . . . She quickly bent over him, noting the color in his cheeks, the steady rise and fall of his breath.

"No," Gabri-elle said gently. "He is in no danger. You understand what Cairn did, don't you?"

On her knees by her father, Brenna shook her head. "Not really, my lady. Just that he saved my father's life." She choked back tears. "And gave his own to do it."

"He poured his life-energies into your father," Gabri-elle said. "We had warned Cairn that we could not keep him safe forever, that if the Enemy learned of him, he would be in great danger. This in fact transpired. When Cairn gave his life to save your father, he could not know it, but that selfless act put him forever beyond Lucifer's reach.

"Your father is restored to physical health from tonight's events," Gabri-elle continued gently. "Yet not even I can halt the disease that is affecting his mind, although Cairn's gift of life has slowed its progress. Your father has lived a good life. I can tell you that he will always recognize those who saved him here tonight, and that when he dies, he will be called to the Light."

Brenna nodded. A mixed blessing, wasn't that the expression? Cairn had saved her father, but at the cost of his own life. No, she tried to tell herself. This was the best possible outcome. Lucifer had no claim on Cairn now or ever. He had gone into the Light.

Gabri-elle looked up as if she had been called from

Above. "I must go," she said. She looked closely at Brenna. "Would you prefer to forget? I can give you that much."

"Forget? Never, my lady," Brenna replied, passionate conviction roughening her voice.

"I am well content with your response." Gabri-elle smiled, a smile as full of mystery and power as it was of mercy. Brenna felt as if she had passed some test, without knowing why or what the purpose.

As for Gabri-elle's question, to the end of her life, Brenna wanted to remember Cairn—beyond, if possible. She would welcome the pain his memory brought as long as she could remember. Which would be every day. Bereft. Alone.

Not alone, came a familiar voice inside her mind. She looked around wildly, saw no one. Gabri-elle was gone. As if on cue, her father opened his eyes.

Or perhaps the angels had conspired to keep George Sirin asleep, Brenna reflected. She wouldn't have to explain anything to him this way, nor would he have explanations to make himself. If her father started talking about angels and demons—well, people might think he was just plain crazy, not ill.

George Sirin sat up without difficulty, looking around him. "Brenna?" he said. "What are we doing here?"

Brenna took a deep breath. "Well, Daddy, you went for a walk and didn't come home."

"But you're in Scotland, aren't you? With that new fellow of yours?"

"New fellow?" Brenna repeated.

"That handsome blond fellow with the Scottish accent. Somebody pulled me out from under the water,

322

and it sure wasn't what's-his-name, the flyboy."

"You mean Jim," Brenna supplied.

"Whatever. Where is your young man?" At his question, Brenna had to turn her face away so he wouldn't see her tears.

"Daddy, we need to get you to a hospital," she said, hoping her fear for her father's health would explain her shaky voice. "You could have died of exposure."

"I'm dry now. So are you, sweetie."

Brenna looked more closely at her father, then down at herself. They were both dry, from their inner to outer garments. A wonderful gift, especially since it had started to snow again. If there had been any footprints, marks, signs of struggle, they were gone now.

Did angels leave footprints? Brenna wondered, stifling a hysterical urge to giggle. Hard on the heels of that thought came the desire to sob.

"You're right, we do seem to be dry. But I'm taking you to Georgetown University Hospital, Daddy, and they're going to do some tests." She hoped this would distract him and he wouldn't ask her any more questions about Cairn. She was surprised he remembered anything at all about tonight. She was certain from his lack of curiosity that he knew nothing about the angels.

"Fine," her father said, agreeing to her plan. Brenna was surprised and pleased. She had assumed her father would resist.

She helped him to his feet and they began to walk up the towpath. A little farther and they would come to Reservoir Road. A few blocks down it and they would reach the large complex that was the hospital.

As they walked, it occurred to Brenna that perhaps her father would be relieved at knowing what was wrong with him and that was why he hadn't refused to go. "We'll call Mom when we get there."

"Of course." Her father was content to walk beside her in silence, seeming none the worse for wear. Brenna found she wasn't especially tired either right now. There seemed to be no physical aftereffects of what they had been through. A final gift from Cairn or Gabri-elle?

The thought of Cairn brought a renewed wave of pain. She concentrated on simply putting one foot in front of the other. This was how her life would be from now on. A struggle to get from one day to the next.

Trust. Believe. The words flowed faintly through her senses. She heard the words again. In what? In whom? But there was no answer.

Chapter Twenty

Her father did not appear to be suffering from signs of exposure to the water, nor did he show signs of pain in his chest or his breathing. Brenna opted for the simplest explanation. She told the emergency room doctor that her father had been gone from the house for a while and that she had found him outside near the river.

Judging from his replies to the doctor, George Sirin did not appear to remember how he had arrived at the riverbank. Moreover, he seemed to have forgotten his tumble into the water and his brush with death. Which made it easier for the doctor to accept that all her father had endured was too much time outdoors on a cold day.

While they were taking her father's temperature and other vital signs, Brenna drew the doctor aside to explain the reason why she believed he had wandered away.

"That's fine, Ms. Sirin," the young doctor said. "After what you've described, I have no problem admitting him to the hospital for the rest of the night. Tests can be done tomorrow as part of a checkup. It's not at all unusual to order tests when someone your father's age comes in with an unspecified problem relating to memory."

Brenna was relieved. Her father would get the medical attention he needed and her mother needn't know that it was at Brenna's instigation. Blood tests were normal on admittance to a hospital. Her mother could find no fault with the procedure. Tomorrow he could be transferred to the Army hospital at Walter Reed where, as a retired officer, his insurance would cover the rest.

Relieved that her father would receive proper medical attention, she went to call her mother. Peggy Sirin arrived less than twenty minutes later, still dressed in her church clothes for the Christmas Eve service. It was five A.M. on Christmas Day.

Her relief at seeing her husband was so great that she asked no questions about how Brenna had arrived in the United States so quickly. Frightened and chastened by the incident, she signed insurance forms and agreed to a wide range of tests without any comment or complaint whatsoever.

Once her mother was installed at her father's bedside, Brenna decided it was time for her to go home. She remembered that her hat and parka were still at Fletcher's Boathouse.

For a moment, she was too tired to care. Then she

realized that the earrings and pin Cairn had given her were in a small velvet box, zipped securely into an inside pocket of her parka. She still wore the ring.

She couldn't leave them there. Someone would surely find her things. The parka was new and enough incentive by itself for someone to steal it. Although her mother protested her decision to leave, Brenna was firm.

"I'll be back later today, Mom," she promised. "I just want to go home, clean up, and get some sleep." She bent over and kissed her father, who was now sleeping deeply.

"Merry Christmas, Daddy," she said softly. She hugged her mother. "Merry Christmas, Mom."

Half an hour later, she walked down the path to the boathouse, the pole-mounted light showing her the way. Even though it was dark and snow still swirled fitfully from the sky, she was no longer afraid. What was there here to be afraid of, after what she had experienced?

Her parka and hat were not where she remembered tossing them aside to plunge into the water. Maybe they had somehow been swept into the water in all the confusion. She walked along the riverbank south to where she and Cairn had brought her father ashore. Nothing.

Then something odd struck her. The rowboat was pulled up to the shore. But she remembered it overturning, sucked under by the current. Who could possibly have pulled it up here? It should have been far downstream by now, perhaps washing up on a bank a few miles down. But it was impossible that it could have come ashore on its own, certainly not in this neat, upright position as if someone had pulled it out of the water and deposited it here.

Brenna turned and walked quickly back in the direction of the boathouse, more puzzled than frightened. She scanned the riverbank as she walked, looking for signs of her hat and parka.

She almost tripped on the flat velvet box. Hearing a sound different than the crunching of gravel beneath her feet, she bent down. Untouched by snow or wetness, the velvet box looked as pristine as the day they had picked out the jewelry. Yesterday seemed like another year.

She forced her attention back to the small box. If someone had been here, and rifled her parka, she was surprised the box was here at all. Maybe the jewelry had already been stolen.

Lifting the hinged cover gently, Brenna was almost afraid to see if anything remained. A homeless person or vagrant could easily have stolen the jewelry and dropped the box.

The top creaked slightly as she opened it. Inside, pinned through the velvet, lay her pin and earrings. When she'd met Cairn near the glen, she had left all her luggage in the rental car, slipping the box from her purse into her jacket pocket at the last minute.

She touched the silver jewelry. As beautiful as it was, she would rather have Cairn. *Trust. Believe.* The voice was a little stronger now, not quite so far away. She shook her head. Fatigue was catching up with her.

Brenna kept walking slowly. A hundred yards away she found her hat. Its crown was damp from the recent snow, but it was intact.

As she looked around for her parka, she heard the voice again, stronger, more vibrant.

Trust. Believe.

"Cairn?" Brenna called. It couldn't be. It wasn't possible. In the darker shadow cast by the boathouse, where the outdoor light did not penetrate, she thought she saw something, a dark shape.

Even as she walked toward the shadow, her heart pounding in her chest, she told herself Cairn could not still be alive. She had seen Rapha-el take him. Hadn't she? Had she? Then why hadn't his body been there?

Maybe the rules were different for angels, she reminded herself. But he had not been a true angel. She knew she had heard Gabri-elle say that. Her head was starting to ache from trying to sort things out.

She was also cold and getting colder. Despite the turtleneck and thick sweater, despite the fact that Washington was far warmer than Scotland had been, she was freezing. If she didn't find her parka in the next few minutes, she was going to have to give up and find a taxi to get home.

Then she realized she wouldn't be able to get into her apartment. She had money in her pocket, but her keys were inside her parka. In that case, she might end up in a hotel for the night, since she didn't want to bother her mother by going back to the hospital and asking her for keys to their house. Her mother would only ask how she had lost hers anyway.

Once again, her foot struck something different underfoot than dirt and gravel. She looked down.

There lay a small heap of puffy fabric. . . .

It was her parka. She shook the dirt and snow off it. As she started to put it on, relieved that this task was successful, she had a very strong feeling that she had not finished looking.

There was something more to find.

Cairn.

Ridiculous. How could she have this bizarre sense of hope when she had seen Cairn die with her own eyes? The angel Rapha-el, who conveyed souls to Heaven, had asked her to give him up.

She hadn't given him up, Brenna realized slowly. She never had. And she did not remember Rapha-el taking him from her arms. Cairn's form had simply disappeared.

Trust, believe, echoed in her mind. Who else could speak to her that way, had ever communicated directly into her mind?

"Cairn, is that you?" she said. "Are you there?" There was no answer. Remembering that she had heard the voice within, she stopped speaking.

Brenna tried to concentrate, using the gift he had insisted was still hers. She was a jumble of tangled emotions. Sadness, hope, disbelief, denial.

Believe. She heard it more strongly this time, elbowing its way through the clamor in her wounded soul. Surely it was not up to her? She clenched her teeth in frustration. There—was something over there in the shadows?

She moved closer to the boathouse wall. This was crazy. *Get a grip, girl.*

But the part of her that had become aware of the possibility of the impossible was now as strong as her rational, disbelieving, modern self. It wasn't all a hallucination. It wasn't all a dream. *You haven't woken up in a cozy bed in Scotland. This is Christmas morning and you're in Washington. How do you think you got here?*

Believe. Believe what? That he was alive?

Believe. All right. She could be as crazy as the next person. She walked boldly into the deepest shadow. Walked straight into a man's body, whose arms closed around her as she fell.

Brenna screamed, remembering the drunk they had encountered earlier. She wasn't afraid of devils, for these were all-too-human hands. Struggling wildly, she kicking out with her legs as her arms were imprisoned. Trying to avoid her flying feet, the man rolled over her. They struggled on the soft, damp soil, rolling away from the boathouse, toward the bushes.

Brenna. The voice rang clearly, if weakly, in her head. *Stop fighting me.* That convinced her as nothing else could have. She stopped struggling. He released her.

Panting, one hand up to shove the hair out of her eyes, she looked at the man she was practically lying on top of. Light from the boathouse shone down on him. Or was it his glow?

She looked more carefully. His blue-gray eyes were unmistakable, the firm, sensuous shape of his mouth achingly familiar.

His shoulders were broad and strong. His powerful body was clothed in brown corduroy trousers and a wheat-colored turtleneck, much as he had been when she first met him. Or met him most recently, she thought giddily.

331

There was no light around him save the weak light of the security lighting above. There were no wings. No wings.

"What are you?" she asked aloud.

"A man, Brenna," Cairn said, his deep, rich voice sounding exhausted. "Just a man."

She scrambled off him, backing away on her knees. "Are you here to trick me? It won't work. Cairn is dead. I . . ."

"Brenna," he said, still speaking aloud. "Come here."

Remembering the circle of fire and the demon, she hesitated, then spoke. "No."

Trust. Believe. The now-familiar litany rang in her head, clear and strong. He repeated the words aloud.

It was Cairn, weak but whole. Not dead, but alive. And apparently restored to mortal form once more. Could another devil have come to deceive her?

"Look inside, Brenna," he said in a low voice. "Feel."

Waves of joy, love, relief, flowed through her. From him into her. From her toward him. There was no way to counterfeit those feelings, no way to feign the current that ran between them, stronger, brighter, hotter than it had ever been.

"Oh God, Cairn, I'm sorry. Are you all right?" She rolled off Cairn immediately.

Cairn sat up slowly. His movements were sure, but not swift. It appeared he had just been regaining consciousness when she'd literally stumbled on him.

"I'm not certain," he said finally. "I was dying. I knew that. When Rapha-el took me, I thought that was it. Then . . . I can't explain this in words." Cairn held out his hand to her in wordless entreaty.

She took it and helped him to rise, moving out of the shadows. As she did so, a series of images flashed before her eyes. Cairn, borne somewhere by Raphael. Not up to the sky, but to a secluded island a little way down the river. Cairn did not know where it was, but Brenna recognized Roosevelt Island, a bird sanctuary and park by day. The pedestrian causeway to the island was locked at night, the only way to get onto the island.

Brenna saw Cairn, who was astonished to find himself in his human form again. She saw him bow low before a green-robed angel whose very wings seemed to contain all-seeing eyes. The angel held a bright, flaming sword in one hand. The Archangels Gabri-elle and Rapha-el assisted Cairn to stand before the great Archangel Micha-el. As his friends slowly raised him to a standing position, the heavy, sodden wings behind Cairn's back disappeared into a gray haze.

The mist cleared away. Cairn looked at himself, at the angels with him. He was wearing the clothes he had on now. Brenna knew from his expression that he was asking them what had happened. There were no words, no sounds, but Brenna understood what they conveyed to him in vivid images that appeared to her closed eyes, as she stood holding Cairn's hand.

He was fully mortal again. He would live a normal life with a normal span of years. It had to do with his unselfishness in saving her father. Because of it, the angels had been able to extricate him from Lucifer's hold.

Once he died, he was no longer subject to the rules

Above and Below. No longer able to wear angelic form, he became human again, a gift from the Archangels. As a normal human, he would no longer be the object of Lucifer's special attention. The angels had masked his transformation from Lucifer. The Lord of Darkness would never find him now.

Brenna opened her eyes, her heart filled with wonder. Cairn's eyes shone in the darkness. "An ordinary human?" she asked, scarcely daring to hope.

"Quite ordinary, I'm afraid. And not very knowledgeable about the time you live in." His voice had a note of hesitancy, as if he feared that being an ordinary human was insufficient.

"You'll learn that quickly." Her matter-of-fact acceptance and assumption that he would remain in her life eased Cairn's mind considerably about his future.

"How old were you when you decided to . . . to wait?" Brenna wanted something resembling hard information to go on, even when a miracle had been at work in her life. Her habits as a fact-seeking reporter were too well ingrained.

Cairn thought a moment. "Twenty-eight, I think. You were twenty-three."

"Is that how old you are now?"

"I think so."

"I do too," Brenna said decisively. Two years younger than she, but given everything that had happened to him, "younger" was no longer a relevant word.

"You look as you did then." The words popped out without conscious thought.

"Do I?" Cairn began to smile. "Do you remember that?"

"I don't know if I remember it exactly, but I just know." She was perplexed at herself. What did she hope to prove?

The answer came from inside herself. He had been restored to life at the moment when it should have been cut off. The angels had allowed him to pick up the thread of his life again. It was that simple. That astonishingly complex and mysterious.

She was a little older than she had been then, but that didn't really matter either. Certainly she, Brenna in the here-and-now, was far more suitable than when she had been the frightened girl Brianna in Scotland. Acceptance of that past reality came more easily too, she found.

Cairn's smile grew wider. He interlaced his fingers with hers. "This transformation suits you?"

"Suits me? This is wonderful," Brenna said. "You're normal, completely normal in every way?"

Cairn leaned toward her, brushing her lips with his. "We'll just have to experiment and see, won't we?" The unmistakably sensual look on his moonlit face sent warmth racing through her system, tingles to the back of her neck. The fine hairs on her arms rose. She felt it even through the layers of clothing she wore.

Brenna tried to ignore the goosebumps, to focus on being practical. "Then we'd better get out of the cold," she said. "You still don't have a coat."

He nodded, but didn't release her hand. He reached for her with his free hand, stroking her cheek before rubbing his thumb slowly across her lower lip. He drew her in to fit snugly within the shelter of his arms.

Brenna caught her breath, not expelling it when he captured her lips with his again. He kissed her slowly, as if he had all the time in the world, savoring the taste of her, reacquainting himself with her mouth as if years had passed since they had last kissed.

All the time in the world. Cairn liked the sound of it in his mind, even though he knew his human body disagreed. That part of him wanted her. Now.

Brenna surprised him by laughing. "Not here. We're going home."

Cairn wondered if the ability to read each other's thoughts and emotions would remain, or fade as time passed in his human form. Were Brenna's abilities linked to his? She had never been anything other than human, but she'd had the Sight.

Human. And his. He liked the way those words sounded in his mind even better.

"So do I," Brenna said shyly, linking her arm through his as they emerged onto the road.

"Can we go see your father?" Cairn asked some time later. They were the only two people out in the very early morning of Christmas Day.

"I just came from the hospital. He's doing fine. The exposure, the fall in the water—you healed him."

"Not of everything," Cairn said, sadness in his voice.

"Gabri-elle told me that. But she also said he would always remember those who helped him on this night. Daddy already approves of you, you know.

He said something about you in the hospital before Mother came."

Her father had been moved to a room of his own. By the time they found out where and reached his room, the floor nurse told them he was asleep. Her mother had gone to get a cup of coffee.

Brenna was frankly thankful her mother wasn't there at the moment. She didn't know how she was going to explain Cairn.

He squeezed her hand. "One thing at a time," he said, as if he sensed her turmoil.

She squeezed back, but didn't say anything. They tiptoed quietly into her father's room. He was asleep, the boyishness of his face accentuated in sleep.

Brenna approached the bed. She bent to kiss her father's forehead. As she did, his eyes opened and focused on her. They were a clear, pale blue, reminding her of when he was younger, of the years growing up, when he was her ideal man. Always ready with an encouraging word, he had given her love and understanding when she had been at her lowest, wondering whether anything she did would ever meet her mother's high standards.

He smiled at her, then turned to see Cairn at the foot of his bed. "So it's you," George Sirin said with satisfaction.

"Yes, sir," Cairn said politely.

"You're the one," he said cryptically. "Are you going to take good care of my little girl?" Brenna felt a hot flush cover her face. She was not a teenager any longer.

But Cairn had moved to the other side of her father's bed to shake hands. "Yes, sir. I would also like to ask your permission to marry Brenna." Brenna sucked in a breath.

Her father chuckled. "Have you asked her?"

"Not in so many words," Cairn admitted.

"It's nice of you to ask, but nowadays the lady gets first say," George said.

Cairn looked at Brenna across the bed. "I had planned to ask her later," he said honestly. Brenna felt her blush deepen, guessing just when he had planned to ask.

"You can always ask me later, son," George said. "After Brenna says yes. Go along now, and come back to see me tomorrow, you hear?"

"Yes, sir." Cairn's deep voice was still respectful, but Brenna couldn't look him in the eye. She heard the promise in his tone just in those two words.

She bent to kiss her father's cheek. "Go enjoy Christmas," George said. "I'll be here with your mother. Call later on."

"Of course, Daddy. Umm, what are you going to tell Mom about your escapades?"

"Tell her what? A forgetful old man like me?" He winked, and Brenna knew she would have a chance to tell her mother about Cairn in her own time. And that whether her father remembered it or not, he was not going to tell anyone about the incident at the boathouse.

"Merry Christmas, Daddy," she said, this time smiling as she had not been able to an hour or two earlier.

"Merry Christmas, Brennabear."

* * *

The all-night hospital staff obligingly called another taxi. By the time they reached her apartment, Brenna was practically asleep on Cairn's shoulder. Only the fact that she had given the taxi driver the address when they first got in kept them from ending up who-knew-where.

"You live near the cathedral," Cairn said, peering through the early morning light creeping over the city, remembering how he had been drawn to this area. He had thought it was the building's nearness to the cathedral, but it had also been Brenna.

"Mmm," she said in sleepy agreement. She started to get out of the taxi.

"Do you not have to pay?" Cairn asked.

"Pay? Oh, yes, of course." She had been expecting him to pay. Probably he hadn't a cent to his name. Did he *have* a name? was her next thought.

She handed the taxi driver a ten-dollar bill, thankful she hadn't changed all her American money in London. She would have to call the hotel later and get their suitcases shipped to them. If Cairn had a suitcase.

Suddenly it hit her. Cairn did not have a name, a home, a place to live, or a living, as far as she knew. And probably nothing to prove his identity.

"They weren't so impractical as all that," he said quietly in her ear as she pushed the elevator button.

"What do you mean?"

"Our 'friends.' In my luggage in Scotland, there is a British passport, identity papers, that sort of thing. Some money."

"You're British?"

"I told you that."

"Well, I know you were originally, but . . ."

"But they didn't exactly have passports in those days. I know. And I believe I am an historian."

She laughed. "Well, that's certainly appropriate."

Brenna turned the key in the lock. She felt as if she'd been gone forever, yet it was less than a week. And she was now sharing her apartment.

"I need not stay," he said, recognizing the source of her anxiety. "Surely there are hotels nearby."

"No, no, it's fine. Look, why don't you take a shower first? It'll take me longer since I have to wash my hair. I'll stick your stuff in the wash while you're showering. Just toss it out the door. There are some old clothes of my dad's here. I was going to take the stuff over to the cathedral for one of the homeless shelters. It's old, but it's all wearable. The stores won't open until tomorrow."

She was babbling and she knew it, so she stopped and sat down to call the Fife Arms. The long-suffering night clerk promised to retrieve the car and her luggage. Cairn's suitcase was still in his room. Brenna called the rental car agency in Aberdeen, agreeing to pay an exorbitant fine because she hadn't returned the car. She didn't care. Her father was well; Cairn was safe. Nothing else mattered.

At last Cairn emerged from the shower, his color high, hair damp and curly. He emanated an aura of physical vitality as visible as the light that had once surrounded him. Her father's old jogging suit was the only thing that would stretch enough to cover his long legs and arms. Nevertheless, he still looked unbelievably attractive.

Brenna was suddenly acutely aware of how dirty

and bedraggled she was from rolling in the mud. "Umm, let me get cleaned up," she said. She looked back at the stacked washer and dryer combination in her kitchen. "Take your clothes from the bottom and put them in the top, that's the dryer, for twenty minutes, OK? It's that knob on the—"

Brenna turned around to find Cairn standing next to her, a damp towel in one hand. She almost ran smack into his broad chest.

"You are very uncomfortable," he remarked easily. "You are certain you do not wish me to leave?"

"No, no, don't. This will just take some getting used to." He was right. She did feel awkward and uncomfortable. She had never shared her apartment with a man, even though some of her suitemates in her freshman dorm had been male. She was acting like a virgin in a romance novel, she thought, all flightiness and nerves.

"Look, I will go," he said. "You get some rest, and—"

"No," Brenna said, this time meaning it. The thought of him walking out the door frightened her in a way she could scarcely name. "No, don't go."

Chapter Twenty-One

Cairn dropped the towel on a chair, pulling her into his arms. "What is it?"

"You can't read my mind?"

"It is more difficult when you are agitated. I think the ability is fading anyway. Perhaps it is not meant to go with a normal human body."

Brenna squirmed away from him self-consciously. "Listen, I'm a mess. We'll talk about this in a little while, all right?" She escaped into the bathroom.

Emerging an hour later, she felt considerably better. She was clean, her hair was blow-dried and bouncy, and for a few brief minutes she had forgotten the bizarre situation that awaited her. An angel in her living room.

When she came out, she noted the set table, smelled eggs and bacon cooking, saw orange juice

on the table, touched the cozy settled on the hot teapot.

That was it, she thought, grinning in relief. She
was definitely in love if the man could cook. "Look
at all this," she said, impressed. "What have you
done?"

Cairn looked at her, his face impassive. "I thought
you would be hungry. I am. It has been—what is the
expression?—an age since I ate."

She couldn't help it. She giggled. Then laughed.
Helpless, she sank into a chair, holding her sides. "It
probably has been forever, hasn't it?" she managed
between giggles.

Cairn had been looking at her in consternation.
Once he got the joke, he smiled, then laughed himself. When she didn't stop, he realized her laughter
had an hysterical edge to it.

He knelt before her chair. Brenna's eyes were
streaming, and she was on the verge of falling apart
completely. He picked her up easily, depositing her
at the table enclosed on one side by her oriel window.

"Sit down and eat. I think you need it more than I
do," he said sternly, but she saw a suppressed smile
on his arresting features.

Half an hour later, she was inclined to agree. She'd
eaten every bit as much as Cairn. She didn't even ask
how he had learned to cook. Maybe being on cam-
paign so much in the old days. Soldiers had probably
had to fend for themselves.

She looked at him covertly as he finished a glass
of orange juice, watching the muscles in his strong
throat work as he swallowed. Vital, alive, he filled her

343

little dining corner with his masculine presence. For the first time, she thought about the future they might have. She had hardly dared to hope since finding him at the boathouse, but nothing she had seen or heard indicated there was anything temporary about his current state.

She awoke from her daydream to find his blue-gray eyes on hers. "Why don't you sleep?" he said. "You must be exhausted."

"That wouldn't be very polite of me," she started to say. Cairn pushed his chair back. He was in front of her in a moment, stooping to lift her into his arms again.

"I am not a guest," he said. The irritation in his tone was unmistakable. He found the door to her bedroom and pushed it open. "Do not treat me like a stranger."

"Aren't you?" she shot back, goaded.

He sat down on the bed, still holding her in his arms. "Perhaps that is what you want me to be, so you can retreat again and make me into something safe, someone you can be distant from. But I am not a stranger, Brenna. You know that. I am your lover."

Before she could fire back another reply, his mouth descended on hers. Firm, knowing, sure. Excitement arced through her, racing along her spine in time with the sweep of his hands up and down her back.

"You know who I am, don't you?" he asked in a low, sexy voice, then gave her no time to reply. He brought his hands up to her face to cup it between his long fingers, kissing her intimately.

Brenna could barely breathe. He pulled back, his

eyes consuming her. "You know what I want, don't you?" he asked, kissing her again before she could respond, his tongue entering her mouth, daring her to meet him.

Fire burned in her. She wound her hand into his thick blond hair, angling his mouth to suit her. He smiled against her mouth, letting her take the initiative.

When she pulled back, breathless, he did not let up. "Who am I?" he asked, still challenging her.

"Mine," she said fiercely. She did not want him to leave, did not want him to stay somewhere else. Did not want him to sleep anywhere else except here, with her.

His hands dropped from her face, caressing her shoulders, moving to her breasts. "You know who I want, don't you?" he asked, starting to unbutton her shirt.

"Me," she said, the brush of his fingertips like melted wax on her skin, thick, heavy, hot. She unzipped his jacket, running her hands across his smooth, broad chest in one sweeping caress.

"What do *you* want, Brenna?" he asked, his breath emerging as a caress on her rapidly hardening nipple.

"I want you," she said, amazed at her own boldness. She didn't stop to consider any of it. She was on fire and couldn't wait.

"Where?" he said.

"Here," she said, pulling her shirt off herself, reaching around to unclasp her bra. Cairn repositioned her on his lap so she straddled him. Through the soft fleece of the warm-up suit, she felt the ridge of his manhood against her jean-clad thighs.

She felt hot and wet between her legs, the ache intensifying when he took her nipple into his mouth. He manipulated the other peak, rolling it between his long fingers, cupping the weight of her breasts in both his palms. Brenna reached for the jacket, eager to feel more of his powerful body beneath her hands, unzipping and pulling the cloth away from him.

He had to remove his hands from her breasts to cooperate. As soon as she pulled his arms free, they sought her again. He suckled strongly on one breast, his other hand at her back, pressing her more closely into him. Brenna arched against him, bracing her hands on his shoulders.

Cairn leaned back until she fell against him, rolling her neatly so that she ended up on her back, feeling his weight across her legs. She sought his hair again, loving the thick weight of it in her hands, the brush of it against her breasts as he caressed her.

Pulling back until he was propped on one elbow above her, Cairn reached for the waistband of her pants. He pulled her jeans down slowly, kissing her navel, then her stomach as he peeled them off. It was hard to imagine anything more erotic, Brenna thought, than being undressed like this.

Her panties were beige, nearly nude. He dropped a kiss on the silky fabric above her nest of curls. Brenna felt herself expanding, readying for him. He moved his lips to the place where her bud was hidden, pressing his mouth against the lace until she felt him there. But he went on, leaving her damp from his mouth, damp from her own excitement. He kissed the tops of her thighs, her knees, where he found an incredibly sensitive place behind each one, which he kissed.

Her calves were not neglected, or her ankles, which also proved more sensitive than she had ever suspected. He kissed her instep, sliding the heavy jeans fabric free of its last entanglement. Her legs felt bare and cool now that they were exposed. Pushing the pants off the bed, he kissed his way back up the way he had come.

When he reached her lacy underwear, he slipped his fingers under the leg, brushing the curls that covered her. Brenna could not keep from moaning.

"Do you want me here?" he asked.

"Yes, oh yes," she said. Cairn ran his hand along her fleecy mound, letting his fingers linger on the seam. She felt him brushing back and forth with slow, agonizing strokes, felt herself open, her legs parting to offer him more.

He slipped into her heat with a groan that Brenna echoed with a sigh. One hand slipped deeper inside her and she grabbed at his head. He shook off her touch, raising his head to look at her, his eyes glowing.

"What do you want?" he said.

"I want you."

"Here?" he asked, pressing deeper inside.

"Yes."

"Just this, or all of me?"

The emptiness ached to be filled. He wanted it all, wanted all of her, and he wouldn't let her hold anything back.

Remembering how wild and free she had felt in the dream when she'd flown, Brenna surrendered the

347

last of her inhibitions to the man she loved more than anything in the world.

"I want all of you." He moved his clever fingers inside her, stretching, teasing, before sliding his hand back up and out in a smooth, liquid motion that had her toes curling.

She moaned when his hand left her, but it was only to slip her panties off. A moment later, she realized he'd divested himself of his pants. She found him a moment later, soft steel, hard velvet. Brenna closed her hand around him with wonder, pleased to hear him groan at her instigation.

Skimming her thumb over the tip, she found a drop of liquid and covered the head with it, rubbing slowly. Cairn took her mouth in a deep kiss as she continued to hold him, exploring his length with curiosity and delight.

Finally he reached down and unfolded her fingers. "I want to be inside you," he said, his tongue flicking at the outer shell of her ear. "Do you want me?"

"Yes, Cairn, yes." Her surrender did not make her weak; it made them equals. He moved over her, his knees gently parting her legs still further. She was wet and ready for him. He barely had to push as he thrust gently into her, pausing when he came up against the barrier.

"This may hurt," he warned.

For reply, she fastened her mouth to his, encouraging him to thrust into her mouth with his tongue. His hips followed suit, short bursts that advanced and retreated, stretching the untried sheath. Deeper, he had to be deeper. She captured his tongue as he pushed.

One long thrust and he was inside. She stiffened, broke the kiss. Cairn leaned his forehead against hers, kissing her closed eyelids, holding himself completely still with great effort.

A tear escaped beneath one of her closed lids. Cairn kissed it, tasting the salt. "Are you all right?" he asked. He did not honestly think he could stop, but he could try. "Do you want me to stop?"

"No, no," Brenna said. "Just give me a minute."

"Try thirty seconds," he countered in a stifled voice. Her eyes flew open and she looked at him, saw the taut lines of his face.

He kissed her nose. "Sorry," he said. "I have waited too long, my love." Even as he spoke, his hips started to move.

"You feel wonderful, but I don't want to hurt you. Oh, God," he said, and with a supreme effort, pulled out of her. He felt like a fish out of water, gasping.

Brenna felt almost as bereft as when she thought he had died. The burning feeling had passed, and all she felt now was emptiness. The emptiness of never knowing his touch, the emptiness to which she had awoken in her dreams. He was here now, real, wonderfully real. She swore to herself that this encounter would not end unrequited.

Brenna moved beneath him to position him over her once more. "It's all right now. Really," she said when he looked unconvinced. Her legs reached up to wrap around him, her arms bringing him close, stroking down his back.

He slid into her gently, pausing to look into her eyes, to make sure she was all right, before starting to thrust slowly.

All she felt was bliss. Brenna kept her legs locked around his hips, feeling him with wonder, thrust deep inside her. His lips were on her neck, her shoulder, her breasts, everywhere he could reach with his mouth, while his lower body gave her shock after shock of delight.

His touch burned, excited, enflamed. Brenna began to rock with him, twisting to feel as much of him as possible against her own body, twining her hands in his hair, pulling his mouth back up to hers.

She knew she was approaching the peak, felt the wild tempest in her body. As she moaned deep in her throat, his lips slid down to cover her throat, to feel the vibrations. "Cairn, I . . ." she cried out, his name as deep inside her as his body.

She did not finish saying "I love you," because at that moment, she shattered. Her muscles tightened, released in an exquisite, consuming fire that licked her head to toe, its burning heart inside her. Cairn called her name, his whole body tightening. She held him blindly as he convulsed in her, feeling her climax and his, beyond speech, beyond thought.

One from two, one together, at last.

When the glory subsided, she would not let him leave her. They remained intertwined. His forehead, damp as his freshly washed hair had been, rested against her equally damp one. He tucked strands of her hair behind her ears, dispensing tiny kisses everywhere he touched. She stroked his back, slick with exertion, marveling at the rippling strength she felt under the smooth surface of his skin.

He lifted his head to look deeply into her eyes, his own a blazing cobalt blue. A tender smile curved his full, generous mouth. She realized she had no idea what was going on behind his eyes, but she hardly needed to read his mind to know.

"I can't feel what you're thinking anymore," she said.

"I cannot either," he confessed. "Does it bother you?"

She thought. "No, not really."

"Me either."

"Why do you suppose that is?"

"Maybe it was a substitute for this," he smiled down at her glistening body, pausing to gently lave a nipple until it puckered again, helplessly, beneath his touch.

"Or maybe it helped us find each other," she suggested.

"Mmm," he agreed, his mouth still occupied.

"Do you miss it?"

"Not when we have this," he said, nudging her gently with his hips. She realized that he had slipped out of her naturally as he had lost rigidity. And that now he was hard against her.

He met her eyes, looking vulnerable yet potently male all at once. "Are you too sore?"

She shook her head, suddenly shy, a blush coloring her face. She looked away from him, over his golden, sculpted shoulder.

"Oh come, Brenna," he said impatiently, "I thought you were over that."

"You have the honor of being with the last virgin in America," she said stiffly. She scooted out from under him. "I've been called sexless more times than I care to recall."

He grabbed her waist, and she shrieked. "That tickles!" But he held on. He rolled her on top of him, lifting her above him with strong hands.

"I love you, Brenna. Nothing can change that. Don't you know that by now? You are beautiful, desirable, sexy—isn't that the word they use now?" He captured a breast, suckled the nipple firmly, quickly, moving to the other one to prove his point. Her aureoles contracted immediately, and she felt arousal coil through a body she had just considered incredibly replete.

"You see?" he said, laughing at her with his eyes. "You are a gorgeous, passionate woman. I want to make love to you forever. I may never leave your bed long enough to ask your father's blessing." His old-fashioned notions of courtesy and his playful loving were an irresistible combination.

Without having to read her mind, he saw her eyes soften. He lowered her slowly until she was straddling him, her hands on his chest. "Show me how passionate you are, my Brenna. You were worth waiting for, always."

He took one of her hands and ran his tongue over her palm, then flicked lightly between each of her fingers. The caress excited her wildly.

Cairn felt her heat against his stomach, wished desperately to feel her close around him lower down. She swayed above him, her eyes drifting closed with the sensuous pleasure of it.

"Show me," he urged, his voice husky. Brenna felt the exquisite friction as she moved down to find him. His shaft quivered as she found him and rubbed against him. His eyes were closed now, groans rumbling deep in his throat.

"Look at me," she commanded gently. His eyes opened, fixed on hers as she lifted herself to begin taking him inside her. She could feel him stretching her, but there was no pain. Once he was sheathed inside her, she began to slide forward and back. He responded to her pace, now fast, now slow, following her lead.

"Look, Brenna," he said, his voice rich and low. "Look at us," he said, lifting up to his elbows to see where they were joined. He thrust strongly, and she felt the friction against her throbbing bud. She moved her hands from his chest to grab the headboard above him, while his mouth sought and captured her swaying breasts in turn.

She rode him fast and hard now. He lay flat against the pillows again, holding her breasts as she rose and fell above him. Finally, it was too good to bear. He could no longer hold to her rhythm. He thrust, his hips rising off the bed. Again, and again.

He felt her convulse around him, her sheath hugging him with her inner muscles, and he came. She had collapsed against his chest while he still surged in her, relishing the feel of her soft hair in a cloud around his shoulders. He turned her face up to him, capturing her mouth with his in his final thrust, feeling closer to her than he ever had.

No, he did not miss the mind-to-mind contact, he thought as he lay, heart pounding, her soft body's curves poured over him. Not when they had this to express their love.

After a little while, he began to chuckle. Brenna

was drifting half-in, half-out of sleep, wondering if her future was staying up all night, then sleeping half the day away with Cairn. There were worse ways to live, she thought, a smile stretching the corners of her mouth. She became gradually aware that his broad chest was moving, not in the rhythms of sleep, but in unmistakable masculine laughter, a deep, rumbling amusement.

"Whazz so funny?" she asked, rolling off him.

"You," he answered, pulling up the coverlet around them, tucking them closely together, face-to-face.

"Hmm?"

"Sexless. Not in a thousand years, Brenna. What is the matter with this century?" He shushed her with a kiss on each eyelid. "Never mind. I should thank the men of this century for being idiots."

Appeased yet still annoyed, Brenna stretched against him like a cat, please to hear him draw a sharp breath when her naked form encountered an appreciative part of his anatomy. "Waiting for you hasn't exactly been easy, you know," she muttered.

He sobered. "I know, love. I am sorry."

"Not . . . your fault . . ." She was fading fast. "Glad you remembered, love . . ."

"I am too," he said into her hair.

Epilogue

They were married in Washington National Cathedral on New Year's Day. Her mother had not accustomed herself to the idea of Brenna having a new fiancé, let alone marrying him "in such indecent haste," as she said.

Brenna was determined not to wait one more minute to be married to Cairn, and told her mother so politely but firmly. Her mother came, in her best dress.

George Sirin did receive a diagnosis of Alzheimer's, but his delight in Brenna's happiness and his strong, instant rapport with Cairn removed much of the shadow from the day.

He presented Brenna and Cairn with the carved wooden figure he had been working on the day he left the house on Christmas Eve. He said his inspiration was a stone-carved angel in a chapel at the National Cathedral, but Brenna privately thought the figure, with its massive wings and powerful grace, looked like Cairn.

Marina flew back a week early from her vacation in Italy to be Brenna's maid of honor. Vincenzo arrived from the airport bearing a traditional Italian wedding cake made at his family's restaurant specially for Brenna and Cairn.

Much to Brenna's surprise, Maud Barrett accepted Brenna's telephoned invitation to the wedding, since there had been no time for the engraved invitations Peggy Sirin wanted. Maud spent half the service looking at Cairn with speculation. When she congratulated Brenna after the ceremony, Brenna wasn't too surprised by what she said.

"Is he the one?" she whispered while Cairn was talking to Marina and Vincenzo in the small receiving line that had formed at the back of the church among the thirty or so friends and family who were there.

"Mr. Right? Absolutely," Brenna declared.

Maud held Brenna's hand firmly in her grasp. "No, it's more than that. You accepted your past. He found you. Together you created a future."

The prophetic sheen faded from her eyes, and she looked almost abashed. "Was I right?" she asked, a shrewd look in her serene blue eyes.

"Oh, yes," Brenna said softly, turning to meet Cairn's glance. He held her gaze with love and promise.

"Here's someone you should meet," Brenna said to Cairn, realizing that she would have to speak or risk missing the rest of the receiving line, lost in Cairn's loving, magnetic, gray-blue gaze. Certainly *he* showed no inclination to break their silent communion.

She indicated Maud, handing her over to Cairn. "I suspect that you two might have met already, in a manner of speaking," Brenna said.

Despite Cairn's quizzical look, Brenna refused to elaborate. Maud shook Cairn's hand, an expression of pure joy spreading across her face as their hands met. Startled recognition filled Cairn's eyes.

Brenna smiled. Her hunch had proven correct. No further introductions were needed.

Author's Note

Dear Readers,
I've been scribbling stories on squirreled-away bits of paper since the age of ten. Fascinated since childhood by Celtic mythology and Scottish history, I was recently inspired by a wild series of "what if" questions. Cairn and Brenna appeared soon after, demanding that I tell their unusual story, in which Cairn, in his quest to find his beloved Brenna, is actually an angel himself for a while. I hope you, too, are swept away by the power of their story, by a love so strong that it binds two people across centuries, overcoming the obstacles of time, fate, and evil.

I love to hear from readers. Please write me at: P.O. Box 1055, Vienna, VA 22183-1055.

Corinne Everett

An Angel's Touch

D.J.'s Angel
LORI HANDELAND

D.J. Halloran doesn't believe in love. She's just seen too much heartache—in her work as a police officer and in her own life. And she vowed a long time ago never to let anyone get close enough to hurt her, even if that someone is the very captivating, very handsome Chris McCall.

But D.J. also has an angel—a special guardian determined, at any cost, to teach D.J. the magic of love. So try as she might to resist Chris's many charms, D.J. knows she is in for an even tougher battle because of her exasperating heavenly companion's persistent faith in the power of love.

_52050-8 $5.99 US/$7.99 CAN

An Angel's Touch

Heaven's Gift

JANELLE DENISON

The last thing J.T. Rafferty expects when he awakes from a concussion is to find a beautiful stranger tending to his wounds. She saved his life, but the lovely Caitlan Daniels has some serious explaining to do—like how she ended up on his isolated ranch lands, miles from civilization. Despite his wariness, J.T. finds himself increasingly drawn to Caitlan, whose gentle touch promises sweet satisfaction. She is passionate and independent and utterly enchanting—but Caitlan also has a secret. And when J.T. finally discovers the shocking truth, he'll have to defy heaven and earth to keep her close to his heart.

_52059-1 $5.99 US/$7.99 CAN

An Angel's Touch

Time Heals
SUSAN COLLIER

Tired of her nagging relatives, Maeve Fredrickson asks for the impossible: to be a thousand miles and a hundred years away from them. Then a heavenly being grants her wish, and she awakes in frontier Montana.

Saved from the wilderness by a handsome widower, Maeve loses her heart to her rescuer—and her temper over the antics of his three less-than-angelic children. As her angel prods her to fight for Seth, Maeve can only pray for the strength to claim a love made in paradise.

_52030-3 $4.99 US/$5.99 CAN

An Angel's Touch

Longer Than Forever
BRONWYN WOLFE

"A wonderful, magical love story that transcends time and space. Definitely a keeper!"
—Madeline Baker

Patrick is in trouble, alone in turn-of-the-century Chicago, and unjustly jailed with little hope for survival. Then the honey-haired beauty comes to him, as if she has heard his prayers.

Lauren has all but given up on finding true love when she feels the green-eyed stranger's call—summoning her across boundaries of time and space to join him in a struggle against all odds; uniting them in a love that will last longer than forever.

_52042-7 $5.99 US/$7.99 CAN

An Angel's Touch

Forever Angels

TRÁNA MAE SIMMONS

Tess Foster is convinced she has someone watching over her. The thoroughly modern woman has everything: a brilliant career, a rich fiance, and a glamorous life. But when her boyfriend demands she sign a prenuptial agreement, Tess thinks she's lost her happiness forever. Then her guardian angel sneezes and sends the woman of the nineties back to another era: the 1890s.

At first, Tess can't believe her senses. After all, no real man can be as handsome as the cowboy who rescues her from the Oklahoma wilderness. And Tess has never tasted sweeter ecstasy than she finds in Stone Chisum's kisses. But before she will surrender to a marriage made in heaven, Tess has to make sure that her bumbling guardian angel doesn't sneeze again—and ruin her second chance at love.

_52021-4 $4.99 US/$5.99 CAN

WICKED
Evelyn Rogers
An Angel's Touch

"Evelyn Rogers delivers great entertainment!"
—*Romantic Times*

Gunned down after a bank robbery, Cad Rankin meets a heavenly being who makes him an offer he can't refuse. To save his soul, he has to bring peace to the most lawless town in the West. With a mission like that, the outlaw almost resigns himself to spending eternity in a place much hotter than Texas—until he comes across Amy Lattimer, a feisty beauty who rouses his goodness and a whole lot more.

Although she's been educated in a convent school, Amy Lattimer is determined to do anything to locate her missing father, including posing as a fancy lady. Then she finds an ally in virile Cad Rankin, who isn't about to let her become a fallen angel. But even as Amy longs to surrender to paradise in Cad's arms, she begins to suspect that he has a secret that stands between them and unending bliss....

_52082-6 $5.99 US/$7.99 CAN

An Angel's Touch

Carly's Song

LENORA NAZWORTH

Carly Richards has come to New Orleans to escape her painful past. She certainly has no intention of getting involved with some reckless musician with an overzealous approach to living and an all-too-real lust for her. Sam Canfield is simply the sexiest man she's ever seen, but Carly is determined to resist being mesmerized by his sensuous spell.

Sam thinks he's seen it all in his day. But one enchanted evening, his world is turned upside down when a redhead with lilac eyes stumbles into his path and an old friend he thought long gone makes a magical appearance on a misty street corner. Soon, the handsome sax player finds himself conversing with an elusive angel, struggling to put his life together, and attempting to convince the reluctant Carly that together they'll make sweet music of their own.

_52073-7 $5.99 US/$7.99 CAN